JUST HIS IMAGINATION?

I ducked into the closed door of Balducci's gourmet food store, ostensibly to light another smoke. I looked back down the street, my first concession to growing paranoia. It was just the weekend crowd in the West Village. *Nothing wrong here. No one is following you.*

I looked again. *It must be me.* Wouldn't be the first time. In fact, paranoia was one of my warning symptoms. Mania returned in stages. Over the years I'd learned the signs. Sometimes I could cut things off before they got out of control. Paranoia was not a "usual" for me, it was a "sometimes." But it was as familiar as a pack of cigarettes and as dangerous as a gun.

I took one last look.

Nothing is there. Just go home.

And so I did, ignoring a mounting inner panic. It was just the nicotine; I wasn't used to it.

I climbed the four flights of stairs to my loft. Everything was okay, as it should have been. And then I reached the landing....

Other *Leisure* books by Charles Atkins:

THE CADAVER'S BALL

THE PORTRAIT

CHARLES ATKINS

LEISURE BOOKS NEW YORK CITY

To Elizabeth Joy

A LEISURE BOOK®

July 2008

Published by

Dorchester Publishing Co., Inc.
200 Madison Avenue
New York, NY 10016

The Portrait is a work of fiction. Any resemblance to persons either living or dead is purely coincidental.

ISBN 10: 0-8439-6084-1
ISBN 13: 978-0-8439-6084-6

Visit us on the web at www.dorchesterpub.com.

ACKNOWLEDGMENTS

The author wishes to thank the following for their support, guidance, and encouragement: Gary Steven Jayson, Sandy Bacon, Kathy Kim, John Strauss, Jaak Raakfeldt, Larry Davidson, Jeanne Steiner, Malcolm Bowers, Barbara Veselago-Turner, Peggy Atkins-Munro, Collin Munro, Cynthia and Jaspard Atkins, Susan Barkin, Ida Marks, Sandra Watt, Priscilla Palmer, Steve Schneider, Robert Cassidy, Laurie Duncan, Jeanette Mitrukiewicz, Sue Kociszewski, MaryAnn Berube, Judith Ehrman-Shapiro, Laura Nesta, Barbara Brown, Barbara Howard, Stacey Asip, Stacey Rubin, Robert Kneitschel, Lydia Capuano, William Curtis, Maureen Briand, Blanche Agostinelli and Carol Cestaro.

THE PORTRAIT

CHAPTER ONE

I took my pills, two of them. I caught my reflection in the mirror over the sink. One day out and I was already looking rough, a thick stubble on my face; my long hair, nearly as red as my dog's, streaked with splatters of acrylic paint. My eyes glittered darkly, the pupils wide from caffeine, the hazel irises nearly eliminated. The image disturbed me, my expression was too intense, the angles of my face too sharp. *Did I really belong out of a hospital?*

I had to call my agent.

"Prescott Unlimited."

"Yeah, this is Chad Greene. Is Pamela in?"

"One moment, please."

A familiar voice. "Chad, how are you doing?"

"Not too bad; pretty good, actually."

"That's great, it's good to hear your voice."

I read the subtext in her intonation. *Is he really okay? Is he high? Is he depressed? Is he going to make sense?* "Look, I wanted to find out how things stand with the show. I know I've not been too available."

"Don't worry," she said, "everything's set. You just need to show up."

Thank God for Pamela, I thought. After eight years

as my friend and agent, she was the glue that pieced my life back together after each time I blew it apart.

"Great, when's the hanging? I want to check out the lights. Maybe we could get together and go over the space."

"I was planning to go in tomorrow," she said. "I didn't know if you'd want to or not."

I let it slide. "I always want to, you know that."

"I know, I just didn't know how you were doing."

"Look, Pamela, I'm fine. No, that's a lie. I'm good enough, a little shaky, but that's the lithium." I laughed; she didn't. "You want to meet for lunch?"

"Okay," she said, not sounding enthused.

"Great. Spring Street Bar at one o'clock?"

"I'll be there."

There it was, the struggling artist fresh from the nuthouse. How historically correct and something of a cliché. I wondered how many people she'd told. There was a time when I would have told them myself. Disclosure was not a problem. I cringed at the mistakes of my youth. Me at seventeen versus me at thirty-five. What would another ten years bring? Would I become one of them? One of the patients?

It was always like this just after discharge, trying to shake the residue of patienthood. The hospital clung to me, like the shell to a chick still breaking free of its yolk. I wasn't one of them. *Yeah, right. Just keep telling yourself that.*

The Portrait

Ching, my beautiful red chow, lapped at my hand and ran circles around me as I headed toward the bathroom. *Got to pee, got to pee.* Lithium, with its endless cycle of thirst and urination, never lets you forget. My tongue always felt dry and coated, and then there were the blood tests and warnings. I remembered mnemonics learned long ago about the danger signs of toxicity. On my first inpatient admission, when I was seventeen, a nurse traced the outline of her hand, like a first-grade teacher would draw a Thanksgiving turkey. Instead of Tom Turkey's tail feathers, each finger was a symptom of lithium poisoning: tremor, slurred speech, diarrhea, confusion, and ataxia. I wanted to color it in.

It was funny, the times I had been in the hospital; they didn't seem quite real. For a while I thought I'd never get out, that this, my real life, would be a memory, like a trick done with mirrors. So many ghosts followed me—quick friendships on locked wards, endless mouth checks with hard-faced nurses. The ghosts filled my paintings, worlds populated with earthbound saints and tormented devils. My own Faustian dilemma became a little clearer each year. If I took the pills, so I was told repeatedly, I could avoid the hospital. I could also kiss painting good-bye. So I juggled. This week I'd be good. I'd take the pills and hang the show. I'd take Ching to the vet for his monthly trim and nail clipping; I'd brush his coat till it shone like a well-curried horse's. I'd wear a silk jacket and turtle-neck to the opening. I'd take an Ativan to keep me calm. I'd ask Dr. Sturges for a prescription.

I looked at the roughed-out portrait I planned of Sturges. It made sense to finish it with lithium in my system. If I hurried I could include it in the show. There should be a psychiatrist somewhere in the gallery.

The phone rang.

Mom's voice searched my own like a diagnostic probe. "How's it going?"

"Not too bad . . . I got out yesterday. I was just try-ing to straighten things up."

"That's good. You have everything you need?"

"Yeah."

Long silence.

"Do you want to talk about what happened?"

"Not right now. Maybe later. I suppose it was my fault, again. But don't worry, things seem pretty stable. You know my show goes up next week? You and Dad coming down?"

"We'd like to. Maybe on the weekend."

"Just let me know; I'll make up the guest room. So how's Dad?"

We talked. Her voice soothed me. The two hundred miles' distance that separated us was essential to her sanity.

Now, whenever I crashed, it was into arms of my

own making. I would not burden my parents. They needed their denial too.

/

The next day I met Pamela for lunch at the crowded SoHo eatery. As we waited for our hamburgers and Caesar salad, we discussed the show and reviewed the catalog.

"What do you think?" she asked, pushing back a strand of abundant auburn hair.

I scanned the glossy brochure, a black-and-white photo of myself on the inside cover. "It looks good. Thanks."

"You nervous?" Her voice was warm, like my mother's.

"A little, not much. I need the money, that's for certain. Isn't that sad?"

"What, that you need money?"

"No, that I have to sell paintings. That somehow the work isn't free from materialistic pressures. Whatever happened to artistic purity?"

"Uh-huh. You got to eat. You got to pay the rent."

"I've got to pay my insurance premiums and all the charges they won't cover at the hospital. God, I'm not looking forward to that. Every time I get one of those bills it just astounds me. Like, how the hell am I going to pay this?"

"How many days were you in?"

"Fourteen."

"That's a lot of money."

"I know. They'll probably cancel my policy. But I better not think about that . . . I sure hope we sell some paintings."

"Any problems with the university?" she asked, wondering if I'd sabotaged my day job.

"No, at least I don't think so. I got sick mostly over spring break. Only a couple people know. I think as long as I get shows they'll continue to renew my contract."

"Good."

A waiter came with our salads and ceremoniously broke the yolks. He ground in pepper, tossed and served.

"Oh, there's going to be one more painting for this show," I told her.

"Really?"

"It's not finished, but it needs to be there."

"I suppose that's okay. It obviously won't be in the catalog. We'll just leave a space for it. Do I get to see it first?"

"It's just a portrait."

"Whose?"

"My shrink."

She paused, her large brown eyes, surrounded with tiny wrinkles, met mine, an anchovy dangled from her fork. "Great . . . now it's my turn. I don't even know if I should bring it up, but it's been bothering me."

"What?"

"It's strange"—she watched me for my reaction—"three of your paintings went on the block at Christie's while you were in the hospital."

"No kidding. How did they do?"

"Well. Actually, better than well. Your high end just doubled. Two of them went for around ten; the third came close to fifteen."

"Jesus! Pity I don't get to see any of that. Which ones were they?"

"That's the strange part." She fixed me with her gaze.

"What?"

"All right. I'll just say it. Are you looking for another agent?"

"What are you talking about?"

"I'm trying to figure out why I've never seen these paintings. They're not ones I brokered." She pulled an illustrated auction catalog from her pocketbook and flipped open to a page marked with a yellow Post-it. "They're definitely yours. Old you. But you."

I took the catalog and quickly located the three paintings. Blood rushed to my head. "Where did these come from?" My fingers tingled. "These were never meant to be sold." I looked across at her. "Where did they come from?"

"I was hoping you knew."

"Did you call the auction house?"

"They wouldn't tell me. They're pretty sticky about that. They did say they would try and inform the seller

7

that I wanted to contact them. But it would be up to them whether or not they got back to me."

"Shit! Look at them. God, they were never meant to be sold."

I stared at the images, violent paintings of shattered glass, with demons and madmen trapped inside the jagged slivers. Next to each, Pamela had recorded the selling prices, not including the taxes and 10 percent buyer's premium that the auction house tacked on: $10,500, $14,000, $9,000. The most expensive one was of a giant mirror being smashed by a robed figure with long red hair. Inside the glass, an army of angels waited to be freed, above it the words: PREPARE THE WAY.

"I can't fuckin' believe this! How the hell did this happen?" I wanted to yell at her. "Where did they come from?"

"I don't know, Chad." She tried to calm me. "In some ways maybe it's a good thing. It does set a high-water mark right before the opening of the show. Of course, we don't get a cent of it. But maybe something good can come out of it."

"They weren't meant to be sold." I tried to stay in my seat, tried to fight back the urge to walk away. "Look at them! Shit!"

She watched me silently.

"God! These are crap. These weren't meant to be seen, let alone sold. I just can't understand where they came from." I looked at Pamela, a fleeting thought: *Would she do this?*

"When did you paint them?" she asked, a trace of fear in her voice.

"Right." I knew exactly when I made them. "Pamela, I can't stay here right now. This has got me too worked up. I need to get away."

"That's okay. Are you going to be all right?"

"Who knows? I'm probably overreacting. Isn't that what I do? Look, I'm sorry, I got to walk or do something." My face was flushed. I needed air.

"Call me if you want."

"Fine. I'll talk to you later." I abandoned my untouched burger and pushed my way out of the crowded restaurant.

That night, I worked on the portrait. It felt a little better, the canvas not quite so distant, so blank. Paint gobbed and squished out of the tubes and onto the palette. My fingers, too clean and flabby, moved stiffly, tentatively. *It's okay*, I told myself, *be sweet. It'll be there*. I felt with the brush, daubing in and out of molten color. My hands still shook, but not as much. I pushed away a pang of guilt.

"So, Chad," he'll say to me, knowing I skipped my meds, "any problems with the medication?"

"No," I'll lie, "it's fine. Everything's fine." I'll smile, let him see that I'm happy—not too happy, happy enough.

"How are things?" he'll ask. "Are you painting? Getting out?"

"Fine, fine, everything's good."

A scream gathered inside; I funneled the impulse through my body and down my arm. My fingers tingled. They jammed and twisted in the paint, the brush thickened with yellow and red. The clarity of primary colors, kindergarten shades, lost innocence as they bled and swirled.

Hours floated by, a primal sense of time as night gave way to the rosy glamour of a newborn sun.

Why have I drawn this?

I sipped another cup of forbidden coffee. Words returned and gave voice to the unformed. "Why did you paint this?" Guilt tweaked my thoughts. "No, I've done nothing wrong." My painted therapist disagreed, his bearded face caught in a split of light and dark.

Why have I drawn him? Do I want him to see it? My painting impresses him. But, it's what I do. He impresses me. It's what he does. I should take my lithium. I shouldn't be drinking coffee. I shouldn't have stayed up all night. I shouldn't have this buzz in my brain and in my body—feels so good.

"Oh God, what have I done?"

Sometime after seven, I finished the portrait and dumped the rest of the coffee down the drain. It was cold anyway. Dutifully, the prodigal son returned to the bathroom, to his pill bottles.

I was a little unbalanced; lithium was a salt, so I was told, it balanced me. Frankly, I liked imbalance, at least parts of it. The downside I could do without, but that always followed, didn't it? "Remember, Chad, you take the lithium so as not to get depressed." Of course, that was only half of it. No thrills, no spills. Couldn't have one without the other. Couldn't lose one without losing the other. At least painting kept me quiet, better than Ativan.

I tried to focus on the still-wet canvas. It wasn't the most technically proficient thing I'd done, but that's what I wanted. The fine tremor in my hands giving testimony in acrylic. The colors warped to the orange, an intentional by-product of incandescent light. It wasn't bad. Pacing around it, I watched the eyes, trying to calm myself. Not bad.

I wonder if he'll go to the show? He never does. What will he think? And again the thought: Why have I drawn this? I want it in the show, no doubt there. But why? I'm not overly fond of Dr. Sturges, he's more utilitarian than inspirational. His eyes, those of a competent psychiatrist, are my barometer. At $175 an hour I watch for their dark reflection, their reading. How do they see me today? Am I manic? Again the avenging berserker armed with the power of God? Will I trust him enough to bring me down from blissful heights?

"So," I said to the portrait, "how am I today? Am I okay? Why am I going to put a price tag on my psychiatrist and try to sell him in SoHo? Hmmm, you say."

I thought of the pictures that had sold at auction.

I felt the seeds of anger. Who could have had them? I hadn't seen them in years. Maybe Pamela was right. Done is done. Nothing I could do about it.

I walked through the loft turning off lights, Ching tagging along at my side. Outside my seven windows facing north on Fourteenth Street, the Empire State and Chrysler buildings glowed white. I stood there, watching them, enjoying the familiar, finally glad to be home.

"I painted your portrait," I told him, not able to look him directly in the eye.

"Really?" The long pause. He waited, his dark, hawk-like eyes watching me from where he sat in his over-stuffed black leather chair.

"I don't know why. I never know what a painting will be until it's finished. Sometimes, I have an idea, or two ideas that link when I start, but I never know exactly . . . I'm hanging it in my show."

"Did you think I'd object?"

"I don't know. I feel sort of bratty, almost juvenile, like a kid drawing pictures of the teacher and passing them around behind her back. I don't think that's it, though. Not all of it. I think it has more to do with going back into the hospital." I looked up at him and mentally traced the lines in his brow. Long ago I had memorized his features—it was a talent. As some people have a photographic memory for things they read, I had one for visual recall. I never forgot a face.

"Tell me about that," he said, intruding on my visual exploration of his earlobe.

"The hospital?"

"Uh-huh."

"What's to tell? I don't really want to talk about it. I suppose it's my fault."

"What do you mean?"

"To get real mechanistic, I could say it was the push to get the show together that sent me over. On some level, I made it happen."

"Explain that."

"I didn't have enough work for the show. I'd sold some pieces privately that I'd been planning to use as focal points. So I had a choice. I could borrow the pieces back for the show, which would have filled the walls, or I could paint some new ones. See, the problem with pictures that aren't for sale is those are the ones that people want, or at least think they want. Like, these *must* be the good ones, or the valuable ones, because someone else has already bought them. We all want what we can't have. So that was part of it. Also, I need the money. But that's not it either, at least not entirely." I paused, not wanting to say what came next.

"What is?"

"My art. Doesn't that sound pompous? But it's true. At times I feel like a total fraud. Painting, at least my painting, is about rhythm and flow. A sort of truth. This is where it gets flaky. I think I started out wanting to get more pictures for the show and somehow something got kindled. I was painting every night, teaching classes during the day and sleeping less and less. I knew what was happening. I was getting high, but the work got better and better. And there was a point, I remember this, where I gave in and let it happen. It seemed more honest."

"The mania?"

"Yeah."

"Could you have stopped it?"

I let the bomb drop. "I could have been taking my lithium."

We looked at each other. I knew he already knew; my lithium level was zero when I got admitted. I had been off it for three weeks.

"You imagine I'm angry with you?" he asked.

"Yeah."

"What about the other way around?"

"I don't follow."

"Are you mad at me?"

"For what? Not stopping me? God, I suddenly got this hit of déjà vu. I've been here before. I've had this conversation. Not with you, with Dr. Adams."

"Your first psychiatrist."

"Right. I can see him, his office, the contours of his face."

"What about him?"

"I miss him. Not that I don't think you do a good job . . . but . . . he saved my life—or at least showed me how to get through it."

14

"What would he say about your being hospitalized?"

"I don't know . . . we'd probably talk about the good parts of being manic. I wonder what it would be like to be high all the time and have people leave you alone. Of course, I tend to break things when I'm manic. But not this time. I just painted. And they're incredible. Almost like I took a calculated risk and went too far. I do that a lot. It's sort of like Adam and Eve."

"How's that?"

"Well, they were in the Garden of Eden, which was pretty decent, but there was something even better and they were told they couldn't have it. I know my work is better if I'm a little high. There's a lot of precedent. But I'm dribbling on."

"We are going to have to end soon. Are you sleeping?"

"Fair." I opted for the half-truth. He didn't need to know I hadn't slept more than four hours in the past three days. "I was wondering if you could give me a few more Ativan. I think I want to take one before the opening and maybe the night before so I get to sleep."

"That's fine." He scribbled on a prescription pad. "I'm going to want a lithium level." He said this without looking up.

"Fine."

"You find it intrusive?" he asked.

"You're checking up on me. Making sure I'm taking the pills."

"What do you suggest?"

"Get the level."

He handed me the prescription. "See you next week."

Halfway to the door, I stopped. "I forgot . . ." I handed him one of the glossy postcard-size announcements for my show. It was a photo reproduction of *Landscape Number Five*, a painting of the view outside my window. In it the buildings were transparent; their occupants, all insane, were trapped in domestic rituals. "I'd like you to come."

"Thank you." He took the card.

I didn't move. A suspicion sprang to life.

He looked at me. "Yes?"

"Some paintings, old ones, came up to auction while I was in the hospital. I don't know where they came from."

"Why are you telling me this?"

He clearly wanted me out the door.

"They were pictures I did ten years ago in an art-therapy group at Bellevue. They were never meant to be sold. Until yesterday, I didn't know they still existed."

"Why tell me this now?"

I knew it was the wrong thing to say; I couldn't stop myself. "You were there. Someone obviously took them and it would have to be someone who was there."

He stared at me, incredulous. "You think I stole your paintings?"

"I don't know. Did you? You always talk about how much you admire my work."

Silence.

He lowered his voice, "Are you taking your pills? You're sounding paranoid."

"Oh. Great!" I hit the side of my head as they do on the V-8 commercial. *"Chad has a problem, so he's got to be paranoid. Fucking great!* What is so wrong about my thinking and so right about yours? Why is it always my problem? Someone made over thirty thousand dollars off my work. Stuff I didn't want anyone to see. Wouldn't you be upset? Wouldn't you be suspicious? Or do you maybe not believe that it happened? Would you like proof?"

"We need to talk about this, Chad." He tried to calm me. "But I can't right now."

"Yes, I know, my hour's up. Do you know where those paintings came from?"

"We can talk about this next week."

"Stop dismissing me! I'm not a child. Just give me an answer. If you know something, tell me."

The telephone rang. We stood there, staring at each other, my breathing too heavy, his too controlled.

He picked up the receiver. "No," he said, "everything's okay. I'm almost done for the day. Bye."

He looked back at me. "We need to stop—now." He stood by the open door, his arms crossed over his chest.

I didn't move. "I want an answer."

"Chad, leave."

"Or what? You'll lock me up?" I knew I shouldn't push it, that I was right on the edge. "Fine."

I stormed out of his office and slammed the door.

CHAPTER TWO

Morning came. I rolled in bed, Ching at my feet, the metallic taste of lithium in my mouth. My mind raced, flitting from anxious thought to anxious thought: *It's the show today, take a bath, your bank account is empty, brush the dog, your school-loan payment is overdue.*

I searched for something to pull me out of the bed, into the bathroom and into the tub. I thought about the gallery, the crush of people expected to be there. *They'll mill about the paintings, discussing them, offering profundities, putting them in reference to things familiar: "They remind me of early Chagall." "No, too much realism, more like Matisse or even Balthus." I'll pretend not to hear. I'll stay calm. I'll pee.*

Ching nipped at my heels and tried to steer me from the bathroom on my left to the kitchen, and his food bowls, on the right.

"All right," I moaned, giving in to his priorities.

I poured fresh water and rattled high-tech kibble into his bowl. He was happy, all fuzzy red and glad to see me after my two-week hiatus. I needed to get the downstairs neighbors something for looking after him. I'd just put it on plastic. Why did I obsess about money so much? *Because you don't have any.* True. And not true. I calculated how much I could make if all my paintings sold, if half sold, if a quarter sold. I set up the coffeemaker, negotiating how many cups to make. I didn't want to be too buzzed, but then again . . . I filled it to number six.

The portrait of Dr. Sturges stood on the easel in the middle of the loft. Wrapped in brown paper, its contents pulsed a peculiar energy. *I can't believe I was such an asshole yesterday.*

I put Mahler's Third Symphony on, poured my tub, and sent Ching running back and forth the length of the loft in pursuit of his red rubber ball.

It started. The opening crowd trickled in. Some of them I knew by face, some by type. My friends soaked up free wine and scarfed down hors d'oeuvres. They whispered catty things to me in passing.

Pamela, dressed in burgundy velvet and Victorian jet jewelry, schmoozed a pair of potential buyers. "Of course, you have to love it," she said, shepherding the well-heeled couple, "but it's also an investment." They nodded. "Chadwick Greene, whom I'd like you to meet, is the youngest living artist with a painting in the MOMA." She rattled off my accomplishments, adding a bit, deleting a bit, never quite crossing to the realm of fantasy. "And for the last three years," she continued, "his work has been included in the Whitney's 'New Artists' exhibit. This is his fifth major show in four years, and he already has a track record at Butterfield's, and Christie's. Which"—lowering her voice—"has been phenomenal—amazing appreciation."

"What about this one?" the woman asked. "It's disturbing."

I liked her quick appraisal of my *Woman and Child in the Park*. I broke in.

"Hi."

"Speak of the devil. This is Chadwick Greene. Chad, I'd like you to meet the Jensens, George and Cynthia."

We shook hands.

"I like this painting," Cynthia said, extending her well-manicured hand. A heavy gold Bulgari leopard bracelet brushed my fingertips. "I like it very much, but there's something about it that's sort of menacing. Do you know what I mean?"

"Something in their expressions," her husband offered.

"I didn't know if that would carry. What do you see?" I asked.

"Excuse me, Chad." Serge, the gallery director, tapped me on the shoulder. "There's someone I want you to meet."

I left the Jensens to ponder the seemingly harmless portrait of a mother and small child holding a balloon. The model for the mother was a woman tormented by paranoid schizophrenia. She believed there were babies trapped inside her. Occasionally she would try to get at them with the plastic cutlery they gave us at Glendale. The child was a little girl I had seen in an emergency room. I didn't know why she was there, but something in her stillness spoke to me of unnameable sorrow.

I nodded in passing to a pair of local artists scoping the scene and was deposited before a balding man in his fifties.

"Chadwick Greene," said Serge, my name sounding like a salad coming through his East-European accent, "this is Harold Schlemer; he reviews for *New York Scene*."

"Nice show," he said. "Your work changes a lot."

"It does." *I never know what to say to critics.*

"Is that intentional?"

"No. It happens." I looked at him closer. "It's part of the process. The work changes and I don't really know how or why."

"Would you mind if I recorded you?"

"That's fine."

"As you were saying?"

"About process, it just happens. You can influence it to a degree, but it's almost automatic."

"What about technique?"

"Has to be there. At least for me. I'm too vain to allow something to not be well-drawn—when drawing matters. There's freedom with strong technique. That's why I teach. A, it's a steady paycheck, and B, I never stop learning. But technique gets buried, like a foundation. When I paint, I'm rarely conscious of technique. It should just be there."

"And subject?"

"I sometimes start with an idea, but it's just a start. Like planting a seed from an unmarked package. You don't know if it's going to be a pumpkin or a summer squash."

"What about this one?"

I looked at *Clara's Portrait*. "It's someone I knew."

"Is that all?"

"No. But let me ask you: What do you see?"

He stood back and stared into the picture. "She's fragmented. It's a whole person, but her pieces don't quite fit. Parts of her are alluring, and others . . . almost repulsive."

"Right. That was Clara. She killed herself. I painted her from memory. I think I wanted to understand more. Who she was, why she suicided."

"Did you find that?"

"I found my explanation. It may or may not have been hers. She felt empty. I think she eventually gave in to that, let it swallow her."

"What was it like to paint that?"

"Odd. Very emotional. I deliberately shifted to a more 'up' painting when I was done. I thought about doing happy clowns on black velvet, but with my luck they would have been evil child-eating clowns."

"What did come next?"

"Excuse me." Pamela draped a crushed-velvet arm

on my shoulder and whispered, "The Jensens are buying *Woman and Child*." She kissed my cheek. "Do you mind if I drag him away?" Not offering a choice, she pulled me back into the growing crowd.

The critic followed. "Would you be willing to set up a time for a full interview? I'd like to talk to you about your work and process."

I resisted Pamela's tenacious grip and gave him a card with my university studio number. "Just give me a call."

"Mr. Greene." One of my undergrads, dressed in army boots, fishnets and black hot pants, flagged me down. She gushed, "This must be so exciting. God, I would kill for this."

"Thanks."

"I saw your piece at the Whitney, but this is so much more powerful. It's out there, just awesome."

"Thanks for coming." Her face glowed with the light of too much complimentary chardonnay.

I looked around and picked out several more of my students, in club-kid black, milling about. It was a good sign. An opening was like a party. The mix was crucial: buyers, artists, agents, wannabees, has-beens, friends, ex-lovers, family, and people who talked too loud. Everyone wanted a piece of the spotlight and some free booze. But, as Pamela said, "The more booze, the better." Nothing finer to fuel conversations and to open wallets.

"No," a middle-aged woman snapped at her befuddled swain, "this has nothing to do with postmodernism."

I caught snippets of conversations, grateful for my height, about six feet three, which kept my eyes and ears above most of the bubbling brew.

Pamela, however, was a woman with a purpose. She dragged me like a pull toy from pillar to post. Tonight's opening would make or break the entire show.

But what's this?

A man and a woman in dark, rack-bought suits and conservative haircuts carved a path toward us.

They don't fit.

"What's up?" Pamela asked, looking up, sensing she had lost me.

"I don't know. I think we're going to find out."

"Mr. Greene?" the man asked.

"Yes."

He flashed a police shield. "I'm Detective Collins and this is Detective Bryant. Is there someplace we could talk, alone?"

My mood plummeted. "There's an office. Could you tell me what this is about?"

Before he could answer, his partner pulled his attention. "Dave, look at that. It's him." They stood in profile viewing the well-lit portrait of Dr. Sturges.

"What's this about?" I repeated.

The woman turned to me, her expression blank. "We should probably talk in private."

I looked at Pamela. "Mind the fort, would you?"

"Sure." Concern clouded her face.

"Come with me." I pushed through the crowd toward the storage room and back offices. I smiled and nodded to well-wishers, my face stiff as a mask, my mouth sucked dry.

Police made me nervous. Invariably I saw them in uniform when I was in the midst of mania and they were carting me away.

"In here." I ushered them into a small private viewing room.

We stood looking at each other; no one spoke. It was a game: whoever said the first word would lose, or at least be vulnerable. I watched them watching me, making their mental observations, fixing their first impressions.

Finally, the woman spoke. "You knew Philip Sturges?"

"Yes, he's my psychiatrist." *Why the past tense?*

"When did you see him last?"

"Yesterday."

"What time?"

"Four. Why?"

"Did you see him anytime later in the day?"

"No. Could you tell me why you're asking these questions?"

Detective Collins answered, his eyes fixed on my face, staring into me, "Philip Sturges was found murdered last night—in his office."

"Oh my God." I flashed on my doctor, his face embedded in my mind, his eyes, his voice. The air rushed out of me, as if I'd had a fist to the gut. "Oh my God."

"Were you close?" she asked.

"He was my doctor."

"But you included his picture in your show?"

"Yes, I did."

"Why would you do that?"

"I don't know. Would you mind if I got a glass of water? My mouth is very dry." *What is going on here?* I poured from the minibar, the tremor in my hands grew stronger, coarser. *Dr. Sturges is dead, murdered. Oh God, what must he have felt?* Images of suffering, Sturges's face twisted in pain, forced themselves into my consciousness. "Do you mind if I sit down?"

"How long did you know the doctor?"

"A long time. I've been with him since I came to the city, probably fifteen years."

"Then you knew him well."

"Not really. How much do you really know about your psychiatrist? They don't say a lot about themselves."

"Could you tell us what you do know?"

"I don't mean to be difficult, but am I a suspect? Should I have a lawyer?"

"That's up to you. At the moment we're just asking questions."

"I see. I suppose that's all right. He was always on time." *God, is that the most I can say for the man?* "It's so weird."

"What?"

"That he's dead. I'm supposed to see him next week

and I can't register that he won't be there to open the door."

"What time did you say you last saw him?" Bryant asked.

"Three. It was always three."

"I thought you said four?" The man pounced on the inconsistency.

"It was four—I mean that I last saw him. The appointment was at three, so I left at four. I always saw him at three." His question flustered me. "My sense was he was very busy. Anytime I needed to change an appointment he rarely had an open slot."

"Why did you go to him?"

"I have bipolar disorder."

"What is that?"

"It used to be called manic-depression."

"And he was helping you for that."

"That's right."

"How would he do that?"

"I'm on medication for it. That, and we talk."

"What kind of medication?"

"Mostly lithium."

"Mostly? What else?"

"Ativan, sometimes; some Trilafon."

"What are those?"

"Tranquilizers." I didn't want to tell them that Trilafon was an antipsychotic. My awareness tuned into the steady roar of humanity in the other room; like a rushing in my ears, the situation flooded me. *Someone murdered Dr. Sturges.*

"Where were you last night?"

"At home."

"Was anyone with you?"

"No."

"Is there anyone who could vouch for your whereabouts?"

"No . . . I made a couple phone calls, took the dog for a walk, that kind of stuff."

"Who did you call? And when?"

"My agent; probably a little after eight. Oh, and my ex-wife called before that, maybe seven thirty. Who else? That might have been it. I'm having trouble remembering. Can I ask you something?"

"Yes."

"From these questions it seems like I'm a suspect. Is that true? He must have had dozens of patients. I don't understand. Do you spend this much time with everyone?"

The woman, her face already burned into my memory, answered. "We have reason to think that Dr. Sturges was going to be here tonight. We also have reason to think that someone didn't want him to attend. But I can tell we've taken up enough of your time. You need to get back to your opening. If you think of anything that might be helpful . . . here's my card. Thanks for your time."

We shook hands and they exited through the gallery.

As I tried to stand my knees buckled.

Somebody killed Dr. Sturges. Why? Angry tears began to fall. And then the awful realization—that I was a suspect—that I had intentionally withheld information about my tantrum with the doctor. My mind raced against the backdrop of the opening's hubbub.

How could I be such an idiot? I'm going to need a lawyer. This sucks.

CHAPTER THREE

A door opened. Gallery noise and Pamela's head pushed through.

"You okay?"

"I suppose. Maybe not."

She looked over her shoulder. "Oh well," she said, and closed the door. "What did they want?"

"Dr. Sturges is dead. He was murdered."

"Your psychiatrist? Jesus!" She sank down next to me.

"Yeah."

"I'm really sorry." She paused, watching me. "What did they want with you?"

"I'm not sure exactly. Questions, mostly. And then the woman"—her card was still in my hand—"Detective Susan Bryant, Sixth Precinct, she said something odd. Like it's somehow my fault."

"What did she say?"

"That they thought Dr. Sturges was going to be here tonight and that someone didn't want him to come. How could they know that? I gave him one of the postcards for the opening. But that doesn't make sense. Maybe he put it in his book. But why would anyone care whether or not he came?"

"I don't know."

31

"This is weird. You know the saddest part is they were asking me what I knew about him. And that's just it. After fifteen years, he knew everything about me and I knew nothing about him. I don't know if he was married. If he had kids. Nothing. Do you think I need a lawyer?"

"You haven't been charged with anything."

"I know, but I feel like I should do something. And there's something else."

"What?"

"The last time I saw him, we fought. Or at least I did. You know those paintings that sold when I was in the hospital?"

"What about them?"

"I did those ten years ago when I was at Bellevue. I haven't seen them since. I thought he might have taken them. I still don't know . . . I want to get his portrait out of the show."

She hesitated. "You can't do that."

"Excuse me?"

She looked at her hands. "It's been sold."

"In the last five minutes?"

"You weren't there. And besides, that's what I'm supposed to do."

"You're right. We're just going to have to unsell it."

"Chad"—I could feel her pull back—"we can't do that."

"Why not?"

"It's gone."

"What! How could it be gone? Paintings never leave in the middle of the show. I don't care if they're sold or not! What were you thinking?"

"I'm sorry. But I know you need the money and he was very insistent."

"Who?" I began to pace.

"The buyer."

"Yes, I realize that, but who was it?"

She didn't answer.

"You don't have his name? How is that possible?"

She looked up, her large dark eyes near tears. "He paid cash. He said the buyer wanted to remain anonymous."

"What? I'm just speechless. How could you do that?"

"It's what I'm supposed to do. Look, Chad. I didn't know what was going on back here. My job, for which you pay me 25 percent, is to sell your paintings. That's what I was doing. And it wasn't five minutes—you were in here over an hour. I kept waiting for you to come out after the police left. I started to get worried."

I let that sink in; *an hour?* "Is he still here? Maybe I can buy it back?"

"I don't think so. He had Serge wrap the painting and he left."

"My head feels like it's going to pop. The cops will love this."

"I'm really sorry, Chad. But this has got to work out, somehow. Can I say something really crass?"

"Sure."

"At least now you have the money for a lawyer."

"How much?"

"After commissions . . . ten thousand."

"No shit?" I felt a different sort of shock; I'd never sold a painting for that much. "Your idea?"

"You told me to mark it up, didn't you?"

"Sure, but I wanted to strike a deal with Dr. Sturges. I'd trade him the painting for a year's worth of therapy. I thought he might go for it. I can't believe he's dead. I need to get out of here. I've got to think." Then I stopped. "Tell me what you do remember."

"About what?"

"The man who bought the portrait. What did he look like?"

"Chad, can we do this later? One of us has to take care of business."

"Just tell me what he looks like, then I'll get out of here."

"All right. He looked like an NYU type, sort of professorial: short, full beard, had one of those Scottish-tweed caps. Maybe in his thirties, maybe forties. He had glasses, I think they were tortoise frames. The thing that astounded me was the cash. I thought it might have been counterfeit, but Serge says this type of thing happens every so often. Someone comes in, no questions asked, and pulls out a wad of money. No mess. No fuss."

"How did he have the money?"

"It was in an envelope, all hundred-dollar bills. I kept thinking it was like drug money or something. But he didn't look the type. Of course, what do I know about that?"

"What did he say?"

"You're not going to let me get back, are you?"

"What did he say? Why did he want that picture?"

"He didn't say. Serge came up to me, said someone wanted to buy the portrait and wanted to know how much. It wasn't in the catalog, and I couldn't find you, so I just picked a number and figured if it was too high we could negotiate later—if he was serious. He didn't argue. I kept looking to see if you were around; it happened very fast. He looked at me—green eyes, very intense, bright, they reminded me of those colored contacts, they may have been. But why would someone wear contacts with glasses? He just looked at me, like he knew I'd jacked up the price, and then he said, 'Fine, I'll take it. Could you wrap it?' And then he started to count out the money. I've never seen that much cash."

"Didn't you tell him that sold paintings don't leave until after the show comes down?"

"We tried. I kept looking for you, wanting to slow him down. But I kept seeing the money. I knew it would pay almost your entire hospital bill. Serge was going great guns; I figured what the hell."

"This is too bizarre. Why that painting? Did he say?"

"I don't think so. I've really got to get out there,

now. We can talk later. And Chad"—she stopped on her way back to the gallery—"I'm really sorry about your psychiatrist."

"Thanks." I watched her leave, sampling the hub-bub of my show as the door opened and closed.

I was still holding Detective Bryant's card; they'd want to know about this. I quickly dialed and was electronically directed to her voice mail after first being instructed: "If this is an emergency, press 'one' now."

"This is Chadwick Greene. Something odd happened. The portrait of Dr. Sturges was sold for cash while you were interviewing me. I thought you might want to know . . . and there's something else . . ." I left my home and university numbers.

My hands shook less and my knees felt a little steadier. Still, a prn [as needed] Ativan would have been nice. Before escaping through the loading bay into the alley behind the gallery, I popped the small white oval and swallowed it dry.

I'm going to need a new psychiatrist.

Outside, it was Saturday night in SoHo. I melted into the trendy crowds on West Broadway and let them sweep me by the front of my show as I headed north to Fourteenth Street. It was a view I'd never seen, like watching my own funeral. All the well-wishers gathered inside, milling about with plastic cups of wine. I lingered briefly, and then slipped away. But I did store the image for future use.

The walk went fast. The late-May night, combined with the Ativan, wrapped me in a comfortable buzz. I was still focused on Dr. Sturges, but it bothered me less as the veil of tranquilizer thickened.

I stopped at the newsstand on Eighth Street. And there it was. On the lower right of the front page of the *Post:* VILLAGE SHRINK MURDERED. I grabbed one of each daily and as I prepared to pay, quietly blurted, "Throw in a pack of Sherman's red box." I considered taking it back, but right then I needed a smoke. One box did not a habit make.

I tucked the papers under my arm, broke the seal on the smokes, inhaled the sweet familiar tobacco, and lit up. So much better, that first taste, like a friend I'd left behind. Maybe I'd go back to smoking—just for a little.

The Eighth Street crowd was thick, rowdy and young. Kids from Jersey and Long Island mixed with NYU undergrads. They spilled half-drunk and stoned out of tourist bars and T-shirt shops. I wove my way through the masses, and at the end of the block cut north up Sixth Avenue.

The more I thought about Dr. Sturges, the queerer I felt. *Why would someone do this? And what were the cops talking about? "Someone didn't want him to go to your show." How could they know that?*

I ducked into the closed doorway of Balducci's gourmet food store, ostensibly to light another smoke. I looked back down the street, my first concession to growing paranoia. It was just the weekend crowd in the West Village. *Nothing wrong here. No one is following you.*

I looked again. *It must be me.* Wouldn't be the first time. In fact, paranoia was one of my warning symptoms. Like an aura that preceded my getting carted off to the emergency room. Mania returned in stages. Over the years I'd learned the signs. Sometimes I could cut things off before they got out of control. Paranoia was not a "usual" for me, it was a "sometimes." But it was as familiar as a pack of cigarettes and as dangerous as a gun. I should have resisted, before suspiciousness blossomed into a fear-filled cage that locked me inside my loft. I'd stay like that, slowly starving myself, certain that my food and water had been poisoned.

I took one last look.

Nothing is there. Just go home.

And so I did, ignoring a mounting inner panic. It was just the nicotine; I wasn't used to it.

I climbed the four flights of stairs to my loft. Everything was okay, as it should have been. And then I reached the landing . . .

"Oh shit." My stomach dropped when I first saw the steel security door—wide open. I heard the sound of a dog, my dog, whimpering. "Oh shit. Ching!"

I ran into the darkened loft and flipped on the lights. "Oh my God. Ching." My beautiful bear of a dog lay in front of the fire-escape window covered in broken glass and blood. "Oh God." I ran to him, kneeling in glass. "Ching, it's okay." I tried to locate the source of the blood. "It's okay." I fought back the tears. My fingers grew sticky as they searched out the contours of a small wound buried in his fur. I ripped off my jacket, wrapped it around his chest and tied the expensive silk sleeves in a knot to apply pressure.

All around me was carnage. Someone had torn the place apart, but it was only things. All I cared about was getting Ching to the vet. I grabbed a thick blanket from off my bed and swaddled him. He made little noise, his breathing was shallow. I bundled his seventy pounds in my arms. *I should call somebody.* But I couldn't think who, and a quick look at my wall phone, torn from the socket, made the point moot.

I raced down the stairs, leaving my loft open. *Don't think. Just get him to the vet.*

CHAPTER FOUR

"Are you going to be okay?"

I focused on the scrubs-clad veterinarian's assistant, and her expression of concern. *Do I look that bad?* "I'm having a rough night." Understatement suited the circumstance. It wouldn't be right to blast her with the truth. My shrink had been murdered; my dog, apparently, shot; my apartment ransacked; and all this with me just three days out of the hospital. "How's Ching?"

"It's too soon to tell. He lost a lot of blood, but the bullet missed his heart."

"How long till I can see him?"

"I don't know. They've got to stop the bleeding. It could be a couple hours."

I sat there taking it in, a numbness in my limbs. *I've got to keep moving.* "Do you have a water fountain and a phone I could use?"

"Sure, I'll get you some water and you can use the desk behind the counter. Just dial nine first."

I settled at the receptionist's ordered workstation, a place for everything and everything in its place. *So what am I doing here? And what am I supposed to do next? It's eleven o'clock; my opening is winding down some fifteen blocks away.*

"Here's your water."

She waited. "Have you called the police about your dog yet?"

"No." And then I remembered. "My phone was ripped out of the wall."

"What happened?"

"I don't know. Someone was in my apartment."

"Did you see them?"

"No, they were gone. Or at least I think they were." I felt a different sort of fear. "But you're right, I need to call the police." I fished out Detective Bryant's blood-smeared card and called. At the recorded direction of "If this is an emergency, press 'one' now," I did.

"Sixth Precinct."

"Hi, this is Chad Greene. I need to speak to Detective Susan Bryant."

"Detective Bryant isn't in. Can this wait till the morning?"

"I don't know. I don't think so. My apartment was broken into tonight and someone shot my dog."

"Detective Bryant is homicide. This wouldn't—"

"I'm sorry," I interrupted. "This may have something to do with a homicide she's investigating. I think she'd want to know. Is there any way you could call her, let her know?"

"I could page her"—he clearly didn't want to—"but it sounds like a routine burglary. I'll send a patrol car. What's the address and phone number?"

I gave him the address. "I'm not there right

now . . . And the phone's been ripped out. I'm at the Village Veterinarian. I could be there in five minutes."

"Is there any possibility that the perpetrator is still in your apartment?"

"I don't think so . . . I don't know."

He paused. "What's the number and address where you are now?"

I searched the desk and spotted a flyer for "The Village Veterinarian's WELL-PUPPY CLINIC." I read him the information.

"I'll send a car to pick you up there."

"And you will page Detective Bryant?"

"I'll page her."

"Thanks."

We hung up.

I looked at the water. I had missed my evening dose of lithium; nothing was worse than taking them without food. I weighed the pain of the heavy pills tearing into my stomach lining versus the risk of "losing it." I opted for pain and swallowed two 300-hundred milligram pale pink tablets.

"What you taking?" the receptionist asked.

A perfectly innocuous question, which still took me by surprise. "Just some medication."

"They're so big, don't they bother you going down?"

"A little. It's better to take them with food, but I forgot."

"You know, I bet we've got something around here. Allen always leaves boxes of crackers and stuff around. Of course, if he were here"—she was warming to her topic—"he could find them himself. Don't you hate that?"

"What?" I didn't really want to talk.

"When people you barely know just ask you for all sorts of favors. Like, gee, I have nothing better to do on my Saturday night than work a double shift. But of course, everyone knows 'Helen is such a *good sport*. Just ask Helen, she'll do it. Helen won't mind'!"

I told her I was fine without crackers; which didn't slow her discourse on "Man's Inhumanity to Helen."

God, I wish I had a cigarette. I was remembering the box of Shermans in the breast pocket of my blood-soaked jacket. The thought turned my stomach, or maybe it was just the pills.

Ten minutes later two uniformed officers walked into the lobby. "Chadwick Greene?" one of them asked, putting an end to Helen's verbal effluence.

"Yes." And so it started, again. They told me their names, we shook hands and one of them flipped out a small notepad and a pen.

"Could you tell us what happened tonight?"

"I came home." My voice sounded hollow and distant. "The door to my loft was open, and then I heard Ching, that's my dog, crying. He was in front of the fire escape, covered with blood; the window was broken. I don't remember much else, but the place was ransacked. There was stuff everywhere. I know the phone was torn out."

"Anything missing?"

"I don't know. I just grabbed Ching and came here . . . Is Detective Bryant coming?"

"She'll meet us at the apartment. You can ride with us."

"Okay, let me think. I need to check on my dog. I'll be right back." I went behind the receptionist's desk into the back. A crack of light seeped from under a single door; I heard muted voices and turned the knob.

Inside was a small operating room. Ching, recognizable only by a bloodied patch of fur, was surrounded by green drapes; his body lay still on the stainless-steel table.

"How is he?"

A tall masked and gowned man answered, an electric scalpel in his hand. "We've got the bleeding stopped; it looks worse than it is, really just a flesh wound. His pressure's holding good. He'll pull through."

"I've got to go with the police. I don't know where I'll be staying tonight. When should I call?"

"We'll know more in a couple hours."

"Thanks." I went back to the lobby and pocketed one of the clinic's brochures.

The officers escorted me out.

I half-expected a waiting ambulance, its lights flashing, ready and waiting to take me to the nearest psychiatric emergency room. Not tonight. I ducked into the back of the patrol car and we pulled away from the curb. I passively watched the nightscape through the bars of the police car. I noticed the doors without handles and felt a familiar powerlessness.

The entrance to my building was cordoned off with a strip of yellow police tape. A few locals and late-night walkers milled about, curious as to what would necessitate two police cruisers and an unmarked car. Flanked by the officers, I went in, up the four flights of ancient stairs and into my mural-covered lobby.

"You paint this?" one of them asked, taking in my version of Bosch's *The Garden of Earthly Delights*. Essentially, it was a glossy jungle scene that covered the walls and ceiling. Hidden in the foliage were all manner of beast and man. It was an experiment a few years back in the use of egg-tempera paint. It was a piece few people saw.

"Yeah."

"It's amazing."

"Thanks."

And then we entered the loft. I'd purposefully not been thinking about this. Denial failed in the face of chaos. It was too much. "Shit!" *Where do I look first?* Every drawer, every closet, every bookcase had been upended and emptied onto the floor.

"Mr. Greene." A familiar female voice.

"Detective Bryant."

"I'm sorry about your dog, and about this." She looked tired. Her suit had been replaced by a baggy sweatshirt and khakis.

"Thanks for coming. I didn't know if I should have

them call you or not. But this is all too strange. This whole day just isn't making sense."

"I'm glad you did."

I stood rooted, trying to take it in manageable bites. I felt her watching me, gauging my response.

"Do you notice anything missing?"

I tried to focus. "There, above the piano, there should be a triptych in a gold-leaf frame. And over the bed I had a series of woodblocks I'd done when I was a student." A pattern arose from the chaos. Blank spots on the wall, bare brick with empty hooks showed shadows of vanished paintings and drawings. Entire portfolio cases were missing, my Victorian print chest had been emptied of its contents.

Systematically she led me through my loft, my home, occasionally admonishing me, "Try not to touch anything until we've dusted for prints." The inventory of missing things, my things, things I never thought much about, grew. At one point she asked, "Do you have any insurance?"

"For my artwork? I don't think so. Maybe a little, I have some renter's insurance. I never thought to insure this stuff."

"What sort of value, dollarwise, would you place on the missing paintings?"

"Just the paintings?"

"No, everything."

"A lot." I looked at the list she'd compiled on a lined pad of paper. "My drawings—pencils and charcoals—have been going for about one hundred to five hundred dollars each. Whole books of sketches are gone; there are probably several hundred pieces there. Most of them aren't very good, but still, there's probably a couple hundred that are salable. Watercolors a bit more, maybe two-fifty to a thousand. There again, there were stacks of them. I often do series of watercolors before doing an oil or acrylic. And then the paintings, they've been shooting up. Someone bought one at the show tonight for over ten thousand dollars."

"Really? Congratulations."

"Yeah, that's something else you probably want to know about . . ." I told her about the sale of Doctor Sturges's portrait.

"Is that the only painting that sold today?"

"I know of one other, and after that, I was with you and then I left. So I don't know."

A uniformed policeman interrupted, "Detective Bryant, there's something I think you'll want to see."

"Excuse me." She was led off to the fire-escape landing.

I watched the officer's latex-gloved hand jiggle an obviously broken doorknob. He gestured to the shattered window, and then they disappeared onto the fire escape. I watched their backlit silhouettes through the windows. *The Empire State Building burns red tonight. I save it away, save it all away.*

A long time ago, when I was a student trying to be

normal, to fit in, my mentor, Jan Hobling, told me to paint into the heart of my pain, to search for emotion and to pursue it. It made sense, sort of like therapy. Only there the goal was catharsis, and with painting it was to capture something of power onto a canvas. As horrible as this night was, I'd save it away, take it out later, and look at it in pieces.

I wanted to call the vet. A second look at the phone told me I had a sixty-dollar service call before I could do that. My loft felt open and unsafe. The smashed window was like an open wound that oozed with the inky New York City night. Ching's blood stained the floor, my shirt, and my hands. I wanted a bath. I wanted my dog. *This will pass. Yeah? When?*

"Mr. Greene?" Bryant's expression was puzzled. "You said the door was open when you came in."

"That's right."

"You're certain of that?"

"Absolutely."

"What's on the roof?"

"Not much. A water tower, little else."

"How many ways are there to the roof?"

"Two . . . no, three, if you count both fire escapes."

She paused. "How many people live in the building?"

"Starting at the ground floor, there's the Indian Grocery, but they don't live here. Although sometimes, I think, one of the children, or somebody, stays overnight in the storeroom. They have a bed back there. On two is Willie's kung-fu dojo."

"Anyone live there?"

"Yeah, Willie and Carol, they have a kid and a couple of German shepherds. Right below me are the Richards. Nice people, they look after Ching whenever I go away . . . You don't have a phone I could use, do you? I want to check on my dog."

"You can use my cellular. Anyone else in the building?"

"The only other floor, the one upstairs, is empty. There used to be a bunch of people up there. It's the same size as my loft, only it's cut up into a lot of rooms."

"How come it's empty?"

"The landlord's trying to sell the building. It's a lot easier if you don't have people in rent-controlled spaces."

"How much do you pay?"

"Five hundred a month." I watched her expression, a mixture of disbelief and envy.

"How did you get it so cheap? This place must be a couple thousand square feet."

"Nah, just over a thousand; it looks bigger because of the windows."

"Still"—she pushed back her short dark hair—"I pay more than that for a one-bedroom hovel."

In the midst of hell night, I looked at her. Perhaps it was the familiarity of another New Yorker caught in the timeless discussion of comparative apartments. We must have been about the same age; she was attractive, but only on second look. She didn't wear

49

makeup and her hair was cut short for function. Her face was arresting (no pun intended). Unconsciously, I dissected her features into lines, planes and shadows. It was a fine face, balanced and intelligent.

She noticed my scrutiny. "On your message, you said there was something you didn't tell us before, something about Dr. Sturges."

"Right." I tried to remember back to the opening. It was only a few hours ago; it felt like days. "I fought with him, not physically, but I was angry about something and I let it out at him."

"What was it about?"

"Some paintings that were sold at auction. I thought he might have had something to do with it."

She asked me questions while a team of criminalists swarmed over my loft. I watched them photograph shattered glass and dust for fingerprints. One of them came out of my closet with a cellophane bag of wadded-up work clothes.

"What's he doing in my closet?"

"We need to be thorough. Which reminds me"—she retrieved her valise from beside the door. "Chad, because this is a crime scene, we will probably want to take a few things to be analyzed. Overall, it makes the evidence better if you've given us permission. This is called a Permission to Search." She pulled out a single-page document. "It's just a formality."

None of this seems real. I don't seem real.

"Chad?"

/ "What?" I realized I had begun to space out.

I met her gaze. I watched her struggle. *What is she thinking?*

I took the pen and signed.

"Thanks. You wanted to use the phone. You might also think about finding someplace else to stay tonight."

"I suppose you're right. I don't think I'm going to get much sleep, anyway. I don't want to leave."

"It might not be safe. We don't know if the motive is just robbery. Whoever's doing this is armed and possibly a murderer."

"You don't think this is a coincidence?"

"It's possible, but clearly, whoever broke in here wasn't on a random burglary. They knew what they wanted."

"They?"

"Too soon to tell."

"I'd rather stay. It'll be daylight soon. I'm going to need to call the locksmith, get some plywood for the window, clean this place up." I looked at her, watching me. *What does she see?* "And, I need to paint."

CHAPTER FIVE

I couldn't sleep. My head buzzed and my body tingled. It was four-thirty on a Sunday, too early to subcontract order back into my life. Nothing was open. The last cop left an hour earlier. Susan—or should that be Detective Bryant?—said good-bye after three. I wondered who waited for her—no wedding ring, no references to a husband, boyfriend or children. I told myself to keep cleaning.

But, there it was, in the midst of the chaos, an old voice, an urge not to be resisted: "Screw this." I let the broom drop and got my paints. I was thankful my supplies were intact; the robber was more interested in the finished product. If it weren't for Ching, I might have been flattered. At least the vet said he was going to be okay.

I placed a fresh canvas on the easel, facing out the broken window. My eyes traced across the shards of glass, the black-iron fire-escape railing and the distant panes glinting with reflected streetlight in the building across the street. My hand moved at my eye's bidding. I painted.

* * *

A knock came at the door. "Chad. Are you home?"

Pamela's voice shocked me out of my trance; I'd been painting for hours. "It's open."

"Oh my God! What happened?" She stood in the doorway, immobile. I watched her scramble through the possibilities of what would have me painting in the midst of a ransacked loft.

"No, I'm not manic," I assured her. "I was robbed."

"When did this happen?"

"Last night."

"You should have called."

I pointed to the wounded phone and put down my brush "It's been a long night."

"I'm so sorry, Chad. What did they take?"

"Paintings, sketches, prints, anything they could find, apparently."

"Then they knew what they were doing." She carefully skirted a pile of clothes.

"Why do you say that?"

"It's what I've been telling you for the last two years. Everything you've ever done is worth something, once you begin to sell. I knew we should have put it in storage. How much did they take?"

"A lot. Most of it is crap, a few things I'll miss. But what can they do with it? If they try to sell it, people will know. Don't you think?"

"Yes and no." She poured herself a cup of coffee. "Want a refill?"

"Sure." I'd lost track after the second pot.

"A lot of serious buyers don't care if a work of art is stolen. Particularly if it's appreciating. Oh God . . ." She noticed the blank space above the piano, "Not the triptych."

"I know. Maybe I'll paint another."

"I'm so sorry." She cleared a space for herself on the couch. "It's true, though, some buyers prefer stolen pieces—it adds mystery. Sure, you can't sell at Christie's, but there are plenty of private markets."

"Really? I could see it for expensive things, but in all seriousness, with the exception of the portrait, and I guess those paintings that went at auction at Christie's, my work tops out at about five grand. It's a lot to me, but is it really worth the effort? I could see it for some old masters, or a purloined Kandinsky; I'm just not that big."

"Yet."

"Robbery on spec?"

"I'm glad you can joke. This is scary."

"What time do you have?" I shifted the conversation away from a direction that was stoking my smoldering paranoia.

"A little after ten."

"Oh shit! I didn't know it was so late. I need to get some workmen in here. Would you mind staying while I make some calls?"

"Actually, yes. I've got a full schedule this afternoon, I'm sorry." She paused. "I've got my cellular in the car; if that helps any, I could let you have it for a couple days."

"I'd appreciate it. I'll pay you back."

"I don't think that's going to be an issue."

"Why's that?"

"Well," she smiled coyly, "that's why I came over. Not that all this weirdness isn't scary, but . . . after you left, your opening turned into a feeding frenzy. I've never seen anything like it."

"Oh God, what else happened?"

"Nothing bad. But after the man left with the portrait, people began asking questions. Then they found out that another picture had already been sold and Serge started dropping casual asides that several more were on deposit."

"Were they?"

She smiled. "Not at that point. But Serge does love the smell of money. It was better than the auction houses in the eighties."

"How many sold?"

She paused for maximum effect. "All of them."

An hour later, standing with the locksmith, I was struck with déjà vu. When I first moved into the loft some thirteen years ago, I was robbed. Not like this; then, it was inevitable. I'd not had that first New York lesson about random crime and how to protect yourself. It took all my money at the time, plus a two-thousand-dollar loan from my parents, to get the best steel window grates and Medeco lock cylinders, not to mention the iron bar, aka police lock, that angled from my front door into a notch in the floor. Also, at the urging of my dad, I got renter's insurance.

"The truth of it is," Burt, from Ace's Total Security, told me, chewing on the nub of an unlit cigar, "if someone really wants in, they get in. I can't tell you how many times I've seen it." He surveyed the destruction. "You might want to consider a security system. Beyond that, you don't have too many choices. The way I see it, we could replace the window with security glass, that'll help a little, and you might want to go with welded bars. Of course those can be sawed through, it just takes longer; sometimes that's enough. Then, on the doors, you see this?" He indicated a two-inch gouge in the frame of the fire-escape door. "That's how they got by the cylinder. It's a good lock, can't be picked, but if you cut around the dead bolt, end of story . . ." He bent down and studied the lock. "That's interesting."

"What?"

"You'd think they would have tried the lock first. Whoever did this knew not to bother."

"How come?"

"No scratches on the lock, no pry marks; it's untouched. Won't need to change it, nothing wrong with it. He went straight for the dead bolt because he knew he'd get nowhere with the lock. Now we can go a few ways . . ."

And for the next half hour I learned about reinforced steel plates, kickplates, and heavy-gauge slide locks to secure the doors on all sides.

"I'll get back to you in an hour with an estimate," he said, having completed my home-security wish list. "Then, if you want to go with that, I could start this afternoon, do it as an emergency. The labor's a little higher that way, but if you're going to stay here, I'd recommend it." He looked at me, deciding whether or not to say something.

"What?"

"Well, it's none of my business, but this wasn't a regular robbery, was it?"

"What do you mean?"

"Well, like the door. Your average punk would look at the lock and the gates and move on. From the fire escape it doesn't take a brain surgeon to see that both the apartment above and below you have much lighter security. I could break in downstairs in maybe thirty seconds. But that doorframe, that's a good five minutes, easy. I know, I have to do it sometimes. And then there's that." He pointed to the dark, chalk-stained outline of Ching's blood. "Someone get killed?"

"My dog was shot."

"God! That's cold."

"He's going to be okay."

"That's something. I'd go crazy if anyone messed with my mutt. Ever think about bulletproof glass? It's real expensive, but maybe for the three windows by the fire escape . . ."

As Burt left, Tom, the insurance adjuster, made his entrance in a well-pressed gray suit.

"This certainly looks like the place," he said, extending his right hand. "Are you Chadwick Greene?" Not waiting for my reply, he gripped my hand. "I'm Tom Barrett with The Mutual." He gave me his card and began to survey the loft. "Made quite a mess, didn't they?" He took pictures of the damage. "Do you have an inventory of what they took?"

"No."

"You're going to need that. Also pictures of any missing items would be helpful. So what exactly is missing?"

My explanation, now on its umpteenth retelling, sounded canned. What had been my private space and life had become an open house.

"You think it could have been anyone you know? Does anyone have a grudge against you?"

My first response was to tell him to fuck off. But he had a point. "I don't think so." My wariness bumped up several notches. "Why do you ask?"

"No reason," he remarked, continuing to take pictures, whistling at the damage to the fire-escape door. "Someone really wanted to get in. That should be covered, and the window as well. To be honest, the artwork just isn't handled by a standard policy; you should have had a floater. But I suppose that's not what you want to hear right now. Do you have a copy of the police report?"

"No, but I can get one."

"Good, as soon as I get that I can give you a partial disbursement. You should make an inventory regardless; whatever we won't cover, which is probably a lot, is deductible as an uninsured loss on your taxes."

"Thanks."

He headed toward the door. "Oh, one more thing."

"What's that?"

"If you decide to use an outside adjuster, the payment will probably be delayed."

"What's an outside adjuster?" I smelled a threat.

"They're a bunch of scavengers who try to get ten percent of people's settlements. They come across with a good line, but generally they hold things up and don't deliver much."

And with that, he left. His footsteps blended into the general murmur of Fourteenth Street.

I closed the door and discovered the newspaper I'd bought last night. How long ago that seemed. I picked it up, poured the last few ounces of muddy coffee into my mug, and read the four short columns on Dr. Sturges. There was an old black-and-white head shot of him in a suit and tie. In it he was younger than I remembered, the beard without the gray. It said he was "found murdered in his West Village brownstone office." It didn't say how. It said he was survived by a wife and two daughters and that the funeral would be "private."

I wanted a smoke. I stared at the paper; my mind drifted.

I started with Dr. Sturges my sophomore year at NYU. It should have been my junior year, but that was another story. That middle year was not much more than a blur. Part of it I was manic and in the hospital; most of it I was depressed and on too much medication, unable to move, unable even to turn on the TV. I spent months in bed, Mom hovering anxiously, Dad screaming at me, trying to understand, fighting off the demons of his own childhood. I couldn't move. It was worse than the first time. If I'd had the strength I would have killed myself.

I was seeing Dr. Adams, then. Every week Mom would trundle me into the car and drive in to his Boston office. He and I would talk, although there were a few months where I didn't say much—I couldn't. Slowly, my mind cleared, as though layers of black gauze were being pulled back from my consciousness; finally I could think again. I'd get myself into the city for Thursday at one o'clock with Dr. Adams, and we would talk. And afterward, I'd wander through Boston continuing the sessions in my head. I was nineteen going on twenty, and there was a fork in the road ahead. I was being given a choice: I could either take some control of my life, be an adult, whatever that meant—at the time I equated it with taking lithium—or I could surrender to my illness.

I laughed now at my younger self, the dichotomy of

youth, the belief that things really could be all one way or another.

But I did choose. I dragged myself out of bed and made decisions. I knew I had to get out of the house and back to school. And slowly the certainty grew that I wanted to be a painter. It made perfect sense to me, a view not shared by my parents. I discussed it with Dr. Adams.

"I know I have talent," I argued.

"Do you think I'll object?"

"Frankly, yes."

"How come?"

"Because I'm supposed to be normal. Isn't that the objective?"

"What's 'normal'?"

"You know—finish school, get a job, something in a bank or office. Get married. Have kids."

"Like your dad?"

"Basically."

"That doesn't appeal to you."

"I don't see how he can do it. I don't see how you can do this. Listening to people complain hour after hour, day after day."

He smiled. "It's what I enjoy."

"But what if the thing I enjoy is wrong? Then it's just another Chad fuckup."

"How do you mean?"

"I feel like I'm being watched, and no, I'm not para-noid, but I am being watched—by my parents, by you, by the dean at NYU, who has to decide whether or not to let me come back. I have this ongoing dialogue: Do I do what my parents, et cetera, want, or do I go with my heart? Or do I go for door number three—throw up my hands and become a total nutcase?"

"Which do you want?"

"I want to paint."

"And your parents have told you not to?"

"Not in so many words."

"How then?"

"Come on. It's what they're thinking, Dad in particular." I imitated my father: "'Chad, you can never make a living at that. Why don't you get a business degree and keep painting as an avocation?'"

"He's told you this?"

"No."

"But you can read his mind?"

"So what's your point?"

"You tell me."

"That I'm making a ton of assumptions about my parents. Which, when you get right down to it, they don't have to live in my body and I do."

"Sounds good."

I got better. Slowly pulled myself out of the depression. Swore to Dr. Adams, to myself, to my parents that "I'd learned my lesson and I'd never go off lithium again." Ain't youth grand—everything so black-and-white.

I think those sessions saved my life, gave me direction.

The Portrait

When I returned to New York, I had a mission. I breezed through the readmission interview, auditioned for the fine-arts program, got in, and set to work.

I had to leave Dr. Adams, although I did consider commuting to Boston for weekly sessions. He, and a total lack of money for the train, convinced me otherwise. He referred me to Dr. Sturges.

In light of his murder, I felt pretty shabby about how I had thought of Dr. Sturges. I didn't dislike him. Maybe Dr. Adams was a hard act to follow. Sturges always struck me as cold. His gray-streaked beard hid his face, his emotions. His eyes, dark like a bird's, watched me, taking things in, mirroring myself back to me. Over the years I'd thought of switching, but I never did. And, in retrospect, whenever I needed him, he'd been there. Twice in the fifteen years I was his patient I had to be hospitalized. Both times he came in the middle of the night and shepherded me through the Bellevue and the City Hospital psychiatric emergency rooms. There were at least another half dozen times he helped me avert a meltdown. It was a pretty good record. How many people stick with you for fifteen years? Sure, it was a professional relationship. Even so. I can't believe I accused him of stealing those paintings. But they had to have come from somewhere.

A knock at the door brought me back to the moment. Pete from the phone company came in, asked a few prying questions, and set to work.

With Pamela's cellular phone I called back the

locksmith, the vet and the glazier, who still hadn't shown. All the while, my mind played with the edges of doubt. I thought of Dr. Sturges, his wife and his two children whom I had never met. And I couldn't help but wonder, *was this my fault?*

CHAPTER SIX

Thirty-six hours without sleep.

My thoughts buzzed dangerously fast, still linear, but barely. I went out, having given up on the glazier and deciding the locksmith could be left by himself. It was late Sunday afternoon and getting workmen was a bitch. There was always tomorrow. Of course I had two classes in the morning. Best not to think about that.

Just move, try not to think.

I couldn't stop; images and ideas sparked through my mind. My skin felt as if it were held together by force of will, as though my body would split away in a million pieces. I wanted to scream, but where would that get me?

A locked room, that's where.

With a sketch pad tucked under my left arm and Ching's red-rubber bone hanging from my back pocket, I headed quickly toward the Village Veterinarian.

The office was quiet, the waiting room empty save for Helen, the assistant who'd been there last night.

"Yes, I'm still here," she said, "three shifts and still counting. Remind me never to do this again."

"How's my dog?"

"Pretty groggy. But Dr. Anderson said he's going to be fine."

"Can I see him?"

"Sure, just be prepared; he looks pretty strange."

She led me behind the counter into a small room with two large chain-link kennels.

"Jesus." I barely recognized him. His head was surrounded by a white plastic bucket and his thick red fur was shaved down to a half-inch buzz cut. He lifted his head. His eyes were blurry. He made an effort to stand and then thought better of it.

"He's still sedated."

"Ching." Crouching down, I opened the kennel door. I touched my forehead to his, feeling the heat. His chest was covered with a thick bandage; a plastic tube snaked out from under the wrapping and ended in a bottle with a small amount of blood in the bottom.

"What's this?"

"It's a drain. The surgeon will take it out in the morning, it's not putting out much. That's a good sign."

"How long before I can bring him home?"

"You're going to need to ask Dr. Anderson in the morning. If the drain comes out, it's going to depend a lot on how much nursing you feel comfortable giving him."

"Whatever it takes. Can he have this?" I pulled out the red rubber toy.

"Sure."

Ching sniffed at his favorite possession and then fell asleep.

"Did they find out who shot him?" she asked.

"Not yet."

"It's interesting. Not to be nosy, but I've seen a bunch of animals with bullet wounds and this is the first time the police have taken this much interest."

"Really?" I closed the kennel door. "Did they come by?"

"This morning. They asked a lot of questions. Took the bullet with them. Spent almost an hour with the doctor, which I'm sure thrilled him after being up all night."

"Anything else?"

"There was a woman officer."

"Detective Bryant?"

"I think so. She asked me a lot of questions about you." We looked at each other.

"What kind of questions?"

"She wanted to know how you acted. Were you upset? That kind of stuff."

"I suppose it's her job. Was there something else?" I sensed there was.

"Some of the questions were kind of odd."

"Like how?"

"Well, she wanted to know if you smelled of gunpowder, and did I notice any burns on your arms?"

"I see." The implication was clear. "Well, I got to

keep going. If you need me . . ." I gave her the number to Pamela's cellular phone.

Back on the street, the phrase "No rest for the wicked" circled my brain. I headed south toward the Village, my body on automatic, my thoughts spinning ever faster. Outside Pamela's apartment building at Fifth Avenue and Tenth Street, I paused, felt the sketch pad under my arm, and remembered why I had come.

She buzzed me into the beaux-arts lobby with its mirrors, plaster gargoyles, and crystal chandeliers. A million prism-born reflections shot back at me. I looked bad; I should have changed, my shirt was still stained with blood, my hair tangled and knotted. I kept my eyes straight ahead and ignored the hint of a whisper gathering in my head.

She waited for me outside her apartment. "God, you look like hell. Have you slept?"

"No." I stood in the hallway. "Can I come in?"

She looked me over, so like my mother in similar circumstances—maybe it was just they were of a similar age. "Sure, have you eaten?"

"No, not in a while. But I'll do that later."

She ignored me and foraged in her cupboards and refrigerator for an assortment of cheeses, crackers and dried fruit. "How's your apartment coming?" she yelled from the kitchen.

"It's a mess. Ching's doing okay." Again, I tried to remember why I had come here, "Could you get in here?"

"What is it?"

"I need you to do something."

"What?"

"The man who bought the portrait . . ."

"Oh Lord, not again."

"What do you mean?"

"I spent an hour with those police detectives. They came right to the office."

"I see. Did they have you sit with someone and make a composite?"

"Come again?"

"Of the man who bought the portrait. I want you to tell me what he looks like. I want to draw him."

"Chad, for God's sake, let the police do this. They're obviously looking into this, or doing an investigation, or whatever it is they're supposed to do."

"Pamela, please. I have this feeling that *I'm* the suspect. Maybe it's just my paranoia, but I'm not stupid. Everything centers around me. Of course, that sounds a little egotistical, but it's true. It makes perfect sense. It's not hard giving me motives, and how good is my alibi? I live by myself; God only knows what I was doing when Dr. Sturges was killed. I am a mental patient, after all." I let that hang in the air. My breathing felt too fast, I tried to slow it down. "I see where this is going." Her expression was worried. "What?"

"You need to get some sleep," she said.

"I'm fine. I'll get some later . . . I promise."

"You're starting to act strange, Chad. Do you know you're yelling? And you're talking way too fast?"

"Oh." I let that sink in, checking off another landmark on the road to mania. "Please"—I lowered my voice—"just do this for me, and then I'll put myself to bed."

"Okay, fine."

I pushed aside the cheese plate and sat next to her on the couch. "Good, now think back." And I started an exercise I'd done for years with my students. "Close your eyes and let an image of the man passively come to you; don't push, just let it happen. Can you see him?"

"Yes."

"Good, now keep that image floating through your mind; don't push it, just let it be there. Got it?"

"Yeah."

"All right, now look at the blank white page and imagine the outline of his head. Is it more rounded or oval?"

"Rounded, but part of that was the beard."

I started to sketch.

It was dark by the time I left Pamela's. Her furtive glances told me more than I wanted to know. I looked bad, maybe dangerously so. Yet, I felt good. Really good. Strange, ain't it? My body moved incredibly fast over the city sidewalks, darting across the streets and the avenues. Lights glittered around me; refracting rays shot long and crisp.

I turned at the sound of screeching brakes. A horn

blared and a foreign-looking cabdriver swore at me. I smiled back, feeling nothing but love. Then I realized I was standing stock-still in the middle of Sixth Avenue, my attention caught up in the lights.

All right, Chad, pull it together; get home and go to bed.

But I wasn't tired. And the words to "I Could Have Danced All Night" sprang to my lips.

Oh brother. At least I'm heading toward a happy mania and not a mean or paranoid one. Maybe you're just overtired, Chad. Yes, that's it. Anyone who's been through what I have would feel the same.

My chest banged up against the shoulder of a man in a black leather jacket and jeans.

"Watch it!" he barked, not stopping, our eyes connected briefly.

Something in my expression caused him to walk away faster.

I reached my door without further incident. There were other things I wanted to do, but for the life of me I couldn't remember.

As I put the key in the lock, I felt someone behind me, watching me. I looked back, and all I saw were the lights of Fourteenth Street, dancing and piercing the night. Dark shadows of moving people broke the beams, but only briefly. I stood there, caught in the beauty of the moment.

"Hey, Chad. Sorry to hear about your dog." Willie, from the kung-fu studio on the second floor, opened the door behind me.

I focused on his broad, dark features and tried not to stare, but the reflections off his forehead and around his nose had a beautiful symmetry. I traced them, mentally reforming them into a cubist design.

"You okay?"

"Yeah, just looking at the night."

"Got to love the weather . . . I heard about your dog and all; you need anything?"

"Right now, I can't think of anything, but thanks. I should probably get some sleep." The thought of Ching helped to ground me. *Stop farting around, get to bed.*

"You look like you could use it. Take it easy."

I climbed the four flights, pushed past the enchantment of my painted lobby and made it into my loft.

I'm not in the least tired. How can something this good be bad? It's a great night to paint.

I looked at the easel with the half-finished canvas. The pull was strong.

Don't start, you know where this leads. You haven't eaten, you haven't slept, do you want to go back to the hospital? Do you want to lose your job? . . . Do you want to go to jail?

Now there's a new one.

"Oh well."

I went to the bathroom and faced my pill bottles. I swallowed the lithium and looked at the Ativan sedatives that Dr. Sturges had prescribed for me to get through the show. There were three left. I took them all, nothing less would touch me. I flashed on an image of Marlin Perkins hunting wildlife for Mutual of Omaha's *Wild Kingdom*; I was the elephant and the Ativan was the dart gun. I tossed the empty bottle. I was going to need more.

Before I knew it, I was halfway across the loft hunting through an old address book. I found the number and quickly dialed ten digits on Pamela's phone.

An answering service took my message. The woman asked, "Is this an emergency or can it wait till the morning?"

I thought about that; the Ativan was beginning to hit, slowing me down. The elephant stumbled. "It can wait, but could he call me early?"

"I'll pass that along. If I could have your number?"

Transaction completed, I stumbled to bed and fell asleep.

CHAPTER SEVEN

I dream. It's a cloudy day and I'm walking on the street; the lines are crisp and men tip their hats as in a Magritte painting. "Thank you so much," one of them says, as he continues past without stopping.

I say, "You're welcome," certain of what he meant. I look down and Ching is there; he wears a tutu and a small, pointed birthday hat. Then we're on top of a building, rain is falling in solid sheets. I want to get inside, but the windows are locked. I look down, toward the pavement, it's too far to jump, although part of me thinks I could make it.

A bearded man appears beside me, he laughs. "Always a coward." And he hurls himself over the side.

I look down, but he's gone; Ching too.

A puff of smoke mixes with the rain. I realize the building is on fire. A siren sounds and then another. If I don't jump, I'll burn; the smoke grows denser, the shadows of flame draw nearer. I close my eyes and fall. Sirens blare louder.

Consciousness grows and the siren becomes a ringing telephone.

Thick with drugs, I told myself, "Get up." *Just do it.*

I grabbed the phone, "Hello?"

"Hello, Chad?"

I hadn't heard his voice in over a decade. "Dr. Adams, thanks for getting back . . ." I tried to collect my thoughts. "I've got a bit of a problem and I'd really like to see you." I was set to launch into a lengthy explanation, to plead, if necessary.

"That shouldn't be a problem. I can clear up an hour at five. Can you make it?"

"Great." I was wondering if this was still part of the dream. "I'll be there. Thanks."

"I'll see you then. Bye."

"Bye."

Five, he said five, that should work out. *What time is it?* "Oh shit!" I realized I had twenty minutes to make it to the studio for my first class.

I scrambled to the bathroom, looked at an unshaven redheaded lunatic in the mirror, swallowed my lithium and ran a dry razor under my chin. I stank. I showered, or at least got wet enough to scrape off the surface grime. Then I threw on jeans, a T-shirt, a blazer, socks, sneakers, grabbed my sketch pad and beat it out the door.

I'd taught in the University's studio-arts program for almost ten years, longer if you counted grad school. I started as an assistant instructor under Jan Hobling, my mentor. It was the administration's unstated idea to put someone in class with Jan as a buffer between him and the paying hopefuls. Tact was never his strong suit. On more than one occasion, we lost an aspiring undergraduate after a searing Dutch-accented critique. Not that he intentionally discouraged young artists, but he told the truth and that could burn. His message was hard for students eighteen, nineteen and twenty years old to hear. "You have to practice, every day, very hard." He would tell them, "You're wasting your money. Why pay for studying if you don't study? Why pay me to teach if you think you already know everything? It makes no sense."

He'd gone now, off to work and teach in Santa Fe. He wrote to tell me that New York was a cesspool and that I was a fool for staying.

After he left, I took over his classes, a natural transition fueled by my growing success. His parting words were, "Always keep a teaching gig. It'll get you through the rough times." And so it had. It paid child support, my rent and enough for starvation food— Gristede's house-brand macaroni and cheese—four boxes for a dollar. And then there was the health insurance, not as good as it used to be, but, thinking of one of Jan's favorite chestnuts, "What is?"

Class over, a rather dull exercise in life drawing, I sank into a window seat on the twelve-thirty Colonial Express to Boston. I spread my Zaro's pastry bag, coffee, and newspaper on the adjoining seat; it was the international train rider's sign saying "Don't sit next to me." The Danish pastry had been an afterthought, but I couldn't recall the last time I had eaten, and truth be told, I was still not hungry. I looked inside the bag; the Danish had been the only thing in the pastry case that looked faintly appealing. I took one out, cheese, and gnawed away at the edges. It was like priming a pump; after the first few nibbles my stomach told my head to send down more.

It was with a sense of relief that I crumpled the empty bag and sat back, waiting for the train to move. The car was less than a quarter full, there were not many commuters in the middle of a Monday.

I opened my sketch pad and looked at last night's efforts—Pamela's recollection of the portrait buyer. I stared at the bearded face. *Do I know this person?* My recall of faces was uncanny; names were another story. I froze faces in my mind, like photographs—interesting ones, dull ones, faces of people I'd seen only once, and I stored them away, taking them out later, playing with them, manipulating them. This one didn't say much: the beard was full, the glasses were thick and distorted the underlying eyes and the cap cut off the dome of the skull and the hairline. It seemed a disguise, but who knew?

Who are you? Carefully, I turned the page and started fresh. Some traces of authenticity lurked in the face—the small lines around the eyes, not hidden by the glasses. Now, if I got rid of the beard I could guess at the jawline, but not really. I'd drawn so many faces, thousands over the years, that my eye and hand automatically filled in the way things should be. There were rules to faces: how they aged, how they changed, how the shape of the cheek informed the jaw, how the angle of the temple betrayed the vault of the forehead.

Time passed. When the train pulled into Boston I'd drawn three charcoal faces.

I asked the conductor for the time; I had thirty minutes to get from South Station to Dr. Adams's Beacon Hill office.

I flowed with the crowd up the stairs into downtown Boston at the start of the commuter hour. Everyone was rushing home to their families, or so I imagined. Men in suits, with bald heads and briefcases—any one of them could be my father. I thought of a Robert Frost poem painfully memorized in high school, something about "the road not taken." And there it was. And here I was, finally making it, financially anyway, but slammed from behind by something unknown and menacing.

The air was warm and heavy, the sky hazy with the threat of a summer storm. I walked fast past the gold-domed capitol down a route I'd not taken in fifteen years. "The horse knows the way . . ." I wondered what he'd be like. Would he still be the same man? Was I? Would he help me? Could he?

My stomach lurched; I could either throw up or have explosive diarrhea. Was it nerves or lithium?

I pressed the buzzer to his office. Nothing had

changed—the same button, the same raised-letter plaque.

WILLIAM ADAMS, MD
PSYCHIATRIST

I was buzzed in. Once inside, I shot for the bathroom. Finally, with my stomach a hair better, I ventured toward his office.

He stood in the open doorway. "Hi, Chad." His hair was gray in places, but still full; his face less angular, the jawline softer; the eyes unchanged—dark and intelligent.

"Hi."

He extended his hand.

On impulse, I put my arms around him, like an anchor. I hugged him. Not something I normally did.

He didn't stiffen. "It's going to be all right," he said.

There was no way he could know that, but it felt good. "You have no idea."

"Probably not, but that's a good place to start." And we took up positions in overstuffed chairs. It was like picking up a conversation that had stopped fifteen years before.

"I feel like I never left," I said, checking out his office, looking for any changes.

"But you have." His voice rang deep and lyrical. "What brings you back?"

"Right to the chase. Where to start? . . ." And I laid out the details of the last few days.

"Jesus," he said, in response to my monologue. "Way too many things at once, really bad things. How do you deal with it?"

"I'm not. I go from one thing to the next. I have no control. Nothing is solid. I'm not solid. My apartment has plywood over three of the windows. I miss my dog. I can't even think about that, like if I do, my insides will just start spilling out." I pushed back the image of Ching, not wanting to cry. I took a deep breath. "Everyone I know is being questioned by the police. They're all speculating, 'Did he do it? Why would he do it?' I don't think it's hard to ascribe a motive. And then there's my history . . ." I realized he had no idea what I'd been doing for the past fifteen years. "Did you even know I got married? That I have a son?"

"I didn't."

"Yeah, he'll be ten in June. I see him two times a year—supervised."

"Can you tell me about it?"

Funny how the thing I usually most avoided popped out like a horror-show jack-in-the-box after only a few minutes with this man. "Do we have time?"

"Yes. You're my last appointment."

"Great. Shouldn't we talk about medications?" I asked, wanting to stall the inevitable.

"What's to say? You take them. I'll refill them.

And keep using the Ativan to get some sleep, at least for now."

"All right, so I don't want to talk about Jocelyn." I sank into the chair, a taste of bile in my throat. "What's to say? Have you ever done something, or had a part of your life filled with regret?" I looked at him and smiled. "Obviously it's rhetorical." I paused. "Every time I think of Jocelyn and Zack, that's my son, it's too much. 'Cause I fucked up. Not a little, not the sort of fuckup that goes away, but something evil and selfish that can't be undone."

"What was evil and selfish?"

"My marriage. It should never have happened. I should have known better."

"You're losing me, Chad."

"God, I don't want to talk about this."

"Try." His voice gently urged me on.

"I don't know . . ." I was listening to the rumblings of my gut. "No, that's a lie . . . I think if I tell you the truth, the whole thing, you'll be disgusted. You won't want to treat me."

"That bad?"

"Yup. Every time I think of it . . . I don't know. It's like a can of worms that whenever it gets opened, it just oozes for days."

"Does it have something to do with you and Dr. Sturges?"

"That's right." I had not realized the connection

was so obvious. "He was there. He saw the whole thing." I looked at him. "Do we have time for this?"

He nodded. "Yes."

"Ten years later and I still feel shame. Where to start? I met Jocelyn in grad school. We were in a class together, we called it Forgeries 101. It was a combination of art history and comparative technique. We'd go through periods of painters, actually have samples on loan from collections and museums and we'd dissect the style. Try to put ourselves in the shoes of the artists, become them, see through their eyes, paint like them.

"She was good at it. Had a whole portfolio, from the Dutch masters to the postmodernists. I'd watch her in class; she was so beautiful, still is. Standing there painting, her hair, this soft, wavy brown, caught in the light like an art nouveau painting." I tried to catch my breath, the image too clear, too painful. "There was a pull between us. It started with coffee after class and it just happened, we became a couple. Our interests, our temperaments, or so I thought, were matched. She was getting a master's in art restoration. I was going to be a great painter. She wanted marriage and children. I loved her and I wanted whatever she wanted.

"Part of me wants to say, 'She knew what she was getting into.' But then, how could she? Really, I mean."

"What are you talking about?"

"I do get pretty vague, don't I. My *illness*." The word burned like acid on my tongue. "I told her about going into the hospital, about breaking every mirror in my parents' house when I was seventeen and again when I was nineteen. I know there were parts I left out, like the magic of being manic, not just the high, but the fantasy part, or whatever. My *delusions*, but that's what other people call it. They're real to me. I did tell her about the paranoia, at least. I don't think it registered."

"What do you mean?"

"If you haven't been through it, how can you really know? For most people, being manic is something they'll never see or experience. Depression they understand, or at least have some idea of what you're talking about. She listened; I even had my mom talk to her."

"What happened?"

"We got married. Big wedding. I almost invited you, but it seemed an odd thing to do, and I was trying very hard to not be odd. I was real good, took all my meds, saw Dr. Sturges once a week. God, it's amazing, thinking back."

"What?"

"Old feelings. A lot of things I wanted from life that I buried ten years ago. But I'm still vague. Okay, here goes." I pushed back hard into the chair. "Jocelyn got pregnant, and nearly lost the baby in the fourth month. She had to go on total bed rest; it meant she couldn't go to class or teach undergrads—half our income. We couldn't make it on just my stipend, so I took a second job, waiting tables at night. It brought in a bunch of money and they pretty much let me work all I wanted. The more I worked, the more I wanted to work. School in the day, work at night. Isn't that the American way? I started to get high, but I figured 'this once' it would be okay. After all, I had to take care of business.

"I stopped the lithium. It held me back. And the rest is catastrophe. I freaked out in the restaurant during Sunday brunch. I thought the devil was trying to get me through the mirrors; the whole place was glass and mirrors. I began to shot-put teapots through the glass. It's amazing I didn't kill someone. I ran out before the cops came. When I got home I smashed the windows. Jocelyn tried to stop me; she tried to hold me back. Something happened." I stared at my hands, I saw the bookcase fall on my pregnant wife. *I can't tell him about that.* "She went into labor. The cops came, ambulances. I can still hear her scream, blood coming from inside of her.

"They took me to jail. I was in a holding tank for two days. Dr. Sturges came down and somehow talked them into taking me to Bellevue. That was a trip . . .

"She gave birth two months early. Zack had to be in an incubator. It was all my fault. He could have died. She could have died. The cops wanted her to press charges, but she wouldn't. She filed for divorce. The restaurant got the cost for the damages from my parents.

"From there on, everything blurs. I stayed sick; I didn't want to come out of it. I spent almost the entire time in hospitals. Jocelyn came once with the baby when he was six months old. She wanted me to see him. She cried the entire visit." I looked across at Dr. Adams, the light outside darkening, his expression obscured in shadow. "Pretty pathetic, huh?"

He leaned forward in the chair. "No." His face looked pained. "I'm so sorry, Chad."

"I should have known better. I try not to think about it. There's more, too, but I don't think I can go into it now."

"It's late. Maybe we should stop, then. If you'd like, I can see you at this time next week?"

"If that's okay?"

"You know to call me, anytime, if things get out of hand?" He looked me dead in the eye, his message clear.

"Yes, I won't do anything stupid. I'll call."

"Good. There's no way around it, this is going to be a god-awful time for you. I'd be surprised if you hadn't thought about suicide."

"It's crossed my mind."

"Anything more than thoughts?"

"No. More like an option if things get too much worse."

"What you're experiencing now has little to do with your *illness*. Anyone, and I do mean *anyone*, in similar circumstances would be gulping for air. You will get through this. But you have to promise that you'll call me if things get worse."

"I will."

"Good." He wrote out prescriptions and an appointment card. "I'll see you next week . . . I'm glad you came, Chad."

"Me too."

He offered his hand like a lifeline; I took it. But finally I had to let go, and head out of his office and back out to sea.

CHAPTER EIGHT

What did I feel? I skirted the edges of Boston's Combat Zone, with its XXX videos and neon signs ALL GIRLS/ALL LIVE/ALL NUDE. Gooseflesh pulled at my arms. In my periphery, I caught anonymous eyes watching me. I moved quickly past the lights and the prostitutes, my feet headed toward South Station and a return trip on AMTRAK. Then I paused and changed direction. With the Commons, and then the Gardens on my left, I aimed for the Arlington Street Station. *Too much unfinished business in this town; baby's coming home.*

Three levels belowground, amid the roar and squeal, I waited for the "D" train. Again I felt the weight of eyes on my back. Nothing new, just a reminder of who I am.

Just this once, I bargained with myself, knowing it was better not to give in. As the ad says, "You can't have just one."

I turned; I looked. Several pairs of furtive eyes met mine. This was not helpful. Just some working stiffs coming home late, maybe been to the bar, maybe took a quick stop in the porn palace.

A light at the end of the tunnel materialized into my train. *I should call first. Too late.*

I looked out the grime-smeared subway-car window, my thoughts on the session. So many threads dangled in my life, debts owed and not repaid; the family I had started and then abandoned; the can of worms newly opened, fresh and slimy. I flashed on scenes of twice-yearly supervised visits with my son Zack. Each time I saw him, it was as if for the first time. Half a year was huge in the life of a child. I didn't know him. He didn't know me. Jocelyn watched from the sidelines, her tears long gone. *"Say hello to your father, Zack."*

"Hi, Dad."

It eats me alive. All that could have been. All I could have had, "the road not taken," the road blown away.

The train pulled into Riverside Station. I held back and watched the other passengers leave. They swarmed like columns of ants through the parking lot. Car doors opened and closed, headlights popped on; the end of the daily commute was in sight.

Still the feeling persisted—of being watched, of being followed. I remembered something I'd read years ago about paranoia, how it was completely egocentric: "I am the center of the world and everyone watches me," something like that. I suppose that was right, or at least correct in a tight-assed, non-knowing academic way.

I will not look. I will not turn and look.

I turned and looked. Oh well. No one there.

I stood frozen in the empty train. In the distance, a conductor with a flashlight swept through the cars ready to kick out vagrants who wanted to spend the night. I took the hint.

I dropped a quarter in a parking-lot pay phone. It rang. *If they're not home, I'll go back to New York.*

"Hello."

"Hey, Dad, it's your son."

"Chad, how you doing?"

"I've been better. Look, I'm at Riverside Station. I wanted to see you and Mom. I know I should have called first, but it was sort of spur-of-the-moment."

"I'll be right out."

"I can get a cab."

"I'll be right out; give me twenty minutes."

I looked around the darkened station and didn't see any waiting taxis. "Thanks. I'll be here."

I drifted back in time, my thoughts on the session, on ten years ago, when, like a tidal wave, insanity swept over my life. In the aftermath, I made decisions: not to remarry, never to have another child, to plow every ounce of my being into my work. It seemed right, but now, farther down the road, when I looked for meaning, it eluded me. I thought of Zack, and what could have been, of Joz and what I had for two and a half years. I pictured a younger me, working to support a family, feeling as though maybe I could fit. The memories pulled like a magnet, even now; nothing resolved, not really. I wondered if other people had a time, a pivotal event, to which everything else was held in reference.

If I could forget, maybe that would be better. I'd met some, over the years, who claimed amnesia for their manias. I'm not sure I believed them. It was possible. For me, I sometimes lied and said, "I can't remember, it's all a blur." I didn't want to explain. But I remembered plenty.

I remembered smelling the holding tank at the precinct station: the filthy drunks ripe with bourbon, the emaciated addicts, the male prostitutes plucked from the piers and the petty hoodlums jabbering in the patois of the street, all thrown together like rats in a cage. We were taken out one by one, questioned, returned and sent on. The cell, with its open toilet, was filled with fallen souls, or so I believed. I had a mission: I had been sent to do God's bidding. I lectured to my unordained disciples until the guards told me to shut up. I walked and paced and hounded my cell mates one by one, arguing for the light, for salvation: "The Lord is my shepherd; I shall not want." I saw the color of their auras and the twisted sneers and sharp talons of the demons that clung to their backs. It was a miracle no one killed me. Of course, few people were likely to start much with a six-foot-three red-headed maniac.

A set of headlights moved toward me.

I waved.

"Hey, Dad." I sank into the front seat.

We awkwardly hugged, a relatively recent development in our relationship. "No suitcase?" he asked.

"Just this." I was still clutching my sketch pad. "It's kind of an impulse trip. I do need to stop at a pharmacy."

He headed toward the highway, the silence heavy between us. "Do you want to talk about it?" he asked.

"It? I don't mean to be flip, Dad, but there's so much 'it' right now, I don't know where to begin."

"Are you running from something?"

"What would make you say that?"

"A police detective called yesterday and again this afternoon."

"Detective Bryant?"

"I think so. She wanted to know where you were."

Dread surfaced. "What did she say?"

"She asked if we had spoken on the phone Friday night. She wanted to know when, for how long. That sort of thing."

"You said she called this afternoon."

He looked at me briefly, his eyes cut through the darkness and searched out my own. "She wanted to know if we knew where you were. What's going on?"

"My psychiatrist, Dr. Sturges, was murdered." I paused. "Somehow I've landed in the center of the investigation. I think they're going to arrest me."

Silence. "Do you have a lawyer?"

"Not yet. I've been avoiding that. Pamela gave me some names. I should call one, but with all that's going on, it would just be one more thing."

"There's more?"

"Lots. My apartment was robbed." I swallowed hard. "Someone shot Ching. That's the worst part of it. Everything else I can deal with, but why would someone do that? At least he's going to be okay."

"We've been trying to call you the last couple days, kept getting a busy signal. I was getting ready to head down and see if everything was okay."

"My phone's out; I've been using a borrowed cellular; it's a different number."

"Do you want us to come down and give you a hand? I could take a couple of personal days."

I thought it over, the ancient relief that Mom and Dad could make everything right again. "That's okay. I appreciate the offer, but right now I just want a night's refuge. Things look better in the morning, usually. How's Mom?"

"Her usual. Worried about you, sewing up a storm for DeeDee's wedding."

"At least that's something to look forward to; the last one of us to get paired off. Of course, mine didn't last too long."

"She asks about you."

"Joz?"

"Yeah."

"How's she doing?"

"Good."

"Could you be more specific? What's she up to? How's Zack? . . . Is she seeing someone again?"

It's one of the weirdnesses of my life—that my parents, after the divorce, became closer with Jocelyn and saw my son far more often than I did.

I pictured my mother ten years ago, tears in her eyes, rage on her face, trying not to scream at me as I persisted in my madness. "My only grandchild," she'd sobbed, "why do you have to be so selfish? And Jocelyn, what did she ever do to deserve this?" I laughed at her, prepared for the perennial "We still love you. We just don't like you very much right now." Or the popular "We're not mad. We're disappointed." But I'd stepped way over the line. It was the only time in my life I felt that she wanted to hit me. In retrospect, she should have.

"I don't know if she's seeing anyone," he said. "She still works at the museum. Zack's a handful, but so were you at that age."

"And every age that came after. How's school going?"

"Fair. He doesn't like his teacher as much this year; isn't working as hard. He's a lot more into sports. We've been going to his soccer games."

"What's he like on the field?"

"Aggressive. He's a good kid, but he's already taller than most of the others, and when he sets his mind to something it's hard to stop him. I took him to buy sneakers last week, he's up to a men's eight."

I listened to Dad's report on life with my son, my vicarious fatherhood. It used to make me crazy; for years

I wouldn't even ask. Now I realized it was the best thing possible. My son drank from the fountain of my parents' love, and they in turn could be grandparents and dote and be proud and watch him grow.

"Does he ask about me?"

"Sometimes. He used to go through your wedding album over and over. He hasn't done that in a while."

I froze at the image of my son looking for his father in a book of glossy wedding pictures. "Do you know what he wants for his birthday?"

"A bike, definitely a bike. He's been talking about 'hybrids.' All I know about them is they have big tires and they're 'awesome.'"

"I can work with that." We lapsed into silence. I had him stop at the pharmacy two towns away from home. I didn't want to see anyone I knew as my prescriptions for lithium and sedatives were filled. My diagnosis, for those in the know, was clearly spelled out by the pills I took.

As Dad made the final turn into our driveway, he said, "You might not want to tell your mother about everything—all at once."

"Agreed."

She handled it well, while trying to coax me into eating a plate of pot roast and vegetables. I'd worn them down over the years, their calm suburban life broken on more than one occasion by flashing sirens, and policemen and paramedics carting away their son. I was the talk of the neighborhood.

She looked at me, her eyes soft. "How can we help?"

"I don't know. Maybe I just want a night off. It feels good sitting here, like nothing bad has happened. Everything familiar, the way it should be. Like home in a game of tag. At least I don't have to worry about money for a while." And I told them about my show and my financial windfall.

"Have you thought about what you're going to do next?"

"Probably nothing . . . Oh"—reality intruded—"you said Detective Bryant called, looking for me?"

"This afternoon."

"I should get back to her."

I dialed in the kitchen, wanting their presence. Her machine picked up. I listened to the by now familiar message, except there had been an addition, ". . . If this is Chadwick Greene, please dial nine and ask the desk clerk to page me."

I followed instructions and waited for the page to go through. With the phone to my ear, connected to God only knew what chaos on the other end, and my parents here, around the familiar white kitchen table, I felt like the rope in a tug-of-war. I listened to the silence and waited for the worst.

"Hello, Chad?"

"Detective Bryant?"

"Susan. Where are you?"

Already this was odd, her voice less crisp, an invitation to use her first name. "I'm in Boston, or rather the suburbs, my parents' house."

"Thank God."

"Why? What's happened?"

"Your downstairs neighbor saw somebody break into your apartment."

"You've got to be kidding. Did they get him?"

"No. He got out through the fire escape."

"It seems the way to go. What did they take this time?"

"We're not certain. We've got the building under surveillance." She paused. "How's your dog?"

"They said he'd be okay. He looks pretty freakish, though. You have animals?"

"Two cats . . . Chad, you might want to stay somewhere other than your apartment."

"Why? Because it's turned into Grand Central, or there's something else?"

She paused. "We have reason to suspect someone might want to harm you."

"Could you be more specific?"

"There was something in your mail."

"What? And what were you doing in my mail?"

"It might be better if you came down and looked at it." The latter question went unanswered. "I'm really sorry about this, Chad."

"I'll take the first train in the morning. I could be there by eleven."

"If you'd like, I could meet you at Penn Station; we could go to lunch."

"Fine." I was a bit taken aback. *Is that something police do? Take people to lunch?* I gave up trying to figure the angles; maybe it was just her lunch hour.

That night, unable to sleep, not yet willing to surrender to Ativan, I searched my childhood bedroom for traces of a younger me. Some years back Mom redid the kids' rooms. Mine was turned into a study/office with a daybed for guests. Even so, there were bits and pieces of my childhood and adolescence that, for whatever reason, never made it into attic boxes. Desk drawers surrendered souvenir pens from Expo '68 and '69, the remains of a bug collection, a stamp collection, a coin collection and a stack of *MAD* magazines.

In the closet was a trapdoor to the attic. I pulled the handle and released a rickety wooden ladder. I climbed up. A bare bulb illuminated a section of rafters where Dad had put down sheets of plywood over the crossbeams and insulation. Through the years, piles of boxes, old baby furniture, and other detritus had accumulated. Everything "too good to throw away" had landed here. It didn't take long to find a stack labeled "Chad's room." I opened the first box—nothing but paperback books and a few lurid horror comics; I took out the latter and set them aside. The next had my bottle collection and a pair of antique bronze lion bookends that my grandmother had given me when I graduated from high school. I put those on top of the comics and I resealed the box.

Then I struck gold; a number-ten carton filled with sketch pads. They were all labeled and dated. I crouched down, so as not to get beaned by a beam, and I pushed the box over to the trapdoor. Somewhat clumsily, I half-lowered and half-dropped my finds to the closet floor.

Mom's voice came from two flights below. "Is everything okay?"

I climbed down the ladder and opened the bedroom door. "Fine, I was just looking at some old things."

"You know it's after two? If you want to get the early train . . ."

"I'll get to bed soon. Good night."

"Good night, dear."

I didn't know it was so late. Mom's concern, her love and the hint of reproach wrapped me like a blanket.

Just another few minutes.

I opened the box and pulled out dozens of large-sized artist's pads. Pamela would have loved to get her hands on these. Apparently, she was not the only one.

I arranged them in chronological order: the first from when I took summer art class in junior high, the last from the time of my hospitalization ten years ago. It was a peculiar experience, like old photo albums recording the progress of my life. It was more too—my development as an artist, as a person and as a lunatic. The books from when I was seventeen, manic for the first time, were filled with thunderbolts and angels, shattered glass and repentant souls. Bible quotes painted bloodred rambled across the pages. One of them, entitled "Prepare the Way," I'd drawn during an art-therapy class in the hospital. It was a crude forerunner of the one done years later that had just sold at auction. Sketched and colored comic-book style, it showed me in a white cape swinging a mallet into a giant mirror. Behind the glass, hordes of demons surged. It wasn't what the therapist wanted us to draw; I remembered insisting, "But it's the truth, and the truth will set you free." At some point, I scared her and she called for security. I don't remember much after that, they probably shot me up with something and tied me to a bed.

What time is it? I stretched my arms and back. "Four o'clock, how is that possible? To bed, Chad."

Come on, just one more. I hadn't gone through a fourth of the books. "What am I doing? Go to bed." *One more, come on, one more.*

"All right." I pulled a pad from the bottom of the stack.

It was labeled and dated, "Bellevue Hospital Adult Psychiatric: May 1985."

"Great." I let out a sigh and opened a nightmare.

I flipped past the first few drawings, all self-portraits. The technique, miles beyond my adolescent efforts, exploded off the pages. Not even florid psychosis and elephant-strength tranquilizers were able to eliminate years of daily practice. But the results made me shudder: over-defined eyes stared back from faces with out-of-focus features; they were mirror drawings. I'd stood watch in the hospital, convinced of the enemy's ensuing invasion through the now unbreakable mirrors. I was later told that I sat for days staring into the glass. They got me to stop by giving me the sketch pad and a whole lot of Thorazine.

What came next was a series of portraits and sketches of life in a locked ward—forgotten men and women, their names lost, their faces frozen and reworked through my eyes, heart and hand. I never forgot a face.

I turned the page—and there he was. My breath caught and my pulse quickened as I confronted a younger, clean-shaven version of the face I'd drawn on the train.

That's not possible.

"No?" I looked around for my current sketch pad and then remembered I had left it in the kitchen.

I stole downstairs, avoiding the one squeaky step, feeling all of twelve, not wanting to wake my parents.

I turned on the kitchen light and looked at the recent drawings. It was difficult to say; the forehead was the same and the nose, too. The cheeks were different, more jowly, but that could be from age or because he had put on weight.

The Portrait

Upstairs again, I put the pictures side by side. The similarities were real. The hair, the glasses, the beard, the eye color were different, but what mattered, the bits that didn't change—the skull beneath the skin, the arrangement of features—they were awfully close.

"Who are you? Or were you?" I searched the earlier sketch for some identification; it was fruitless. I was always careful to leave my fellow patients their anonymity, a sort of hospital etiquette.

It was now five-fifteen.

"You did it again, didn't you?" It would have been easy not to sleep at all, my mind raced. "Go to bed. Do it now."

I swallowed two Ativans dry and repacked the box. I kept out the last book. *You're just imagining the connection; in the morning it'll look different.*

My mind slowed, my body relaxed. By the time I'd brushed my teeth and talked myself out of flossing, I was ready for bed and the dreamless sleep of the drugged.

CHAPTER NINE

"Chad . . . dear, it's time to get up. Chad"—a gentle push on my shoulder—"you're going to miss the train." Mom's voice softly intruded into my chemical sleep.

"What time is it?" I forced the words through parched lips, my eyes shut tight, the majority of my brain still soundly snoozing.

"It's six o'clock. If you're going to meet that detective at eleven o'clock, you have to get moving."

"You're right." Figuring the math: a four-hour train ride, twenty minutes to get to the station . . . maybe just a few more minutes . . . I sank back into the arms of sleep.

"Chad, please get up. Don't make me do this."

That did it, Mother's guilt, better than an alarm clock. "All right, I'm up."

"Good, there's coffee on downstairs. Your father is ready to go whenever you are."

I struggled to sit up in the too-small daybed, listening to her footsteps as they vanished down the stairs. *You can sleep on the train.*

I dressed and gathered up the ten-year-old sketch pad and the one I'd brought with me.

Downstairs, I swigged back two cups of coffee, 600

milligrams of lithium, and, with Mother's gentle guidance, a steaming bowl of oatmeal.

"I got some boxes out of the attic last night."

"What were you doing in the attic?" she asked.

"I don't know, just looking at some of my old stuff. Anyway, there was a big carton filled with sketch pads; I want you to put them somewhere safe. Maybe even rent a couple large safe-deposit boxes. I'll pay you back. And also lock up all the artwork I've given you over the years, at least for the time being."

"You think someone would come here?"

"I don't know what to think, but I started looking through the old books and I don't want to lose them."

We got to the station as the train roared in. Dad and I quickly embraced.

"You need any money?" he asked.

"No, I'm fine, thanks." I half expected him to slip me a twenty, "for emergencies," but that time had passed.

I fell into the first empty window seat and wedged the sketch pads between my body and the wall. Outside, Dad stood on the platform as the train pulled away, lost in his own thoughts. Once again I had brought chaos into their well-ordered lives. *Don't think about that.* I drifted off to sleep.

"Sir, Pennsylvania Station."

I opened my eyes and met those of an AMTRAK steward.

"This is your stop, sir."

"Thanks." I knew I had to move fast, my body ahead of my brain.

I stepped out onto the platform.

"Chad," a woman's voice called out.

"Detective Bryant, hi." She smiled and headed in my direction. I watched the figure she cut moving through the crowd in her corporate skirt and jacket— awfully warm for that—and then I noticed the gentle swell of a holstered gun.

"I was afraid you missed the train." She swept back a stray bang.

"Almost."

"I'm glad you made it." She looked around at the grime and hubbub of the station. "We've got a lot to talk about, and I'm famished. You have any preferences?"

"I'm not too hungry, anyplace quiet."

"Agreed."

She walked quickly toward the exit; I followed in her wake. Even though I was nearly a foot taller, it was an effort to keep up.

"You walk fast."

"I know." She stopped outside a small Thai restaurant just opening for lunch. "I hate getting stuck in crowds. People get out of your way if you've got a good head of steam. This okay with you?"

"Fine."

The smell of stir-fry and spices reawakened my

hunger. We took a corner booth. I looked briefly at the menu. Thai food was one of my favorites and I already knew what I wanted.

She put her menu aside. "So. What were you doing in Boston?"

It caught me off guard. "Is this an interrogation?"

"Just some questions. We need to get a few things out of the way first."

I thought it over. I wanted to confide in her, to let her know I had nothing to hide. "I went to see a psychiatrist who treated me when I was a teenager."

"Why not someone closer?"

"He helped me when I was younger, and right now I'm not in the mood to go hunting for a new doctor. I want someone who knows me, who I can talk to . . . who believes me."

"Can you give me his name?"

"Yes." Liking this less and less.

She pulled out a notepad and pencil.

"It's Dr. William Adams." I gave her his phone number.

"What time did you see him?"

She systematically pumped me for details, taking notes of my itinerary for the last twenty-four hours.

"Look," she said, "I don't mean to come off like a hard-ass; but your whereabouts, if they can be confirmed, could go a long way toward getting you off the hook. Up to now your alibi is full of holes. Which is a problem, because, while I may believe you and your doctor may believe you, there's a lot of circumstantial evidence piling up against you."

"I know . . . You do believe me?"

Again the smile, almost as if we had known each other for years. "Yeah, but I've been wrong before."

"What about your partner?"

"You'll have to ask him."

"I didn't mean to give offense."

"You didn't. We just work better apart, then we come together and compare notes. It's more efficient. We don't pollute each other's thought processes."

Still hung over from the Ativan, I tried to focus on why I was here. "On the phone you said my place was broken into. And there was something else."

"Yeah. We have a couple stops to make later. I need to show you something at the station and then I want to walk through your loft with you, see if anything is missing."

"That's fine." Not certain if it was. I felt a gnawing resistance, wondering if I was just being used.

"Good."

"It's so weird," I said.

"What is?"

"Everything." My thoughts were interrupted by the sweet aroma of skewered beef in peanut sauce. "There's something else you should know." I was not certain if I should share my amateur sleuthing with her.

"What?"

"The man who bought the portrait. It's possible I know him, or knew him."

"You didn't mention that before."

"I'm still not certain." I cleared off half the table and laid out the sketch pads. "This could all be total bullshit." I pulled out the first drawing of the bearded man with glasses. "I drew this with Pamela, tried to get her to remember as much as she could. Not much to go with, really, like a disguise."

I looked at Susan, tried to read her expression. "Of course it could all just be my paranoia; I don't know," I said, opening to the series of drawings from the train. "Here I tried to take away everything extraneous to the face. It's not that hard to do if you've got a few solid landmarks."

"You think you recognize the face?" Her tone was skeptical.

"No, not really, more like a sense that I've seen it before. Faces and bodies are an overlearned skill with me. I do it all the time. I could draw your face from memory; it would be completely recognizable. I could draw your partner's face even though I can't remember his name."

"It's Collins, Dave Collins . . . Show me."

"Whom do you want me to draw?"

"You met Dave once; draw him."

I took out a soft lead pencil and opened to a blank page. I flashed back to the night of the opening. Staring at the whiteness, my breathing deepened and I fixed on an image of Detective Collins. A surge of fear rose in my belly and I started to sketch. The rest was automatic, my mind's eye was trained in sync with my hand.

"Jesus!" Her voice pulled me back to the present. "That's amazing. May I look at it closer?"

I handed it across the table.

She studied the sketch. "That's him. That's totally him, the eyes, you got his mole, the wrinkles here, his cowlick. I've never seen anything like it."

I smiled, enjoying the praise, remembering something else.

"What?" she asked.

"You just reminded me of my teacher, the first time he showed me how to do this. It was like magic. I thought, how can anyone be that good? You know that saying, 'Those who can't do, teach'? That's bullshit. How can you learn from someone who hasn't mastered the craft? But I'm rambling, there's something else I want to show you." I pulled out my find from the attic. "I drew this when I was twenty-five." I opened to the portrait of the man in Bellevue.

She studied the picture, the comparison obvious. "Who is he?"

"I don't know. It was such a long time ago and I really wasn't in the clearest frame of mind."

"What do you mean?"

"I drew it on a psychiatric ward."

"This was after your divorce?"

She caught me by surprise. "You know about that?"

"It's my job."

"Right . . . No"—I was unable to meet her gaze—"this was closer to the time of my breakdown. The divorce came later, although it sort of blurs together. I was only at Bellevue for ten days. Dr. Sturges somehow maneuvered me there and out of the Sixth Precinct holding tanks."

"Why there?"

"I suppose because he was working there. I never thanked him for that. I think on some level I wanted to go to jail."

"Why?"

"I'd rather not go into that." My cheeks burned as I stared at the tablecloth. "Let's just say I treated my wife like shit, and no one should have to go through what I did to her."

"Where did you go from Bellevue?"

"Glendale Psychiatric."

"What about the man you drew? Was he still there when you left?"

"I don't remember. I don't even remember why I drew him; although I was so high I was whipping off sketches and acrylics left and right. Some of them got pretty bizarre."

"Acrylics? The paintings that sold at auction?"

"Right." I was finally able to look her in the face. "That's when I made them."

She checked her watch. "We should get moving."

We settled the check—Dutch—and headed outside. "Do you mind walking?" she asked.

"Don't they give you a car?"

"Yeah, but if I don't need it I'd rather walk. It's too hard to park in this city."

We moved quickly down Sixth Avenue. "This is pretty close to the vet's," I said. "If it's okay, I'd like to see Ching."

"Sure, we've got a little time."

An hour later I was in Susan's windowless office at the precinct station. I'd signed half a dozen documents: the typed copies of my report from the night of the robbery, a second consent to search, a receipt for my sketch pads, God knows what else. A variety of officers were pulled in to witness them, looking me over, signing their names below mine.

She went down to the evidence room in pursuit of something they found hanging out of my mailbox. In her absence, I studied the office: no personal pictures, a cluster of framed diplomas and credentials, two thriving philodendrums, a blue coffee mug and a desk buried in a sea of papers. Not much to go on, like an Edward Hopper interior, bleak and devoid of natural light.

"I need you to look at this." She closed the door and placed a small sandwich bag on the desk.

Inside was one of the color lithograph postcards for my show. On the back was a Magic Marker drawing of

Ching with blood pouring from his chest and the words "Prepare the Way" written in letters cut from a glossy magazine. My stomach turned as I looked at the image.

"What does this mean?" she asked.

I felt the weight of her stare and realized—she doesn't believe me. "It's a bad joke." The truth filled me with fear.

"Did you draw it?"

"Look! You know me so well"—my anger rose; I pushed back in the chair—"you tell me!"

"It's okay, Chad," she said in a soothing voice, her eyes darting to the door.

"I'm sorry." *Stay cool, Chad. Just stay cool. It's her job.*

"If this is getting to be too much, we could try again tomorrow."

"No, I'll be fine." I sat back down, trying to breathe. "Let me look at it. I can tell you something about who *did* draw it." I focused on the picture. "The technique is about two steps better than the average person who stops drawing at the level of a twelve-year-old. There's more detail and some sense of perspective, almost in a cartoonish way. Like teenagers who draw favorite pictures over and over."

"My brother used to draw cars."

I looked across at her, still fighting the sense of betrayal. "Exactly; it's where most people stop. It's a very intellectualized type of drawing where the thing, the product, is the goal. But here"—I pointed to the detail in Ching's mane—"you can see there's some trace of a developed eye, but the overall effect is primitive."

"An artist?"

"Not a good one." I didn't want to state the obvious: that someone tried to reproduce a style of drawing I used many years ago.

"And the words?"

A vein throbbed on my temple. "They're mine."

CHAPTER TEN

We walked in silence. The last half hour had firmed my resolve to get a lawyer. Frankly, after what I'd just learned, I didn't know why I was still a free man. Was she dogging me into a confession? "There were two sets of fingerprints found on the postcard," she had said. "Yours and Dr. Sturges's." It must have been the one I'd given him at that last session. My fingerprints, I'd learned, were already on file at the precinct, yet another reminder of my ten-year-old arrest. I kept waiting for her to read me the Miranda warning, bring out the handcuffs, lock me away, something. She just watched me. It was a look I knew well. Like someone who tolerates a child's stories: "Yes dear, of course I believe you. Now what color did you say the dragon was?"

We turned the corner onto Sixth Avenue and Fourteenth Street. She stopped and stared across at my building. The windows of my loft were fully visible, the sheet of plywood nailed over the fire-escape door had been pried back, my privacy once again violated. A man with gloved hands appeared through the opening. He scraped something from the twisted doorjamb into a sandwich bag. I glimpsed movement, like a swarm of ants, in one of the intact windows. The crime-scene team was already hard at work. *Why do I feel so afraid?*

"How long has the top floor been empty?" she asked.

"A while. Sometime last fall."

"Have you ever been up there?"

"Yeah, a couple times."

"What do you know about the people who lived there?"

"Not much; I never went up when they were there. I'd see them in the stairwell; didn't even know them by name."

"You've been in there since?"

"A few times." I decided my occasional visits to the deserted loft couldn't get me into any more trouble. "It's an incredible space, the lighting is better than . mine. I painted there a few times."

"How did you get in?"

"Through the fire escape."

"You said the landlord was trying to sell the building. How did he get them out?"

"I'm not certain, probably bought them out. We all . got offers. I guess they're the only ones who took it. I can't blame them, they looked pretty young; I know at least a couple of them were students at the Fashion Institute."

"How much were you offered?"

"Twenty-five thousand."

"Seriously?"

"Yeah."

"Lot of money to empty out a building."

"Is it? I think there were plans to tear down half the block; we weren't the only ones to get offers. The shish-kebab man on the corner said he was offered a hundred thousand for his space."

"That was in the fall?"

"Yeah."

"Why didn't you take the money?"

"Where would I go? It wasn't enough money to buy a loft and if I rented something equal, the money would be gone in a year or two. I figured I'd just stay and take my chances. And there was always the possibility that he'd go higher. I even looked at a couple spaces down in SoHo. But to buy something even close to what I have is around two hundred thousand, and that's not including monthly fees which, on most of those places, is higher than my rent."

"That's why the others stayed?"

"I guess. A few of us talked it over; I thought the Richards might take it, move out to the suburbs, but I guess it wasn't enough."

"Anything since the fall?"

"No, it's been pretty quiet. And there don't seem to be a whole lot of vacancies." I scanned the buildings across the street. "It would be a shame to tear these down. Some of them have historical value. Even mine is supposedly the oldest iron-fronted building in the city.

It used to be a doll factory in the eighteen hundreds. If you go on the roof of the next building you can still see part of the old painted sign on the brick."

We crossed the street and climbed the stairs to my loft. At the outer door she turned to me. "I want you to go through and look at everything; take your time. And here"—she took out two pairs of thin latex gloves from her pocketbook—"put these on, and try not to move anything around, at least for now."

"What are you looking for?"

"I don't know." She smiled. "Answers."

From inside the loft I heard the tinny ring of Pamela's phone. The door was open; at first glance nothing was too abnormal other than it felt less and less like my home. Two strange men looked up as we entered; they nodded to Susan and continued with their work.

As I leaned my gloved hand against the door frame, a film of sticky powder came off on my fingers. Ignoring the persistent ring of the phone, I watched the progress of these men, with their brushes and baggies and tweezers, like ants swarming over my belongings, sampling them, taking bits and pieces back to the nest.

The phone didn't stop.

"Do you want to get that?" Susan asked.

"I could," I said, not really caring one way or the other. I picked it up, trying to avoid the thin coating of fingerprint powder.

"Hello."

"Hello, Chad?"

"Yes." I didn't recognize the male voice.

"God, I've been trying to get you for days. You really need an answering machine."

"It's not working right now. Who is this?"

"I'm sorry. It's Harold Schlemer; we met at the opening."

"Right, you're the reporter."

"I wanted to get to you before my *Newsday* piece came out; I just couldn't reach you."

"How did you get this number?"

"I had Serge call your agent."

"What about *Newsday*? I thought you worked for an art magazine?"

"I do, *New York Scene*, but after what happened at your show I decided to pitch the idea to *Newsday*, for their 'Hot and Not' section. I didn't think they'd bite, and when they did, I couldn't get in touch with you to see if it was all right. Anyway, I needed the money and I went ahead."

"Why did you want to get to me before it came out?" I asked, getting the strong sense that he was holding something back and wishing I hadn't picked up the phone.

"It's kind of sensational; they changed it all around. You can barely tell it's my copy."

"How much did you get for it?"

He hesitated. "A thousand bucks for the words and five hundred dollars for the picture."

"That's pretty good. I can't blame you. But, what picture?"

"Just of the outside of the gallery. I really hope you don't mind."

"When does it come out?"

"It did—today."

"Not much I can do about it, is there?"

"You're mad?"

"Look, Harold," I said, as I watched Susan's gloved hand forage through my paint box, "I don't know what I am. I suppose it's okay. Does Pamela know?"

"Who?"

"My agent; it doesn't matter." I tried to end the conversation.

"Look." His voice picked up speed. "I know you're probably not into it, but at the opening you said you'd give me an interview. Is there any chance we could still do that? I'd like to make up for the *Newsday* thing, do something serious. I'll show you the galleys before it goes to press, whatever you want."

"Here." I gave him Pamela's number. "Give her a call, tell her what you want, and if she says it's okay, have her set up a time."

"Thanks, I really appreciate it. And maybe the *Newsday* thing isn't too bad, your 'fifteen minutes' and all that."

"Yeah, I got to get going." And I hung up.

Susan, now systematically scanning my bookshelves, looked up. "What was that about?"

Is it really any of her business? "Some reporter. He was at the opening and apparently there's something in this week's *Newsday* about it."

"What's his name?"

"Schlemer, Harold Schlemer."

She wrote it down, "You have his number?"

"No. I told him to call my agent; he wants an interview."

Standing there, in the middle of my loft, I felt a wave of despair. *This isn't my home anymore. Every aspect of it violated, and Susan, just one more of the ants, maybe the queen of them all, ferreting for scraps.*

"Do you notice anything missing?" she asked.

I tried to focus on the task. *How can you tell? Yes, my privacy, my peace of mind, they're all gone. But the objects, the things of my life, except for the artwork, it all looks the same.* "I can't really see anything." I wandered through the space, my mood blacker with each step: the empty walls, the bloodstained floor, the corner of plywood ripped back. Dark-suited men gave me surreptitious glances as they cataloged and labeled. I could almost hear their thoughts—*guilty, guilty, guilty.*

"Take your time; look at everything," she said.

I stopped by my easel, still set up in the center of the loft. "Right. There's something."

"What?"

"I'd started a painting; it must have been Sunday morning; it's not here now."

"Are you certain?"

"It was on the easel."

"What were you painting?"

"That." I pointed to the plywood and the street scene beyond.

She looked out the window and wrote something down. "You really can see into the building across the way."

"I know." I was not able to muster a joke about one of New York's favorite pasttimes—spying on the neighbors.

"They must get a good view of what goes on in here."

"Probably, unless the lights are off."

"Anything else?"

"Nothing that leaps out." Internally, a decision coalesced: *It's time to leave. Let the ants have it; I've got to get to safer ground.* "Susan?"

"Yes." She turned to look at me, notepad in hand.

"Are you going to arrest me?"

Our eyes locked; *I will not look away.* I watched her struggle for a response, each second's delay ripe with information.

"Not now." She broke her gaze.

"Then I'd like to leave."

"Where will you go?"

"I don't know yet. Maybe a hotel."

"Are you okay?"

I looked at her, and reminded myself, it's her job. "I'll be fine."

She stood rooted, watching me, struggling with

something. It's a look I've seen in countless hospital therapy groups, the stifled secret, embarrassing and powerful.

"What?" I wished she would leave, wished they all would leave.

"You will take care of yourself?"

"I'll be fine." *Now go.*

She didn't budge. "I have a sister like you," she said.

"And?" An edge had crept into my voice.

"And she acts like this before she gets sick."

"Like what? I'm a little stressed right now." My tone was too sarcastic. "And what do you do? Make sure she gets locked up? Get her carted away before things get too messy?"

She flinched. "That's not what I meant. But I can see I've overstayed my welcome." A coolness descended. "Be sure to let me or Detective Collins know your whereabouts. Try to get some sleep." She went over to one of the men. They conversed in voices too low for me to hear. And then she left.

I fought the impulse to run after her and apologize. I could be a real shit sometimes, but right now I couldn't tell if it was warranted or not.

I stood there, turning slowly. *What do I want? My things seem increasingly foreign. Like some gloved space traveler, I don't fit here. Even my paints, all jammed together in an oversized tackle box—they're not really mine anymore. There are traces of white fingerprint powder over the latch and handle; it all belongs to the ants.*

I heard one of the men in my closet rifling through my clothes. The other had started on my books; one by one he turned them upside down, fanned the pages and looked down the bindings.

A voice, not a thought, spoke from inside my head: "*Prepare the way.*" It rode on a wave of euphoria—a whiff of real madness. "Chad, get out of here," I said out loud. "Just go."

The man by the bookshelf looked up. Our eyes met.

"I want to leave," I said, wondering what he thought of my talking to myself.

"That's fine. We'll secure the space when we're finished."

"Thanks." I felt the stare of his gimlet eyes. I turned and walked away, taking only the cell phone.

CHAPTER ELEVEN

I wandered the heart of the Village, where the streets twisted and turned in defiance of the otherwise orderly layout of Manhattan. My thoughts raced as I headed toward the piers.

Usually, this was a walk for Ching and me, he bounding ahead, clearing the way, looking every inch the Imperial Palace guard dog.

Earlier, with Susan looking on, the vet had said, "Another week; he's developed an infection around the surgical site, and some sort of complication caused by the anesthetic; he's not waking up the way he should. He needs a course of intravenous antibiotics, and we've got to let the sedatives leach out of his system."

I touched my forehead to Ching's; his eyes were cloudy, barely seeing. "Please don't die," I whispered. He tried to lick my face, but his tongue felt too dry and too hot. *This is all my fault.*

Back on the street, a man and woman glanced at me anxiously as they passed.

I turned and watched them hurry away, suddenly realizing that my lips were moving and a steady stream of words was pouring out. What was it they had seen?

"Oh shit!" I hurried toward the docks.

I dodged eight lanes of speeding traffic on the West Side Highway and came abruptly upon the relative peace of the newly paved walking park that overlooked the Hudson River. Half-naked Rollerbladers swerved out of my way and drug dealers called out to me: "Nickel bag . . . smoke, smoke. Good Shit. Crystal, 'ludes, acid, rock, check it out. Check it out."

A new ten-foot chain-link fence topped with barbed wire had been erected to block access to the piers. But as with its many predecessors, a large tear had been snipped in the mesh. I peeled back the fencing and stepped onto the ancient wooden structure. A few late-afternoon sun-worshipers, mostly men, mostly gay, dotted the runway-sized pitted surface. Appraising eyes followed my progress as I walked to the end of the pier.

I stood at the edge staring into the water, polluted, black and viscous. A breeze swept off the surface and brushed my face. Traces of rotted fish and chemical waste seeped into my nostrils. I sank down on the splintered wood, my head in my hands.

"What are you going to do?" I cried, not caring if anyone heard me.

I felt the walls close in.

You could just give up. It's easy.

"It's not that easy."

Sure it is: Stop the pills, give in, lie back and let it all happen.

I patted my jacket pocket, felt the reassuring rattle and roll of my pill bottles. "You've got your pills, you've got your wallet and you've got a cellular phone. How about some direction?"

If you go crazy, you could cop an insanity plea.

"No. I didn't do anything. It's not my fault." I pictured Dr. Sturges.

It's your fault.

"No. No. No." My breath came faster, acid pains rolled in my belly. *All your fault.* Images raced in my head: Ching and Joz, Zack and my mother. *All your fault.*

Kill yourself. Make it easier for everyone.

That one thought, like a bucket of cold water, shocked my brain into silence.

You have the means. Lithium, a month's supply, more than enough to do the job.

The idea grabbed me. As if I'd overlooked something basic, I suddenly realized that no matter how bad things got, there was a way out—death. And that wasn't so bad; everyone had to die; and it was always an option. My parents would be sad, my sister too. They'd get over it. "It was probably for the best. He suffered so," they'd reason. I'm sure they'd take care of Ching. And for Zack, he barely knew me; could I hurt him any worse than I'd already done?

I took the pills out of my pocket, the bottle full. There were probably four or five lethal doses in my hand. I pushed down on the safety cap and looked at the chalky-white tablets. Saliva gathered in my mouth. *So easy.*

I put two pills on my tongue and swallowed dry. I pictured them scraping the lining of my throat as they descended to my stomach. I felt their weight in my belly as I worked up the next mouthful of spit.

The muffled squeal of the telephone broke through the lining of my jacket. I froze, catching an image of myself in the black water.

It rang again.

As though watching myself from afar, I put down the bottle and pulled the cellular out of my pocket.

"Hello?"

"Chad, it's Pamela."

"Hi. How are you?" My voice sounded canned, not quite real.

"I'm fine. I'm a little worried about you, though."

"No need; things couldn't be happier."

"You sound strange. Where are you? I need to discuss some things, and I have a great big fat check for you."

"Sounds good." I looked at the bottle. "Where's home?"

"What are you talking about?"

"I don't have a home right now; too many ants."

"You have ants in your loft?"

"Huge ones; '. . . just crawl all over you, take everything away. Go up your nose and in your toes, cart away your Christmas bows.'"

"Where are you?" Her voice was insistent.

"Pier nine."

"Are you on something?"

"Not a thing; just love, death and happiness."

"I'm coming to get you. Wait for me."

"No need, I'm fine."

"I'm coming anyway."

"Okay."

"You be there." She hung up.

Now why should she be upset? Thinking it through, I'd skyrocket to fame if I killed myself. Prices would shoot through the roof. Of course, Pamela wouldn't see much of that, she only made her cut on the new stuff, not on the secondary markets.

My gaze drifted to the swirling waters, my face darkly reflected and distorted in its oily surface, the open bottle of pills by my side.

Wait a minute. I struggled to retain a train of thought. "What was that?"

Something about money. Pamela said she had some money.

"No, that's not it."

Your paintings, worth more with you dead.

"No shit!" The thought knocked me back.

How could I overlook something so obvious?

I put the cap on the pills, the hard plastic firm against my palm.

I don't want to die. I don't want to go crazy, and I don't want to go to jail.

Perched on the dock with Pamela's cellular telephone, I punched in a number.

I caught Dr. Adams between patients.

"Sorry to bother you, but things are unraveling, my threads are coming loose."

"How bad?"

"Hard to say. Or else I don't want to say. I heard a voice today . . . and there was no one there. First time in ten years. The same one I used to hear."

"Do you have it now?"

I stopped and listened, turning inward, scared, not wanting to tempt fate; it was quiet, just the city behind me and the water below me. "I don't hear it now."

"Good. Has anything happened since yesterday?"

"Just the same. I've left my apartment; it got infested."

"What do you mean?"

"They're all over everything. Taking me apart piece by piece. And I just figured the most important thing; I'm worth a lot of money dead."

"What are you talking about?"

"My paintings. All of my stolen paintings. It's like the stock market, they go up and down. But in art if you really want to make something golden, kill the goose."

"Where are you?"

"At the piers, trying to clear my head."

"Just so long as you're not thinking of jumping off."

I paused. "That was a few minutes ago."

"Chad, you're scaring me."

"Join the club. That's why I called."

"To scare me?"

"No, I'm scaring myself, and just about everyone around me. I don't want to lose it. And I don't know if I can stop myself. Also, there's no way I'm going back to the hospital."

Silence on his end. "All right, a few things. Is there anyone you trust and can stay with?"

"I think so, sort of, my agent."

"Where is she?"

"She's coming to get me." Turning my head, I found Pamela's scarf-draped form in the distance.

"Good. I want you to look at the different things stressing you out right now and make some sort of decision about each. Like this policewoman; it's beginning to sound like you should have some legal advice."

"I know."

"Good, then get some. Now about medication . . ."

Pamela picked her way down the rutted surface. Her heels were wedging in the cracks, threatening to topple her. Her hair broke free of its combs and whipped violently around her face.

"What the hell are you doing here?" she demanded, cautiously coming to my side, peering over the edge.

"Hold on," I said into the receiver. "Pamela, I want you to meet Dr. Adams; he's my psychiatrist."

"Of course," she said, taking the phone. "Hello?"

As she talked to Dr. Adams, I felt an urge to run away. My cheeks burned with humiliation. *I'm thirty-five years old and shit like this still happens. Like Baby Huey, overgrown, yet hopelessly stunted; why the fuck can't I do this by myself?*

"I see," she said, and searched in her purse for pencil and paper. "We'll stop on the way home. You could call it into Brexall's Pharmacy; I've got the number here . . . Uh-huh . . . right. Let me have your number . . . Okay . . . I know someone . . . Right, I thought he should have done that when this whole thing started . . . Great, thanks . . . Let me give you back to him."

She handed me the receiver.

"Chad," he said, "it's real important that you not miss any doses right now. Also, I know you don't like to, but I think a low dose of an antipsychotic would be useful, try to keep the voices from coming back."

"It was only the one time." I wasn't really sure if that was true.

"I don't think you should risk it."

"They make me feel like shit."

"I know. I'm going to call in a prescription of Trilafon for before bed. Just a few milligrams; it'll help kill the edge."

"More likely it'll kill me." I sounded every inch the petulant adolescent.

"Better to stop it now. You know that."

"Right." Tears pushed through. "I won't be able to paint at all. My hands will shake too much."

"It'll just be for a little while. I think you should do it."

"You're right." I tried to regain my resolve, tried to push back my rage. "I'm going to make it through this."

"Yes, you will. Now I've got to see my next patient. You have my number; I'll let the service know to reach me if you call."

"Thanks."

"You're welcome."

I looked at Pamela. "I'll try to be good."

"I know, sweets. Doctor thinks I should find you some pills and a lawyer. What do you think?"

"Yeah." I got to my feet, again feeling like the rope in a tug-of-war. I wanted to run, to jump in the river, to race screaming down the pier. "It's time for my medication."

CHAPTER TWELVE

What had I done? My resolve wavered as I paced the boundaries of my new rectangular home, Pamela's, really, her spare room. Not much more than a closet, which by New York standards gave it a price tag of about two thousand dollars a month. Location location location; after all, this was Fifth Avenue.

Until thirty minutes ago, this had been the gathering ground for her clean laundry. Now, excavated from piles of dry-cleaning bags and Laundromat baskets, it was my temporary shelter. Minimally furnished, it was the one room she never got around to decorating, the pink forget-me-not wallpaper a vestige of one of her daughters, now grown. Its one window faced south on Washington Square Park, just a hop, skip, and a jump from work. If I still had a job; I never called to cancel morning classes.

Is this how it happens—again? The life I spent years building had been blown apart in the space of a week. Like a juggler thrown off balance, I had first let one egg fall and then they all came smashing down. I felt the weight of the lithium in my stomach; after all, death was only a pill swallow away.

At least it was safe here, the comfort of four close

walls, twenty stories above the city. *Maybe I could squeeze in a small easel, park it in front of the mirror.*

"You okay in there?" she asked.

"Yeah, fine." I opened the door. "This is really good of you."

"Don't mention it. Let me show you where everything is."

I took the tour, got shown the linen closet and the microwave. She gave instructions on how to tease hot water out of the shower. All the time I watched her, my unlikely friend.

We had met ten years ago at my graduation show. She introduced herself, said she liked my work and thought she could promote it. I thanked her kindly, not certain what this large, persistent woman in vivid-batiked cotton meant or wanted. She stayed for hours, circling the gallery, mingling and chatting. She'd occasionally stop, catch my attention and smile. It was fascinating, so much social grace, like a brightly plumed bird soaring in and out of conversations. Near the end, she caught me from behind, tapped me on the shoulder while I was talking with Jan.

"Have you thought about it?" she asked. "I take twenty-five percent of everything I sell."

I introduced her to my teacher. "So, you represent artists?" he asked.

"Yes." She handed him her card, ignoring the condescension in his voice. "Of course you're already taken, but should you ever get tired of the McCormicks . . ."

"I see." He took the card and was on the verge of saying something rude.

"Of course," she continued, not giving him a chance, "why should Mr. Greene sign with me? I'm totally unknown, new to the business. Doesn't make sense, does it?"

Obviously rhetorical, "Let me demonstrate," she said, and before either one of us could respond, she'd flown off in a flurry of billowing skirts and descended on a pair of men who'd been viewing my paintings.

We watched from a distance, as my eye automatically traced the perspective, the relatedness of forms. A few minutes later she came back. "Come with me; it's time for the kill."

Jan shrugged, clearly curious, wanting the show to continue.

She introduced me to Mark and Dean as though they were her old friends, and we chatted about the painting. She goaded them to ask questions. "He doesn't bite . . . you'll thank me for it later," she said. She spoke of provenance and told them to place a small label on the back of the painting stating when and where they had bought it. "You'd be amazed what that will do for the resale. Just don't put down what you paid for it." She turned to me, not wanting me to speak. "I told them you'd take a thousand for it, but nothing less."

I was speechless.

"Was that okay?" She wanted me to play along, to be the reluctant suitor.

"I don't know; I hadn't really thought of selling it."

She flashed an approving smile. "I'll work on him," she told them, "but let's be frank. If you have the money in the bank, it's earning what? Four percent? Now a painting you enjoy, all well and good, and very important; I would never encourage anyone to buy a picture just as an investment. But, if you buy carefully and have an eye for what will do well, the potential for appreciation is immense. Chad is going to be a major artist; he's already got representation by the Prescott agency . . ."

It was my first sale. She sold two others from that show, an unheard-of achievement for a student exhibition. Even Jan gave his blessing. A few weeks later, as he made plans to leave New York City for Santa Fe, he told me—besides advising me always to keep the teaching job—"Don't ever get rid of that woman."

"Are you listening to me?" she asked, catching me staring out the bathroom window.

"Not really."

"Jesus, Chad. I don't want to come back here and find water over everything." And she demonstrated the correct technique for placing a pan under the leaky "L" pipe. "You got it?"

"No problem."

"Great," she said, clearly not sure it was. "I've got to finish up at the office. You sure you'll be okay?"

"I'm fine, Mom."

"Good. I'll see you later."

I watched her exit in a sweep of color; odd that I'd never painted her. I stored the image for future use and wandered through her apartment.

Years ago, when we had first met, this had been her office. "I sank everything from the divorce settlement into this place," she'd explained one night over frozen margaritas. After twenty-three years of marriage, she had caught her husband with another woman. "There was nothing to talk over; I left. I always told him I would if he cheated. He probably thought I was bluffing or, I don't know . . . middle-aged-man stuff." She fixed me with an accusing stare. "I try not to think about it too much. And, in the end, after a year of crying and taking antidepressants and having to deal with two grown daughters who couldn't quite forgive me for "not giving Daddy a second chance," and a sister who kept wondering why my marriage couldn't be more like hers, I got on with things. I realized Long Island was killing me. I couldn't take the tennis-club-and-martini set. So I dusted off a very old dream, sold everything I could and moved to the city."

"That was quite an awakening," she said. "Not many people looking for forty-three-year-old housewives with vintage bachelor's degrees from Wellesley. But I can be real persistent." She smiled. "Finally, after two months of daily hounding, the business manager for the Cartwright Agency took me on as a secretary. It was either that or call security to cart me away. So I became a secretary, and then an administrative assistant, and then the office manager; I just kept pushing. It's not hard if you know where you're going. Like all those gurus into visualization, I pictured my goal. They gave me a couple clients . . . actually, I kind of gave them to myself, but by the time they figured that out, I was bringing in money. The clients were happy, didn't want to go back to the status quo, and generally, money talks."

"Why did you leave?"

"I never intended to stay. I wanted my own agency. It was like going back to school—on-the-job training. After two years I left; I'd learned what I needed to, had a telephone book filled with contacts, and knew that I could find and develop fresh talent; it just takes legwork."

Now, wandering through her apartment, looking at the artwork, some of it mine, some from other clients, I realized how far she had come. She had her own suite of Madison Avenue offices, eight employees, and a clientele that included two best-selling authors, a Broadway playwright, and a visual artist whose work garnered as much as six and seven figures. Even Jan left his previous agent and, for those rare occasions when he wished to sell a painting or hang a show, had Pamela broker the deal.

I looked at her framed family photos on the wall next to the kitchen and I saw a woman who'd reinvented herself. A twenty-year-old picture with her daughters set against a sunny day on Long Island

Sound acted as the "before" shot. I could almost smell the surf and taste the promise of a picnic lunch. In another, she was in her early thirties, her hair in a conservative housewife's cut, smiling broadly, her head resting against that of another woman, their faces similar, probably her sister.

"Where are the men?" I muttered aloud, realizing my sex was represented by a single mustached figure, probably her grandfather, in a turn-of-the-century black-and-white wedding photo. She had his nose. I spent a few seconds tracking features through the family.

On the carved coffee table were a name and number she'd left for me. She had said, "I got him from my own lawyer. He said, 'If you can get beyond his personality, there's no one better.' You might want to give him a call."

What the hell. I dialed.

"Attorney Aronowitz's office. May I help you?" The nasal twang of Queens.

"Yes, I'd like to speak to Mr. Aronowitz."

"Who should I say is calling? And what is this in reference to?"

"I'm looking for a lawyer and he was recommended."

"Hold on. I'll see if he's in."

Through the hand-muffled receiver I heard, "Marvin, pick up the goddamn phone."

"I would if you knew how to transfer the goddamn call!"

"Fuck you!"

"I already do."

"You're such a shit."

"Yes, but I'm your shit."

The hand came off the earpiece. "Hold on and I'll transfer you."

I listened to the clicking of the phone, wondering what strangeness was about to be transmitted into my head along the wires.

A pressured baritone with the receptionist's Olive Oyl vowels greeted me. "Marvin Aronowitz. What can I do for you?"

"I'm not sure. I think I need a lawyer and you were recommended."

"All right. That's a start, can I ask for a vowel?" he said stealing a phrase from a popular game show.

"I think I may be arrested for my psychiatrist's murder."

"A vowel! I didn't want the whole puzzle. All right, you need a lawyer; I'm a lawyer, might be a match. I'll give you back to Velma and have her set up a consultation tomorrow. I'm sure I got a spot in the afternoon. Hold on." Not giving me a chance to reply, he said, "Hey, Velma, what's tomorrow look like?"

"You've got court all morning, and the afternoon's full."

"What happened to three o'clock?"

"I penciled in Bronski."

"I told you, I don't want to see that desiccated turd

until after the arraignment! Reschedule him and put this bubee in at three."

"I can see you at three," he told me. "Just give Velma your vitals. You got a name?"

"Chad."

"And a last name?"

"Greene."

"There we go. Chad Greene, what is that? English?"

"Welsh."

"All right, Chad Greene, I'll see you at three. And *heeeeere's* Velma."

The receptionist shot a couple dozen questions at me, obviously filling out some sort of database. Finally I got a chance to ask, "How much will this cost?"

"It depends. You got to work that out with Marvin. His usual rate is two hundred fifty dollars an hour."

"Jesus!"

"Well," she replied, in the voice of the conspirator, "with lawyers you get what you pay for. You pay shit, you get a shitty lawyer."

"Right."

"But don't worry, the first meeting is free. It's more to see if he likes you."

"What about the other way around?"

"Well, that too," she said without conviction. "So tomorrow at three."

"Thanks."

"Don't mention it." She hung up.

The Portrait

1   I went to the bathroom and popped a Trilafon, wondering what it would do on top of the extra lithium. Within minutes, like a runaway train that's suddenly braked, my thoughts started to slow. Or maybe it wasn't the medication, but relief at doing what I should have done two days earlier. Hard to figure.

I forged ahead with damage control. I dialed my department head.

"Hey, Chad." The receptionist's sunny disposition and innate curiosity greeted me. "What happened to you today?"

"Don't ask. Is Kevin around?"

"He just left . . . hold on, I think I see him by the elevators."

Pamela's black marble, Victorian mantel clock ticked loudly; it was four-thirty. *Where does the time go?* I heard footsteps and voices over the line.

"Hello, Chad. We missed you. Still hung over from the show?" Kevin's tone was too affable; he should have been pissed.

"Something like that. I'm really sorry. There's been a lot going on. I should have called."

"Don't sweat it. Everyone's allowed one fuckup. By the way, congratulations on the show. I thought it was great and that piece in *Newsday* really was something."

"So I heard. I haven't seen it yet."

"We've been getting all kinds of calls for you today."

"Really?"

"It's good business, Chad. Publicity like this is what makes an artist a household name. It pulls you out of the faceless masses."

"I suppose. Anyway. I promise I'll be there in the morning. Thanks for being okay with today."

"Don't mention it. I'll see you then."

Now that's odd. He should be pissed, or at the very least, whiny and sarcastic. My vision was jaded by years of seeing him through Jan's eyes. My mentor did not suffer fools lightly, and he'd suffered Kevin not at all. Whenever a staff meeting was called, Jan would mutter, "Idiot, what does he think we are? A bunch of nursery-school teachers? He doesn't listen anyway." Jan usually gave some implausible excuse and I would attend in his place.

To be truthful, the majority of meetings left me with a vague uneasiness. Somehow the theme always turned to flagging enrollment, or the threat of flagging enrollment, and what could we do to keep "our little studio, embedded within this massive university," solvent.

I didn't exactly expect a chewing-out. Kevin was more oblique. He generally went with the veiled threat. Maybe having a successful show and some sort of article were enough to cover my unexcused absence. I pictured Jan's response, "But of course, he's always been form without content."

I sank into the sofa and looked out the view through the picture window. It carried me west toward the Hudson River and the smokestacks of New Jersey. How long had it been since I had been thinking of jumping in? *It's okay, forget it.* My head cradled into the soft curve of the armrest. I kicked off my sneakers and drifted toward sleep.

CHAPTER THIRTEEN

I woke from the twisted sleep of pent-up dreams. I searched for clues as to my whereabouts, sucking in the diffused rays of morning sun and the gurgle and the gasp of a drip coffeemaker as it completed its task.

"Morning." Pamela's voice came from behind the couch.

"What time is it?"

"Six thirty. I thought it was better to leave you sleeping than risk getting you up."

"Thanks."

"What day is it?"

"Wednesday."

I pushed myself to a sitting position. My lower back twinged and my neck shot daggers when I turned it to the right. My clothes, the same khakis and T-shirt, were hopelessly wrinkled; a faint musk rose to my nostrils. *You missed your evening pills.* Oh, well. At least I slept.

"Here, have some coffee." She handed me a steaming mug.

"Thanks." I inhaled the fumes and savored the first dark gulp. "I have no clothes."

"I noticed." She sat next to me.

"I didn't know if I could take anything from my loft. If it was like a crime scene or something."

"Did you ask?"

"No. I just wanted to get out of there. You have a T-shirt I can borrow?"

"Sure."

"I'll buy some things after class."

"Bloomie's is good," she offered.

"Too expensive."

"Not for you."

I turned, wincing slightly, and looked at her profile. A Mona Lisa smile played at the corners of her mouth. "So how much came in from the show?"

She met my gaze, her brown eyes twinkled brightly. "After my percentage and Serge's fees it came to . . ."

"Out with it."

"I want a drumroll."

"I'm not in the mood."

"God, you can be a stick-in-the-mud. All right, it came close to three hundred thousand."

I watched her expression, the steady gaze, the half-smile. "You've got to be kidding." I could see she wasn't. "How is that possible? That can't be right." I was certain there must be some mistake in her arithmetic. Maybe thirty thousand or forty thousand, even that would be over twice what my last show brought.

"That's not even the half of it," she said. "My office is flooded with calls. People from the show. People who saw the article. I've started to book you for portrait sittings; I hope you don't mind."

"It depends who they are. Anyone interesting?"

"*Rich* and interesting. Do you want to know what you're charging?" Her dismay over my lack of enthusiasm was obvious.

"Sure."

"Fifty thousand dollars."

"Jesus!"

"What? That's what Warhol was getting for those silk-screen jobbies. I was thinking of going higher, but I'm going to hold off until after the next Christie's."

"You lost me."

"Well, unlike some people who've been gallivanting around the piers, I've been doing my job. Right now you're it, Mr. Hot New Artist. And whenever that happens, people want to cash in. I know it's crass and distasteful and art should be pure and holy, but that's for you and not for me. Anyway, I just wanted to see what action the show stirred up. So I put out a few calls and sure enough, one of the paintings from the show has already been consigned. I suspect a number will go on the block within the next few months. Hopefully, not too many. Don't want to flood the market."

"But who would do that? If you don't like a painting, why buy it?"

"Chad, it's a business. It has nothing to do with whether or not you *like* the painting. You should know that. Haven't I taught you anything? At least half the pictures from the show went to dealers. Some of them will try and turn a quick buck. So now we sit back and see where things go. Like water finding its mark."

"Paintings as pork bellies?"

"Basically. If things play out the way I suspect they will, money may never be an issue for you again. Which reminds me, that reporter, Harold . . . oh shit, Harold whatever wants to do a follow-up interview. I told him yes and set him up for tomorrow after your classes. Is that all right?"

"I guess. I never did see the *Newsday* piece."

"Not to worry." She got her voluminous black leather pocketbook off the kitchen counter. "I bought a dozen copies. Here, you read and I'll dig you up a T-shirt. Oh, and Chad . . ."

"What?"

"You might want to take a shower."

"Thanks."

"Just trying to be helpful. Although unwashed and smelly isn't necessarily a hindrance to the successful artist."

"I'll keep that in mind."

The cover of the glossy weekly magazine had a picture of an emaciated child in front of a wooden shack. Across her rag-covered body a vivid red banner proclaimed, STARVATION IN AMERICA. I flipped through the familiar publication, heading to the gossipy "Hot and Not" section, always two pages in from the back.

A feeling of dread rumbled through my belly as I scanned the page. My eye caught an exterior shot of the gallery, my name in the window. Below it . . .

SOLD OUT IN SOHO

Like sale day at Filene's Basement, a consumer frenzy swept through Chadwick Greene's opening at the prestigious Gordman Gallery on West Broadway. Entitled "Genuine," many felt the show was a much needed body slam to the increasingly fraudulent trends in contemporary art. Simply put, it was a tour de force.

Mr. Greene, who teaches painting at the prestigious Washington Square Studio, combined virtuoso technique with images that both disturbed and seduced. Many of his themes dealt with personal madness (the artist's lifelong struggle with manic-depression) and a city that breeds insanity.

Almost as soon as the doors opened, pictures began to sell. At one point, an impromptu auction was held as several buyers fought over the last remaining pieces. One painting, which started with a price tag of $4,500, was finally hammered down at $37,500. Its new owner, a major Manhattan dealer who wished not to be identified, stated what became a familiar sentiment, "I could sell it tomorrow for twice that."

"*What is this?*" My mind skittered over the details. Did I really want everyone to know I had manic-depression? Did I really tell him that? I didn't recall . . . $37,500? How was that possible? Could he really sell it for twice that?

I read and reread. I wasn't trying to "body slam" anyone. "Genuine" meant something else; how easily people twisted the deliberately ambiguous into something concrete and nameable. *Maybe that's okay. But do I really want to meet with this man?*

I looked at it again, maybe it wasn't so bad. I suppose it was complimentary—just sort of cheap.

"Done is done," I said out loud.

"So," Pamela asked, a T-shirt from last year's Halloween parade in her hand, "what do you think?"

"It's weird."

"Really? I thought it was pretty good, but then I am thinking about the finances of the whole thing. It doesn't say anything bad, and it lays it on pretty thick about *quality*."

"I suppose. But do I really want everyone to know about my 'lifelong struggle with manic depression'? It sounds like a made-for-TV movie: *The Chad Greene Story: Artist on the Edge*. It's pretty personal. At least it was."

"It's going to get worse. Unless you totally disappear. 'Cause I suspect you're about to be flavor of the week. There's no denying that it's going to be a trade-off."

"What are you talking about?"

"Well, why is it that so few artists, regardless of talent, ever make it? And then, those few that do, generally do best, from a financial standpoint, after they're dead."

"Because it doesn't matter," I said automatically. "The money, at least while you're actively creating, just isn't an issue. I paint because I have to."

"Granted, but what about those very few who become successful in their lifetimes? Like Picasso, Dalí, Warhol, de Kooning—what sets them apart?"

"I don't know. But I suspect you're going to tell me."

"Think about it. It's all about exposure. People buy the art for its value, the signature, the scent of fame. Your paintings are going to bring much more at the end of the year than at the beginning. Is that because you've become a better artist?"

"It's very odd." I refilled my coffee.

"Not at all; it's business—supply and demand." Her eyes caught mine as I sank back into the couch. "And that's where I come in. Things have started to move. The question is . . . how far do you want to go?"

"Is it that simple?"

"At this point? Yes. You tell me how famous you want to be. But there's a price."

"My privacy."

"At the very least."

"I can't have one without the other?"

"Not today. To sell the paintings you have to sell the artist."

"And I know you mean that in the nicest way." I laughed in spite of myself.

"It's true. The work matters, but I suspect, for a while at least, it becomes secondary. People want to know what a million-dollar artist looks like. What sets him apart? How did he do it? How can I do it?"

"All the more reason for the work to be solid. Otherwise you're scamming people."

"That's another subject. I'm not so sure people don't want to be scammed. Then you've got all that fine moral outrage. Half the fun of building someone up is ripping them down."

"Something to look forward to?"

"Forewarned is forearmed. Well"—she got to her feet—"I should head to the office. I'll cut you a check later today for about half, the other half will have to wait till all the checks clear."

"Good."

"And, Chad . . ."

"Yeah?"

"I know you've got a lot on your mind, but think about what I said. This is a crossroads. If we're going to push things, now is the time. But I won't do it unless you give me the go-ahead."

"Thanks."

"Of course it will kill me not to."

"I realize."

"We could make *so* much money. Well"—she hoisted her pocketbook—"think about it, and I'll see you later."

The door closed behind her, bringing silence. I sat there, thinking—*What do you do with that much money?*

It was now eight o'clock. Normally, I'd be finishing my morning paint, having already walked Ching. My rhythm was off. So, what was today's goal? I thought, harking back to one of the endless therapy groups from the last hospitalization—Goals Group. The object, or as far as I could discern, was for every patient to formulate an objective for the day, something to shoot for. Then, at the end of the day, in another group, you had to evaluate how you did. It seemed stupid at the time, just another turn of the wheel in what people thought was therapeutic. But now, where everything was upside down, a single goal was attractive. If I could do just one thing today, what would it be?

Get a lawyer.

Fine, then. My goal for today would be to get a lawyer who would keep me from going to prison. And my other goal was to take a shower. A round of phantom applause met my pronouncement, my inner nurse, a distillation of a long line of smiling concerned faces, beamed on. I'd done well.

In the bathroom I was greeted by an unshaven and unkempt man. My resolve faltered as I realized I didn't have a razor, clean underwear, or a toothbrush. *Not your goals.* I reminded myself feeling a strange comfort in the stupidity of black-and-white logic. *So what if you don't shave? And who needs underwear anyway? At least you've got your pills.* I dutifully swallowed the pre-scribed amount.

The shower was bliss, steamy water and heady smells of unfamiliar soap and shampoo. I sank down, letting the flow course over me, thinking back to the conversation with Pamela. What did I want? Money was all well and good, but it has never been my objective. *Dad would go for it.* I imagined his arguments: "You could put it aside for Zack's college tuition, buy your own home and then invest the rest. You're not in the most stable of professions."

So what was the downside? I immediately thought of the *Newsday* article: "Sold Out in SoHo" and "life-long battle with manic-depression." And Pamela's flavor-of-the-week comment and the loss of privacy. Is that what I wanted?

Did I really have a choice?

I breezed into the studio and taught my morning classes, trying to ignore the subtle, and not so subtle, differences. The student who shyly asked me to sign a copy of her catalog from my show. As soon as I had agreed, several others, who'd apparently been waiting for my response, came out with flyers and catalogs and even a copy of the article for me to sign. One of them giggled to a friend, "This is going to be worth money someday."

As I prepared to leave, Kevin's eternally cheerful

secretary, Lois, snagged me in the hall. "Chad, do you have a minute? Kevin *really* wants to talk to you."

"Well, I'm on sort of a tight schedule." My mind was already several blocks down the road, heading toward Ching.

"It shouldn't take long."

Before I could make good my escape, Kevin's balding head popped out of his office.

"Chad, good to see you." He grabbed my hand and threw an arm around my shoulders. He steered me into his office. "You got a minute?"

I was snared. "Sure."

"You want some coffee?"

"No, thanks. What's up?"

"Right, I wanted a chance to talk to you before contract time. I know with all your success with the show and everything you might be looking at teaching with a different eye, and I just wanted to feel you out about that."

"About what?"

"I just want you to know that I think you're very important to the studio, and I'd hate to lose you."

"Who said anything about that?"

He looked at me closely. "I've been getting vibes that maybe you might be thinking of quitting. And I hope before you make any decision, you'll come and talk with me. I've already been speaking with administration about moving you onto the tenure track. I should have done it a long time ago."

Suddenly, this was interesting. "A professorship?"

"Eventually. You're a real asset and I'm a real ass for not seeing this coming."

I decided to shut up about having no intention of leaving.

"It's how I lost Jan," he said. "Anyway, promise me you won't make any decisions without talking to me first."

"No problem. But I really got to go."

"Sure." He opened the door for me. "And I'll get back to you by the end of the week with what we were discussing."

"Great." A professorship—not part of my daily goal, but interesting nevertheless.

CHAPTER FOURTEEN

I walked quickly through the preserved realm of sixties bohemia on West Third and Bleecker Street, on my way to the Village Vet. Images from Saturday night intruded into my thoughts, like a film loop that played over and over; I couldn't stop it. I saw the open door to my loft, Ching in a pool of blood, the rush of despair thinking he was dead. I walked over, or did I run? I heard his whimper and saw the faint rise and fall of his chest. I thought he was going to bleed to death.

I tried to shut it out, but part of me wouldn't let it go. "Look at it," I told myself, "look at it closer." For someone who professed to be so observant . . . I was missing something. And then, standing at the corner of Sixth and Eighth Street in front of the Indian-owned newsstand where I'd bought my paper and cigarettes, I remembered: the triptych was there! When I picked up Ching, I had briefly looked for something to wrap him in before bundling him in my jacket. I remembered looking at the paisley scarf, a present from Pamela, draped over the piano, and behind it—the triptych was still on the wall.

The realization sank in: *There was someone in the loft with me.* I reeled at the thought. I was being watched.

A new emotion struggled to be born—a smoldering hatred, the beginnings of rage. If I had known, whoever it was would have had to kill me, because nothing would have stopped me from tearing him apart, save for the bite of a bullet.

It's better I didn't know; at least this way I got Ching to the vet.

I stopped outside the low white building—*please, let him be okay*—and went into the waiting room. The receptionist, the long-suffering Helen, smiled as I entered.

"Mr. Greene, I'm glad you're here. Doctor Anderson wanted to talk with you.

My stomach turned. *Something must be wrong.*

"I'll tell him you're here."

"Thanks." My eyes met briefly with those of an elderly woman and her Siamese cat, both sets blue and dulled by the milky haze of cataracts. A black shar-pei puppy strained at its collar, snorting and whining, wanting to sniff me. Its owner pulled back on the leash. "Down, Reggie. No!"

I tried to smile, but a weight pressed on my heart. *Please let him be okay.*

"Mr. Greene, if you could come with me, the doctor will see you now."

It was like watching a car accident in slow motion, knowing the crash was coming, unable to stop it. She led me into Ching's room. I went over to his still body, small and crumpled in the corner of the chain-link kennel, his head still encased in the white plastic collar.

I knelt down. "Ching. Ching." For a moment I wondered if he was dead, and then he snorted and opened his eyes, trying to focus on me.

"Mr. Greene." Dr. Anderson's voice broke through.

I turned around, still kneeling by my dog, and looked at the tall man dressed in scrubs and a lab coat.

"I wanted to talk to you about Ching," he said.

"What's wrong with him?"

He crossed his arms. "On the surface he's been doing okay; he's just not waking up."

"What do you mean? You mean you're not giving him something to sleep?"

"Not since the operation."

"Then what's wrong with him?"

"I don't know; I'm guessing it's some sort of idiosyncratic reaction to the barbiturate; he doesn't seem to be metabolizing it."

"How is that possible?"

"It may be that he just doesn't have the enzyme that processes the parent compound. I've never run across it before, but it is possible."

"So how do we wake him up?"

"I was thinking we'd give him another twenty-four hours to wake up on his own, and if that doesn't work I think we should dialyze him."

"What's that?"

"It's basically a machine that filters the blood. We could remove the drug that way. It's fairly expensive and I'd want your permission before we went ahead with it."

"If you think it will work, just do it."

He crouched beside me, his eyes fixed on Ching. "I just can't understand it."

"What if it's not that?" I asked.

"What do you mean?"

"What if it's something other than the drug?"

"It's possible." He opened the cage so that I could stroke Ching's head. "But we've been checking the level of the drug in his blood, and it's very high. Has he ever had any surgeries before? Or allergic reactions to anything?"

"No, just when I had him neutered, and you have the records for that here. He was fine afterward, a little grumpy, but no problems. Then he had a couple kidney infections, but that's been it."

"It's odd. Otherwise, he's doing well. As soon as we get him to wake up, you can take him home."

"If I had a home."

He looked at me questioningly.

"Long story."

He nodded. "It really sucks when stuff like this happens."

"Yeah. Well, at least he's getting good care."

"Thanks. I just wish it was better news."

"The way things have been going, this wasn't half as bad as I expected."

I left the vet and headed northeast toward Gramercy and the office of Marvin Aronowitz. The afternoon had turned hot and sticky. The air hung thick with car and bus exhausts trapped in the humidity. It was a portent in May of the steamy New York heat that sent every New Yorker who could afford it packing each summer for destinations like Montauk, Fire Island and the Hamptons.

A bronze plaque embedded in the side of a four-story brownstone on the north side of Gramercy Park let me know I had arrived. Hundred-year-old trees shaded this block with its private, locked park. The hint of a breeze was found here and nowhere else. I stopped, knowing I had a few minutes to kill, wanting to give the sweat dripping between my shoulder blades a chance to dry.

An uneasiness formed in my stomach; I didn't like lawyers. Not that I'd had all that much to do with them, but it had always been bad—always me behind the eight ball.

Is that what I was expecting now? To be told I'd fucked up, that this was somehow all my fault?

Scenes from my past came in snippets: my divorce, my arrest, a commitment hearing when I was eighteen and demanding to be let out of the locked unit.

My lawyer then, appointed by the city, did nothing to prevent the lies and twisting of the truth that kept me locked up. It probably was for the best, but the feeling of impotence, of listening to my parents, the tears in my mother's eyes begging the judge not to let me go were still with me. The doctors and nurses gave testimony, using the things I'd said—weren't they supposed to be confidential?—to bolster their case. My words and actions were characterized, vilified and labeled. "He's floridly psychotic with auditory hallucinations and paranoid delusions revolving around hyperreligious themes. He still represents a significant danger to himself and to others."

Needless to say, I wasn't released, and worse, for the next six months, my father became my conservator. Despite having turned eighteen, I was not to be considered a person. All autonomy had been stripped from me and awarded to my father. I wouldn't speak to him for months afterward. It was all in my best interest, they said. I still could feel it—the sense of emptiness, of not being real. And worse, this lingering residue, the certainty that nothing had changed—that it could happen again.

I imagined Dr. Adams's response: "And that's what you're feeling now?"

"That's right." Everything was moving out of my control. I was being jerked like a puppet on a string.

Inside, I let the first rush of cooled air blow over me. I took in the marble floor and crystal chandelier, all the glory of the last century. A carved oak staircase swept gracefully upward, leading me to the second-floor offices. At the landing, a massive gilt-framed mirror reminded me that I needed clothes, my T-shirt and wrinkled khakis weren't the right statement, but too late now.

I followed the muffled clicking sound of a computer keyboard. A phone rang from inside an open door. "Attorney Aronowitz's office" answered the same nasal voice I'd heard on the phone. I followed it.

A woman in her fifties with frosted-blond hair teased into a meringue continued to type, a phone wedged between her shoulder and left ear. "Uh-huh . . . right . . . You're gonna have to clear that with Marvin . . . right." She smiled at me, rolling her eyes. "Uh-huh . . . like I said, you're gonna have to talk to Marvin . . . right. Look, I'll let him know you called. I got to go . . . I know . . . I'm hanging up now . . . right. But you got to talk to Marvin . . . Bye . . . I don't care . . . bye." And she hung up. "Geez, some people."

"Hi. I have a three-o'clock appointment."

"Right, you called yesterday. You're the artist."

"That's right."

"You know," she said, abandoning the keyboard, "I saw that article about you in *Newsday*. That's pretty hot stuff. You want some coffee?"

"No, thanks."

"How about a bagel? You look like you could use it. Me, I got to watch it, but ya know, every once in a while . . ."

"No, really, I'm fine."

"Nervous, bubee?"

"A little."

"Don't be. He's a pussycat. Great lawyer, but a pussycat."

"Velma!" a man's voice bellowed from behind us.

"What?" She returned his call decibel for decibel in a catlike screech.

"Where's my three o'clock?!"

"He's out here!"

"What the fuck's he doing out there?!"

She turned to me, smiling. "He's ready to see you now." And as if the prior yelling match had never occurred, she led me into his office. "Attorney Aronowitz, this is Mr. Greene."

The smell of stale cigars hit me first, making me wish I'd taken that bagel to settle my stomach. Salty saliva rushed into my mouth; I felt bile rise in the back of my throat.

He motioned me toward a black leather armchair, sizing me up from across his paper-strewn desk.

I sat down and tried to breathe through the nerves and the nausea.

"Velma!"

"What?" Her head reappeared in the doorway.

"Where's his file?!"

"For God's sake, Marvin." She burrowed through his desk and quickly came up with a light-blue folder. "Your highness."

"Thanks, Velma." His round, water-blue eyes twinkled with amusement. He settled his substantial bulk back into his chair. "So, Mr. Greene, you think you need a lawyer? What gives?"

"How much do you want to know?"

"Just start talking and if it's too much I'll let you know."

For the next hour I gave forth, pretty much a monologue, with him occasionally interrupting for further detail and clarification. At one point he lit up a half-chewed stogie. The room filled with fresh waves of acrid yellow tobacco smoke. When I recounted the various meetings with Detective Bryant, his interest increased. He leaned forward across the desk.

"Did she have you sign anything?"

"Yeah."

He had me try to remember every document and report.

"Did you read the reports thoroughly?"

"Yeah, although they were pretty long and I'm finding it hard to concentrate for more than a paragraph or two."

"Because of your illness?" His eyes narrowed, evaluating and judging. "Insanity pleas rarely work. I wouldn't recommend it."

"What are you talking about?" I felt the heat rise. "That's not what I was getting at."

"Then why tell me?"

"Because it's a statement of fact. This time last week I was still on the inpatient unit at East Side Psychiatric."

"You don't seem crazy to me"—he leaned forward across the desk—"and that's fine, but if indeed you get charged, it's gonna matter a whole lot. Now listen, this detective—Bryant—has she ever recommended you seek counsel?"

"No. When I asked her if I should get a lawyer she said it was up to me. Was that wrong?"

"From her point? No. She gets pretty close to the line, though." He grew quiet, looked me dead in the eye. "Do you want to fuck her?"

I stared back at him. Not sure if I had heard right. "What has that got to do with it?"

"Well, there's got to be something, 'cause you keep giving this bitch the farm."

"I'm just trying to help. Like maybe if I do they'll catch whoever shot my dog and keeps breaking into my loft."

"Or they'll get tired and just charge you. Which, bubee, is exactly what I'd do."

"That bad?"

"Not good, and you're making things a whole lot worse."

"How?"

"By *helping*. It's the oldest ploy, and she knows it."

"What? Being helpful?"

"That's right. Only two people are as *helpful* as you: the guilty and the incredibly anxious. For the sake of argument let's say you're in the former category. Look at all that can be gained from being close to the detective: You can try and pollute the evidence, convince her you're innocent, maybe you could sleep with her—that would give the jury pause for thought. But the downside, which is what she's banking on, is that you give it away. You know, through the little things, the comments between the lines. The things that won't add up when everything's put together."

"Oh shit. But I didn't do it." I sounded like the worst TV cliché.

"That may be, but it also may have no bearing on the case, at least the case they're building now. One thing you got to know is that the law has nothing to do with right or wrong or what's fair. And she's just doing her job."

"So what am I supposed to do?"

"For starters, you should stop these little tête-à-têtes with your Detective Bryant. If she wants to talk to you, I want to be there."

"You'll take the case?"

"Yeah"—he repositioned the cigar—"it sounds interesting and it sounds like you probably didn't kill your shrink. Or else, in addition to being crazy, you're a real good actor. Either way. Now I got a few more questions . . ."

By the time I left Marvin's office, my head spun and my stomach churned. So, I fucked up—no surprise there. Goddamn. Even my revelation that there must have been someone with me in the loft on Saturday night was met with "So?"

"But shouldn't I let Detective Bryant know that?"

"Probably. But let's think how that's going to look in court. You make one statement. Sign it. Think about it for a few days and then ask to make another. On one hand, sure, people forget things in the heat of the moment. But on the other hand, it looks like you're trying to build a conspiracy case."

"So, I don't say anything?"

"Not yet. Just cool your jets. Let them do their work. If they need to speak to us, then we'll make whatever corrections to the record. Remember, you're not a cop; you're not a detective; you're an artist."

"Right."

"So let's talk about my fees . . ."

And that blew me away.

"So, you do pictures, of people?" he asked, leaning back and flicking his ash.

"Yeah." I wasn't sure where he was going.

"What about me and Velma?" He bit down on his cigar.

And that was the agreement, dutifully written up in triplicate with a fair amount of screaming back and forth between him and Velma.

It wasn't a bad idea, money aside. They're the kind of subjects I liked. The trick was to capture both the strong exterior and the inner person onto the canvas. And, if I could paint my shrink, albeit now my dead shrink, why not my lawyer and his secretary?

CHAPTER FIFTEEN

Life had changed. That night, over ribs and corn on the cob, Pamela gave me a black leather date book.

"If we're going to ride this thing out, we've got to get you organized," she said.

I knew she was right, but appointment books and beeping watches were things I'd avoided in principle. Even my answering machine was a concession that I rationalized based on the paranoiac feature of call screening.

"You've been busy," I commented, as she spread out an assortment of potential commissions.

"A lot of it's been the gallery. Serge is being good about referring people back to me. I think he wants you to do another show next year. Not a bad idea, but we might want to move uptown. Anyway, I've gone ahead and penciled in a few appointments. I hope you don't mind, but I knew your school schedule and I just worked around it." She looked up, catching something in my expression. "None of this is written in stone, so if you're having second thoughts, let me know now. And if you don't want me arranging your life like this, speak up."

"It's fine. I'm just distracted."

"We can do this tomorrow." Her eyes narrowed.

"No, let me see what you've got."

For the next hour I tried to listen as she laid out each of the prospective clients. There were already requests for five portraits at fifty thousand dollars a head.

"That's nothing," she said. "People are trying to squeeze in now while the prices are low. Just wait until after some of the paintings hit the auction block."

"Money their owners will get, not me."

"True, but at least you're alive to see it."

I looked at her closely.

"What?" she asked, feeling my scrutiny.

"Something you said. How much *does* a painter's work appreciate when he dies?"

"It depends. Sometimes a lot, sometimes not so much, and if the work was overvalued, sometimes it goes down—like with Warhol. His estate took a bath after he died, nothing went for anywhere near the appraised value."

"What about my work?"

"Don't get morbid, Chad."

"No, seriously. If I were to drop dead tomorrow, how would that affect the selling price?"

"It's hard to say, particularly now. You're on the launching pad as a major artist. I wouldn't be surprised if you don't have paintings topping the million-dollar mark within five years."

"You're insane."

"Not really. And based on that, your early work is

extremely undervalued, and there's just not a lot of it around. If you were to die, everything would shoot through the roof."

"So all the stolen paintings? . . ."

"Way up," she said. "I can't even think about it, the whole thing makes me sick."

I couldn't sleep. My mind battled against the stillness of this monk's room. I sat up, feeling the sedative, the tranquilizer and the lithium. My body vibrated with a fine chemically induced tremor. And despite the drugs, my thoughts flew at lightning speed. I'd never get to sleep this way.

I stared out the darkened window veined with shadows and reflected light. I needed to paint, but had nothing here. A superstitious fear materialized, like a bone-crushing, canvas-stealing troll from the Brothers Grimm. I imagined gnarled hands reaching for my paintings. "Well, that's just silly," I told myself, the sound of my voice gruff in my ears.

The illuminated dial of the Big Ben alarm clock read 3:15. I wasn't going to sleep tonight; maybe I could get some work done.

I threw on clothes and sneaked silently out of the apartment. One of the joys of New York was that you could get whatever, whenever, if you knew where. I walked quickly toward West Third Street and the All Night Artist. Inside, one of my undergrads, a thin, punky-looking adolescent with a shock of blue hair and an earring in his lower lip, manned the counter on the graveyard shift.

He looked up from his book. "Chad, hi."

He was one of the more talented students in my Life Drawing course; still, it took me a moment to come up with his name. "Jud, how's it going?"

"Quiet, but that's why I like nights. You're out kind of late."

"Yeah, I need to get some work done, but I'm missing a few things."

"What do you need?"

"Let me walk around and think a bit. You got something to put things in?"

"Sure." He handed me a red plastic basket. "Can I ask you something?" His voice was tentative.

"Go ahead."

He came out from behind the counter. "How do you do it?"

"Do what?" I headed down the aisle, savoring the art store with its endless possibilities buried among neatly stacked paint tubes and bins of brushes.

"The whole thing." He followed at my side. "How do you make it as an artist? I mean, you're really doing it. I have such incredible respect for that. But how do you do it?"

I stopped and looked at him. "It's what you want?" I saw a burn in his dark eyes, an earnestness easily overlooked, obscured by iridescent hair and facial piercings.

"It's all I want."

We moved on in silence, stopping at the display of acrylic paints on my left and the oils on my right. Decisions, decisions. I thought about my greatly confined work area and began to pull out tubes of premium Windsor and Newton acrylics. Much as I loved the smell of mineral spirits and oil, I'd probably asphyxiate myself in my present digs.

"I hope you don't mind my asking," he persisted, "but I got to know. How do you do it? You know, really live as an artist?"

I ran my hand over rows of soft-bristled brushes. "It's a lot of things. And then again it comes down to a few basics. You have to be committed. You have to work. Your work has to be *the* most important thing. It has to consume you."

"What about people? Don't they matter?"

I laughed, a little too hard, a little too cynical. "Sure, but you're asking about art. No matter how you slice it, to be an artist is to make sacrifices. Relationships go first. I don't mean to be facetious or discouraging, but it's true. Everything comes after the work. You may think that doesn't matter so much, but give it some thought. Do you want a wife and children?" I asked rhetorically. "They come *after* the painting. How many women are going to put up with that?" Scenes from my marriage flashed before me: Jocelyn putting her arms around me as I painted, only to be met by my screaming at her to go away; all the parties she wanted to go to, the friends she wanted to make;

all the things I wouldn't do for her because I had to paint.

"But you've made it," he said. "Doesn't it get easier?"

"I don't know, probably not with the way I work."

"How's that?"

"You really want to know?" I paused in my selection of an easel.

"Chad, I came to the studio specifically to study with you. The only class I've been able to take is the Life Drawing because everything else is booked up semesters in advance. Like no one, other than the graphic artists, is teaching. I mean," he spoke too quickly, afraid that I'd get away, "there are instructors, but none of them are real artists . . . I want what you have. And then I look at your work, and it's like, God, I could never do that. It blows me away."

It was like a mirrored reflection of me as a younger man, albeit without the generational decorations. His hunger was palpable. "And now everyone's saying you're going to leave the studio. So I feel like, great; now what?"

That got my attention. "I have no plans to leave. Who's been saying that?"

"Pretty much everyone."

"It's a rumor. I'll tell you something my teacher once told me, 'Always keep a teaching gig.' I used to think that had to do with paying the bills, but as time goes on it seems more about other things. Like staying fresh and reminding yourself of what matters in painting." I grabbed several pre-stretched canvases. "Could you wrap these up?"

The bill rang up shy of a thousand dollars. I put it on charge. "Jud, if you're serious about wanting to study with me, tell Kevin to put you in whichever of my classes you want. Tell him you cleared it with me."

"Thanks."

"Don't mention it."

I hailed a cab from in front of the shop. He helped load my instant art studio into the backseat and trunk.

"Do you always buy this much stuff?" he asked.

"Nah, just replacing some things that got stolen."

"That's a drag."

"No kidding."

As I stumbled back to my room, trying to make the least noise possible, I thought of the conversation with Jud: the expression on his face, the tenor of his voice. "I want what you have." After more than ten years of constant striving, me at my art and Pamela at her deal making and promoting, I'd achieved something rare. Not only could I support myself as an artist; I could do well at it. It wasn't my goal, at least not consciously, but the fact of my newfound wealth raised some interesting possibilities. I could send Zack to college, buy my own loft, maybe join the rest of New Yorkers on their yearly exodus out of the city when the mercury rose and the blacktop softened.

But there was something more; I saw it in Jud's

face—envy. It was part of the world in general and Manhattan in particular. This city didn't let people slide. You couldn't coast with what you have; you lost it if you did. People who didn't live here had trouble understanding the forces at play. There was always someone who wanted your job, your apartment and your lover. It was a town of nearly eight million souls competing for a dozen golden apples. I'd broken free of the unnamed hordes and grabbed something luscious. Jud merely had put into words what others thought.

Is that what this was all about? Was that why Dr. Sturges was murdered? Did he have something precious, something worth killing for? Did someone want his brownstone, his money, his patients? Is that why Ching was shot and my paintings stolen? Nothing came easy here. I remembered a Harlan Ellison short story about the "God of New York City," an invisible deity who demanded blood sacrifice. Perhaps this was all payment for goods received.

I set up my new top-of-the-line, aluminum-alloy easel. I laid out the tubes of paint and stared into the blank white canvas glowing in the darkened room. My mind drifted, skittering from thought to thought. Images formed from shadows cast by the moon and by the city lights. With a fine lithium tremor, I began to paint.

A knock at the door broke the spell. "Chad, are you up?"
"Yeah, come on in."

With her hair unbound and wearing a floor-length red velvet bathrobe, Pamela looked like a model for some medieval master. She took in my improvised setup and the new painting materializing on the canvas.

"Did you sleep at all?" she asked.

"I couldn't." Daylight, with its fuller spectrum of color, had replaced the constricted palette of the night.

"That's not good."

"I know."

She examined the half-formed painting, a swirl of human figures tied together, their boundaries blurred, their hands reaching upward and their faces twisted with hunger and desire.

"Interesting."

"Yeah, sort of my ode to Manhattan. Either that, or the first bit of Dante's *Inferno*, where all the souls are swirling about. Did you ever see those drawings?" I asked.

"Which ones?"

"The old ones by Gustave Doré, a sort of nineteenth-century arch-Romantic. The kind of thing Blake would have done if he could have drawn better."

"It's good," she said. "Powerful." I watched her struggle, the agent versus my friend. "It's really good. But do you always have to skate so close to the edge?"

I saw myself through her eyes, my face rough with stubble, my one pair of pants dotted with smears of fresh paint. "It's better close to the edge."

"I know." She sat on the side of the bed. "Maybe it's my fault." A frailty had crept into her voice.

"What are you talking about?"

"I push too much. You should be trying to take care of yourself and all I can think is, 'That's a really good painting, we'll have no trouble finding a buyer.' Can't you do both?"

"I'm trying. But this is how it is for me. Sometimes I manage and sometimes I lose it."

"What about those pills?"

"They're not magic. And they have a big price."

"What are you talking about?"

"They help, and probably, although not definitely, if I took them all, as I'm supposed to, I'd not be cracking up as much. Which is also not to say that I feel bad right now. I just know it's not good for me to go without sleep. I probably could have taken some sleepers and knocked myself out, but then this wouldn't be here; I would never have painted this picture. But that's how it's always been with the pills. And not just the sleeping pills. I would be a better painter if I didn't take anything."

I watched that sink in. "You're serious."

"Yeah. On every level, they slow my thinking, dull my vision and make my hands shake."

"I had no idea. I thought they were just like taking anything, like aspirin."

"I wish."

"So basically you'd be healthier if you never painted."

"No, I'd kill myself if I couldn't paint. The trick is"—I tried to lighten the mood, wanting to see her smile—"just staying a little crazy."

"Great . . . You want breakfast?"

Surprise, surprise. I have an office. Wonder what this will cost? Or perhaps it's prepaid.

Kevin waylaid me between classes and steered me into a freshly painted, double-windowed room.

"What do you think?" he asked, smiling a bit too broadly.

"It's a room with a desk and a couple chairs."

It was obviously not the response he wanted. "I can get you some better furniture, whatever you need, but do you like the space?"

I wasn't being deliberately dense, but none of the instructors had offices. "You're giving me an office?"

"Yeah, I should have done it a while ago." He closed the door behind himself and lowered his voice. "I already spoke with the board and it shouldn't be a problem getting you on the tenure track, but they can't do anything until the new contracts in September. So, I thought, in the meantime I could free up an office and a little extra money and give you the title Artist in Residence. What do you think?"

"That's a lot"—I didn't want to look a gift horse in the mouth, but I couldn't stop myself—"but why?"

"Because I want you to stay."

I remembered Jud's comment and things Kevin had said before. "Who's been saying I'm leaving?"

He hesitated and looked out the window. "You know, people talk."

"Right, but who?"

"Forget about it. That's not important. Do you like the space?"

"It's great. But if people are talking about me, I'd like to know who."

"Chad, forget it. It's just a rumor. You know how things get around here; once something gets started it's impossible to trace it back to the source."

"True." I had the uncomfortable feeling that I wasn't being told everything.

So here I sat, nursing my paranoia and waiting to give an interview in my very own office. Fellow instructors offered me congratulations as I emptied my locker in the staff lounge. Smiling faces struggled to conceal pea-green jealousy. I imagined the comments: "It's all luck. He's not even that good a painter."

That I'd always stayed away from studio politics and after-hours socializing didn't help. I came into the studio as Jan's protégé and had followed in his "outsider" footsteps.

I wondered how much of a favor this was. Although, walking over to the windows, my windows, and looking out on an unobstructed view of the street performers and drug dealers in Washington Square Park, there was something to be said for all this.

The intercom buzzed. "Chad, your twelve-o'clock is here."

I looked at the phone with its many buttons and pushed the one labeled "talk." A high-pitched whine erupted from the receiver, and rather than try again I went into the hallway and met Harold.

His back was toward me as I approached. I overheard Lois tell him, "Yeah, it's all the buzz." Then she saw me. "Oh, there he is."

Harold turned, smiling, his hair carefully arranged over his balding crown. His clothes—a summer-weight tweed, white shirt and tie—were crisply pressed. He looked more like my father heading to the bank than a reporter. "Chad, thanks for seeing me. I didn't know if you'd want to after that *Newsday* thing."

"My agent liked it."

"Yeah, agents are like that. Publicity is publicity. And twenty-five percent is twenty-five percent."

"I suppose. You want to do this in my office?" I liked the sound; it tripped off my tongue.

"Whatever is easiest for you."

"So"—I closed the door behind us—"what would you like to know?"

"How much time do you have?" He popped a cassette into his recorder.

"Let's go for an hour."

"Great. So what's it like to hit the big time?"

"Is that what we're going to talk about?"

"Let me level with you, Chad. You're in a unique position right now, something that doesn't happen often. You're a young artist in the process of being thrust into the mainstream of the art world. You and I both know this didn't happen overnight. I've been following you for years. What's happening now is the logical result of talent, persistence, luck, and some good strategic maneuvering. But people want to know 'Why you?' and, 'What is it like?'"

I looked at this man, probably twenty years my senior, and wondered what sort of life he was living on the out-skirts of the artists' world. "Do you paint?" I asked him.

The question took him by surprise. "I used to."

"Why did you stop?"

"I couldn't get good enough."

"Do you ever paint?"

"Never"—he laughed it off—"now it's all vicarious. I suppose writing takes care of those needs."

"If you want to know what it's like to be getting recognition, money, fame, whatever, it's two-sided. I paint because I have to, and like you, if it's not good enough, it shouldn't see the light of day. That I am getting recognition is real nice, but it almost doesn't matter. I say 'almost' because I can use the money. I don't feel guilty about it, because the work is solid.

And that's not a small thing for me to say. Taking the step from creating for yourself to creating for others is huge. For me to hang a painting in a show I have to ask myself, Is this valid? Is it good enough? Is it honest?" My mind strayed. "I was robbed recently. The night of the show, to be exact."

"I'm sorry."

"Yeah, I don't want to go into it a whole lot. It was pretty awful. But just now it got me thinking. They took my artwork, lots of it, indiscriminately. All the things I wouldn't put into shows—either because they weren't good enough, or, for whatever reason, I wanted to keep them. And now they're all out there. I suppose if I wanted to be purely theoretical, it's probably better."

"How do you mean?"

"It's more honest. Maybe artists aren't supposed to edit. Maybe it's good that all my mistakes eventually pass into the general domain. Then again, maybe I should have burned them long ago. A lot of people do that."

"It's been quite a roller-coaster ride." He paused. "Let me ask you this: Why did you paint Philip Sturges?"

My adrenaline surged. "How did you find out about that?"

"If you'd rather not talk about that?"

"I want to know how you found out."

He didn't answer.

"Look," I said, trying to keep the anger from my voice, "the portrait was untitled; how did you find out?"

"I'd rather not say." He was clearly wishing he'd never raised the subject.

"That may be, but if you want to continue this interview, you'll tell me."

His eyes darted quickly, unable to meet my gaze. "I asked Serge."

"He didn't know who it was."

"He said it was your psychiatrist."

"Yeah, I suppose I told him that. It still doesn't tell me how you knew it was Dr. Sturges."

"Once I knew it was your psychiatrist, it wasn't hard to find his name."

"Be specific."

"Look, I'm a reporter; it's my job to find things out. At the time, I swear I didn't know."

"Know what?"

"That he was murdered . . . it was in all the papers."

I looked at him closer. Small beads of perspiration had cropped up on his broad forehead, and his breathing was heavy. "What is it you really want? These aren't the usual art-critic sort of questions."

"I want this story. Your story."

"Who else have you been talking to?"

"It's not important."

"Look, if you want any sort of story from me, you may as well tell me. I'll find out anyway."

"Just some people here. I tried to speak with your

agent, but she kept referring me back to you. The cops wouldn't give me much."

I counted to ten, on the verge of throwing him out, and then I remembered. "You were in the gallery when the portrait was sold."

"That's what got me started," he said. "I thought it was at least noteworthy that an uncataloged painting was one of the first things sold and at a price well above your normal."

"You saw the man who bought it?"

"Briefly. I didn't know what was going on until I saw them take it off the wall. You have to admit that's pretty rare."

"I know, and not my doing. But you did see him?"

"Yeah."

"Who was it?"

"I didn't recognize him." His expression revealed nothing, other than fear that I might terminate the interview and whatever ambition he had pinned to this story.

I grabbed a pencil and piece of paper and quickly drew the face from memory. "Did he look like this?"

"Yeah, that's about right. I didn't get a real close look, but that could be him."

An idea began to form. "Where exactly were you thinking of selling this story? I thought you worked for *New York Scene*."

"I do their reviews. But mostly I freelance."

"Could you get the story into one of the dailies?"

"Maybe; I'd need an angle . . . Why?" He sensed all might not be lost.

"I want to know who bought the portrait. If you help me with that, I'll let you have whatever story you want."

CHAPTER SIXTEEN

Acrid fumes arose from the scorching asphalt, plugging my nose with the tarry smell. I forced my body with its sweat-clinging shirt through the last of the day's tasks—shopping. So far, knock wood, things had gone better. Ching was finally on his feet, still drowsy, but improved. They wanted to watch him for another forty-eight hours, just enough time to break the news to Pamela. I wondered how he'd take to new digs.

I stopped at the precinct station and signed the last report. Despite Marvin's warnings, I tried to see Susan. She was out. I wanted to retrieve the sketch pad. And, if I was honest with myself, I wanted to see her. My feelings in that area were pretty mixed. Marvin's "Do you want to fuck her?" was part of it—maybe. But there was something else, something reassuring—that she knew her job and would push this chaos away from my life. Maybe it was trust.

On the way to Bloomie's, I stopped at my old building. I looked at my loft with its boarded-up windows. It seemed derelict, like buildings look after a fire or before the wrecking ball. I went into the stairwell and unlocked my mailbox. A couple bills, a credit-card

application—"$5,000 Credit can be yours instantly"—
and . . . another postcard.

Maybe because I'd seen the other one made it easier,
or else I'd grown numb to the grotesque. It was similar to
the first one, a mailer for the show with a Magic Marker
cartoon drawn on the back. Someone was definitely trying to reproduce my style. This one was drawn better
than the first, as though they had practiced. It showed a
man with long red hair hanging from a noose. No words.
I stood there, sweat trickling down my back. I resisted
the urge to shred it. The postmark was from the East
Village. The proximity told me nothing, only that I
walked the same streets as this entity, that we could pass
each other daily, that he could be watching me now. I
stared out the glass-fronted door and telescoped through
distant perspectives, all the vantage points and windows
from which someone could observe me.

I examined the drawing more closely—again that
odd mix of dimensional accuracy with cartoonish
symbolism: Xs through my eyes, a tongue protruding
through my lips, but care taken with the hands, and
the ratio of the proportions. "Frustrated artist," I muttered. What did that mean? I thought back to the interview with Harold: "I used to paint . . . I wasn't good
enough."

Yeah, him and how many others? Downtown Manhattan was peopled with aspiring artists. Every waitress,
every clerk, every secretary and ice-cream vendor har-
bored a dream. And then something happened to

them, or it must, because the Village never aged. At some point, the vast majority up and left, their dreams gone, their lives headed in different directions, their apartments repopulated with the next wave of hopefuls. I saw it with my students, the undergraduates in particular, when, somewhere near graduation, reality hit. The artist's life, divorced from Mommy and Daddy's checkbook, was too much: too much poverty; too much rejection; too much work with no assurance that it would ever pay off. So they switched, lured by the advice of others, and their own insecurities. My father's words, when I was twenty-five, echoed again: "Why can't painting be your avocation and something reasonable, where you can support yourself, be your vocation?" As usual, I wasn't reasonable.

The card held my gaze—a vision of death, the hanged man. *Is it suicide? Am I murdered?* I stood, waiting for fear or some more powerful emotion to surface, but nothing came. *I should bring this to the precinct, show it to Susan.* But I didn't feel like it. I was tired and hot and I smelled like a goat. I crammed the card into my back pocket. Hell, I'd already covered it with fingerprints; what difference could a few creases make?

The air-conditioned lobby of Bloomingdale's department store was like a mountain stream on a summer's day. I wandered past sparkling displays of perfume and jewelry and headed toward the men's department. I tried to ignore the ill-concealed scrutiny and the sideways glances of customers, salesclerks, and navy-jacketed security officers. Well-lit mirrors dotted my progress; one look reaffirmed the necessity of this visit. If clothes made the man, what did my stained and sweat-soaked grubbies say about me? God, I hadn't even shaved. Taking a closer look, my eyes were darkly ringed and my hair was stringy and tangled, with the odd lock jutting out at an unlikely angle. I looked like one of those chronically mentally ill who roamed homeless through the streets. There but for the grace of God . . .

A beautifully dressed man in a dark Italian suit with neatly combed blond hair disengaged himself from a cluster of salesmen huddled around the center register. His voice was soft as he carefully approached. "May I help you?"

I sensed more pity than condescension, as if he were asking, "Can I help you to the men's shelter or the nearest soup kitchen?"

"I need clothes—pretty much everything."

I watched him struggle, his livelihood no doubt tied to commissions. He wondered if I was some insane vagabond out to scam him, at worst; or just to waste his time, at best. I sensed him picking up on my body odor—that of a raunchy farm animal. Even I could smell it. My face reddened; this might have been a bad idea.

"Do you know what you'd like?"

"Mostly casual. I was robbed." I quickly added that

in, hoping to explain my presentation, not wanting to go into a lot of detail.

"This city can be disgusting." His posture relaxed, a smile broke over perfect teeth. "Do you know your measurements?"

I'd never been one for shopping; then again, I'd never had this much money. A pile of purchases steadily grew, from crisp white cotton boxers to an English-cut tweed jacket. My reflection, still rough, transformed under the ministrations of my salesman.

He knows color well, I thought as he deftly selected oxford shirts and silk ties in shades from the same palette as my hair and eyes. Like the lion in the *Wizard of Oz,* I was getting my Emerald City makeover.

As I tried on pants, he chalked in the cuff length. "I could give these to the tailor now if you want?"

"How long would it take?"

"Not too long . . . you could go visit our salon in the meantime."

"I know, I look pretty bad."

"True, but I have a feeling you clean up well. I could call upstairs and see if they could take you now." He flashed a smile. "I'll tell them it's an emergency."

"Thanks." I didn't relish the thought of leaving the cool consumerism of Bloomingdale's and returning to the heat outside. I remembered a "Twilight Zone" episode where people lived in a department store. Actually, they may have been mannequins who came to life; regardless, the idea of another hour in this oasis appealed to me.

/ When I finally left, laden with packages and garment bags, I caught a glimpse in the mirror. I wasn't usually given to personal vanity, but damn if I didn't look fine. My hair shone, free from knots, and broke evenly along the shoulders of a natural linen shirt. For the first time in days my face was free from stubble, but the eyes, as I looked closer, were still too bright, with the look of the hunted.

The man in the mirror smiled back. I remembered the venomous postcard still wedged in a pant pocket, the whole thing crumpled into the bottom of a bag. And then it hit, a realization so obvious I couldn't imagine how I missed it . . .

I have to go back. My stomach lurched.

I have to go back. Images from the past flooded over me. They threatened to break through the elegant glass, its surface shimmered and warped. I thought of the ten-year-old sketch pad now in the possession of Detective Bryant, its pages of rambling bloodred apocalyptic warnings: "Prepare the Way."

I have to go back.

I pushed through the thick glass doors, back into the steamy heat. I hailed a cab.

Why didn't I see it before? Why hadn't Susan seen this? Or maybe she had and had dismissed it as the ramblings of the lunatic. Why should she be any different?

I thought of the *Newsday* article and why it had bothered me—"a lifelong struggle with manic-depression." It stirred my guilt and shame at having a mental illness. Yes, I know it wasn't my fault; I didn't ask for it, but there was always that sense: it must be something I had or hadn't done. That's how the world viewed it, viewed me: defective, weak, someone to be shoved to the periphery, and "Isn't it a shame that all of the long-term state hospitals have closed their doors?"

I tried not to think about those things, always ripe and not too far below the surface. The times I'd been handled like a rabid animal—hustled to the ground, restrained, and shot up with large doses of tranquilizers. I flashed on the panicked feeling of bodies tackling me, pushing my face to the floor, pulling down my pants and then . . . the bite of the needle.

"Stop it," I said, trying to quiet my thoughts.

The cabdriver looked back, a flash of concern visible in his mirrored reflection. "You said Fifth and Eighth?"

"That's right." the normalcy of the exchange sufficed. *But isn't that always the way? I just want to pass. Maybe that's why the obvious has eluded me. Where I have to go, and what I have to do fills me with fear. It is the antithesis of all I've worked for.*

I have to go back.

CHAPTER SEVENTEEN

Do I look normal? I splashed cold water onto the face reflected in the grime-coated mirror. My heart beat fast, my knees threatened to buckle, and the tremor in my hands had coarsened to an embarrassing level. *I've got to calm down.* I steadied myself against the sink in this gray place of steel partitions and mildewed tiles.

I'd dressed the part: gray slacks, navy blazer, white shirt, and quiet tie. The net effect got whistles from Pamela, snickers from my Friday classes, and a sense of increased panic from Kevin, who was convinced I was headed to a job interview.

Oh God, maybe this wasn't a good idea. *Whoever said it was? You can't stay here forever. Make up your mind.*

"Right." I patted back my hair, looking every bit the yuppie businessman. "Do it."

I left the safety of the institutional washroom and headed to the lobby, each step threatening my tenuous equilibrium.

A group of eight patients was herded past me by two psychiatric aides, no doubt headed for a "therapeutic walk" (aka a smoke break). Everyone was dressed in street clothes, but there was no mistaking the players. I heard the shuffling feet, saw the glazed, out-of-focus eyes and the ill-fitting clothes. The staff talked cheerfully to their charges, not deliberately condescending, but their tones were those used with small children.

A hulking man with dark hair and nicotine-stained fingers pleaded with his keeper, his voice low and mumbled.

"No, John, you can only have two cigarettes. Come on, don't argue. Remember your treatment plan."

I stood frozen, letting them pass on their way to hundred-degree heat and the promise of a smoke. One of the women looked up at me; our eyes locked. Her face was twisted in a mask of inchoate rage. I pictured her scream. *What does she see as she looks at me?* Without changing her expression—no social smile—she turned and shuffled off with the rest. I exhaled, realizing I had been holding my breath as they passed.

At the elevators I pressed eight and allowed myself to be delivered up to the locked door of the adult psychiatric ward.

A video camera stared down on me in the empty hallway. Behind me, the elevator doors slammed shut. *No turning back.* I pressed the buzzer to be admitted.

A voice came through an ancient, square speaker box. "Yes?"

"Hi, this is Chad Greene. I have an appointment with Carol, the Charge Nurse. I called yesterday."

"Hold on, I'll check."

I read the handwritten sign in front of me:

The Portrait

I tried not to pace, knowing I was being watched, wishing my hands would stop shaking. *Just calm down. Breathe.*

The door clicked open, spilling out the scent of something familiar and impossible to forget. In ten years, nothing had changed. I entered the patient lounge with its easy-to-wash orange and mustard-yellow chairs, its scarred piano, and its wire-laced, suet-smeared windows. To my right and to my left stretched long, silent, door-filled corridors.

A woman in her forties with short, silver-blond hair and crisply pleated slacks approached. With a polite smile she greeted me. "Mr. Greene?" She searched my face. "Do you remember me?"

"I'm sorry." Her question took me by surprise. "I don't think so." So much for never forgetting a face.

"You probably wouldn't. I was working nights when you were here." Silence. "But that was quite some time ago."

"Ten years."

"So how are you doing?" She led me past a pair of patients aimlessly pushing checkers across a board.

"Not too bad." I remembered Marvin's admonition to keep my mouth shut.

It had taken some late-afternoon phone calls yesterday to get this arranged. She was being polite, but

195

my presence did not please her. I had no idea it would be so hard to see my records; they were mine, after all. When I first called I was flatly told, "We don't allow patients to see their charts; it's policy." I asked to speak to the supervisor and was given to this woman, who was now unlocking a door into the nurses' Plexiglas observation booth. She had been curt on the telephone and tried to explain how psychiatric records were confidential and can be "upsetting" for patients to see. My blood simmered as I again lost my personhood and became a "patient." I thanked her, knowing that to argue would gain nothing. I called Marvin.

"Shmendrick, of course you can see your records. But what are you doing?"

I tried to explain: the second postcard, the lines of connection ten years in my past.

"Uh-huh, you'll be lucky if they don't get the nets. I hope you're not planning to go into all of that."

"Hadn't planned on it."

"Good. Don't."

He called me back five minutes later. "It's all set up."

"How did you do that?"

"Jungle law. The minute a doctor hears that there's a lawyer on the phone they shit themselves. It's not hard to get what you want. The only problem is they tend to panic, sometimes "edit" bits and pieces of the chart."

"You don't think much of doctors."

"Bubeleh, it's human nature. Everyone wants a piece of ass and wants to save their own. Now be careful. I don't want to get a call saying they've locked you up for some sort of paranoiac reaction."

"I'll keep my mouth shut."

"Always best."

Sue opened a door into a small windowless conference room. On the circular table lay a thick manila envelope with a colored bar code and my name in large handwritten letters on the side.

"Make yourself comfortable. I need to have you sign a couple forms before you see the chart."

"What kind of forms?" I hoped my internal panic didn't register.

"One is a release, and the other is like a 'hold harmless,' it basically states that we informed you of potential risks."

"Fine."

"You sure you want to do this?"

"Yes."

"Okay. Would you like a cup of coffee?"

"Thanks."

She smiled. "Sorry I was such a hard-ass on the phone."

"Just your job."

She left me alone with my records.

I let out a sigh and pulled the heavy folder toward me. My heart pounded as I opened it. With shaky hands I pulled a small notepad and pen from my breast pocket. Behind them, I felt the other pieces of stiffly folded drawing paper. *Maybe later.*

The first page was demographics: name, date, Social Security number, insurance carrier, next of kin and attending physician of record—Philip Sturges. I wrote down the admission and discharge dates—ten days in May—and then I was shipped off to Glendale.

Next came three pages of blue-lined paper with a barely legible, but familiar scrawl.

ADMISSION HISTORY

Identifying Data: Patient is a twenty-five-year-old married white male who carries a diagnosis of manic-depressive disorder.

Chief Complaint: "Prepare the way . . . the devil knows all."

History of Present Illness: Patient, who is well known to myself, was brought by ambulance, with police escort, from the Sixth Precinct jail, where he has been held for the past forty-eight hours. I evaluated him there at the request of his family and made recommendations for his transfer. In brief: Patient purportedly discontinued all medication approximately two months ago. He has become increasingly expansive and hyperverbal, with pronounced irritability. Immediately prior to his arrest he went berserk in a downtown restaurant where he was employed as a waiter. Police were called at that point, but did not catch up with patient until he had returned home and assaulted his pregnant wife, who subsequently went into labor.

Per the police report, patient was noted to be "agitated and assaultive." He resisted the arresting officers and backup was required. The report also states that patient "wasn't making sense and kept talking about people coming through the mirrors." This presentation is compatible with past episodes of mania where Mr. Greene stopped his medication and subsequently became psychotic and assaultive.

Per his mother, Judith Greene, patient has been under increased stress of late, related to his wife's pregnancy and their financial difficulties.

Past Psychiatric History: Client has had two previous inpatient admissions. The first when he was seventeen. He has been followed by myself for the past six years.

Family Psychiatric History: Significant for a maternal grandmother with manic-depressive disorder and a cousin who committed suicide.

Alcohol/Drug Abuse History: Non-contributory

Medical History: Non-contributory

Medication: Lithium carbonate 600 mg twice a day

Mental Status Examination: Patient is a tall,

well-developed man. At the time of his admission he was dressed in a torn T-shirt and jeans. His hair was long, his face unshaven, he was malodorous and disheveled. He makes staring and excessive eye contact. His affect is labile and hostile. His mood is angry. Speech is loud and pressured, at times screaming and shouting. Thought processes are disconnected, with flights-of-ideas and loosening of associations. Thought content is markedly psychotic, with delusions based around hyperreligious themes. He states that both God and the devil are currently conversing with him and that he is to be the conduit for some sort of Messianic visitation. He refuses to answer questions around any suicidal or homicidal ideation. At one point he made threatening advances to myself and required physical restraints. Formal cognitive testing could not be performed, as patient was too agitated and disorganized.

Impression: Acute exacerbation of mania secondary to medication noncompliance.

Plan: 1. Involuntary admission.

2. If patient refuses to sign in voluntarily, will need to move toward conservatorship. His parents have already indicated they would be willing to take on this responsibility.

3. Medicate aggressively. Restart lithium. Use Haldol and Valium to diminish psychosis and

agitation. Medicate against client's will, if necessary.

    4. As patient does have private insurance, would recommend transfer to Glendale once he is somewhat stable.

Philip Sturges, MD

As I finished Dr. Sturges's note, Carol returned with the coffee.

"I didn't know if you wanted milk or sugar."

"Black's fine, thanks." My thoughts swam.

"Are you okay?"

An innocuous question—a clinical overture? "It's just a little strange, that's all." I wished she would leave. But I reminded myself of my objective. "Carol?"

"Yes."

"Could I ask you a couple things about my hospitalization?"

"Chad"—she sat down next to me—"it was ten years ago; I won't remember much. Although I'll never forget how you came in. It amazes me to see how well you look."

It's obvious she meant well; I overlooked her prejudice, so common with those that work with mental illness, the assumption that we never get better. "Thanks, I sounded pretty bad; I just read Dr. Sturges's note from the day I came in."

"Philip Sturges—God, that's a blast from the past. I almost forgot he was the attending. I wonder how he's doing?"

I hesitated. "He's dead."

Her eyes widened. "But he was so young, we were both the same age."

"It was unexpected."

"That's horrible. His children must still be pretty young; they were just babies when he worked here."

"You knew him well?"

"I liked him. You know how it gets when you work with someone."

I assured her I did, aware, more and more, of playing a role.

"You know, I do remember *some* of what happened when you were here. Like I said, I worked nights; I just remember things were chaotic. We had three or four patients in restraints most days." Her eyes avoided mine.

"For a while, I was one of them."

She smiled. "You have to admit the man sitting here is far different from the one I knew ten years ago."

"I hope so."

"Let me see the chart."

I slid it over.

She flipped to a section of blue-lined paper covered in various-sized notes written by multiple hands. "Here's one of mine . . . 'Patient continues in four-point restraints throughout shift. Noted to sleep fitfully for about two hours. Verbally abusive and threatening to . . .' You sure you want to hear this?"

"It's okay." I ratcheted down a sadness that welled up behind my eyes.

She read on: "'. . . threatening to kill all who stand in the way of the Lord God Jehovah. Calmed slightly following the administration of prn [as needed] Haldol and Valium.' Pretty strong stuff."

"Yeah."

"You want me to go on?"

"It's helpful." Unable to say more lest my voice crack and tears fall.

"It looks like the next morning they tried to take you out of restraints: 'Patient with slightly improved behavioral control, although still floridly psychotic— "Prepare the way; the Lord God Jehovah comes." Appears to be responding to internal stimuli. Became acutely agitated and combative when his parents came to visit. Likely precipitant was a discussion of upcoming conservatorship hearing. Patient returned voluntarily to four-point restraints without incident, prn medications administered with good effect.' Then comes my note: 'Patient slept through majority of this shift. Taken out of restraints at 6 A.M. and put on room restriction. Good behavioral control despite persistent psychosis. Continues to benefit from use of prn Haldol and Valium.'

"This next note is Philip's." She paused. "Do you know how he died?"

"No." I rationalized my lie of omission; I didn't know *exactly* how he died. I'd rather not say he was murdered. She'd find out on her own. I looked over at the page. "His handwriting is miserable."

"All doctors are the same. I think they teach them that. Let's see if I can decipher it: 'Patient persists delusional and paranoid, with auditory hallucinations and referential thinking. He is less pressured and was reported to sleep the night. Now out of restraints for four hours with good control. However, still refuses to sign in, or to agree to transfer. Will precede with conservatorship hearing and eventual transfer to Glendale. Continue with liberal use of prn medications.'

"Then the day nurse writes: 'Patient noticeably calmer throughout the shift. Advanced to full-ward restriction with close monitoring and fifteen-minute checks. In the milieu, patient noted to interact with others in a pressured and disorganized manner. At one point he was noted to be giving a religious sermon in the dayroom. He was requested by staff to stop and he acquiesced without argument. After lunch, patient requested art supplies be brought by his parents. Subsequently, he spent several hours drawing and painting. Of note, client states he is an artist, and indeed his pictures are quite remarkable.' Do you still paint?"

"Yes, it's what I do for a living."

"Really? You know I still have the picture you did of me."

"It's worth money."

"Seriously?" I watched her struggle, she was wondering if I was delusional, if it was all made up. After all, "grandiosity" is one of the hallmarks of manic-depression. Then again, people who get manic have been known to write symphonies in a day and novels in a week. Or, in my case, major paintings overnight. I think it just pisses everyone else off.

"Do you have a copy of *Newsday* on the unit?" I asked.

"Probably."

"Look in this week's issue under the "Hot and Not" section. There's an article about my last show."

"No kidding?"

"You should probably do it. Otherwise you'll just be sitting here thinking I made the whole thing up."

"Is it that obvious?"

"It's not just you. It's anyone who's seen me when I'm sick."

"Would you mind?"

"Some, but I'll get over it."

"Then I won't."

"You sure?"

"Yeah, but you know the minute you're gone I'm going to look."

"That's fair. So what comes next?" I tried to steer her back to my chart.

"It's funny, but some of it is coming back. I remember we had a staff meeting where we talked about your painting. Once you started, you wouldn't stop. It calmed you, which was fine, but you started doing portraits of all the other patients. There was this whole confidentiality discussion. We don't allow people to take photographs on the unit and here you were making these wonderful pictures. They were kind of wild but you could definitely tell who they were. I don't think we ever reached a decision—you weren't here that long. But let's see"—she turned the page. "Me again. I was thrilled when they finally took me off nights. Anyway: 'Patient noticeably calmer this evening, although still hyperverbal and delusional. Patient's parents attempted to visit; he refused to see them, stating, "The devil will come dressed in the clothes of the lamb." At one point, he wrapped a sheet around himself like a toga and attempted to give a sermon in the dayroom. Other patients asked him to be quiet as they were watching television. Patient complied and spent the rest of the evening drawing. In one-to-one discussion with this writer, he expressed concern over upcoming conservatorship hearing. Also became tearful and guilt-ridden when discussing his wife and news that their son is in neonatal intensive care. Prn Valium was given at bedtime with good result. Patient slept through the night, getting up only twice to urinate.'" She continued without looking up.

"The next note is from Philip—Doctor Sturges. 'Client acutely agitated and increasingly psychotic this morning, focused on religious themes—angels and devils. Has clearly placed myself and his parents in league with the devil. As his judgment and thought processes continue markedly impaired, we proceeded with probate this A.M. Temporary conservatorship (six months) was granted by the court to Chad's father, George Greene. In the midst of the hearing, patient threatened the judge with "a rain of fire and death"; he was subsequently excused from the rest of the proceedings.

/ " 'Later, when speaking with patient, he appeared calmer and remorseful, asking for news of his wife and son. When informed of his transfer to Glendale he appeared paranoid, stating, "It's best, they all want me dead here." ' " She turned to look at me. "He goes on to talk about your meds and stuff. This must be really strange, hearing this."

"Yeah."

"Can I ask you something?"

"Sure."

"We don't get many patients wanting to see their records. The only times I can remember is if somebody is going to sue. Is that what's happening?"

"No."

"Then why?"

It was a reasonable question. I dissembled, aware of the half-truths, not wanting to deceive outright. "I need to know what happened. It's a time when everything fell apart. I was in Glendale for months. When I came out, everything was gone. I'd lost my wife, my son, my freedom. It can't happen again. But unfortunately, I'm going through a lot of trouble right now. I don't want to go into it, but I'm worried that I could go backward, lose everything I've worked for. I need to remind myself of what I'm trying to prevent."

"I understand. Do you want me to go on?"

"If you don't mind; this is helpful."

"Okay, let's see . . . me again: 'Patient is anxious and pacing. His affect is fearful and paranoid, he refused dinner, stating, "They're putting poison in my food . . . His names are minion." With reassurance, he was able to drink two cartons of milk and a sealed juice. He was unwilling to leave his room and go into the patients' lounge for evening activity. Prn medications were administered, with some slight decrease in his anxiety. Patient spent time painting in his room and then slept through the night without interruption. The plan is for transfer to Glendale.'" We flipped through the pages, skimming the notes of the days that took on a sameness.

"Not much left," she said, coming to the end of the blue-lined pages. "Here's Philip's transfer note . . . that's weird."

"What is?" I moved my chair closer, looking at Dr. Sturges's scribbled cursive.

"It's almost like he wrote the wrong note in your chart: 'Patient clearly malingering. Obvious secondary gain to be achieved with continued psychiatric hospitalization and diagnosis. Current panoply of symptoms appear contrived and have been noted by nursing staff to disappear when patient believes himself to be unobserved. Have conferred with hospital lawyer, who recommends he be returned to police jurisdiction ASAP. To this end, have spoken with Lieutenant O'Connor of the Sixth Precinct, who will arrange for a police escort this A.M. As the patient will likely respond adversely to this chain of events, and may well act out, would strongly urge he be closely monitored with full suicide and elopement precautions. Detective O'Connor assures me that this level of supervision can be provided.' Shit!"

"That wasn't me. At least I don't think it was."

"No, it wasn't. This stuff happens. You're sitting with a stack of charts trying to get through them and you put the right note with the wrong patient. Usually, we catch it. But he must have been discharging a couple patients and got the charts mixed up. And look . . . it's the last entry in the progress notes. Probably no one went back to read it."

"So where's my note?"

"Probably in this person's chart."

"Do you remember who it was?"

"Unfortunately, yes."

I held my breath, knowing not to push. I sensed more emotion in Carol than was merited by the mix-up in charts.

"Certain people you never forget," she said. "It's one of the things in working in psychiatry; you just do better with certain types of patients. And then there are some patients, and diagnoses, that just push all your buttons."

"Like what?"

"I hate working with sociopaths. It makes my blood boil."

"The man in that note was a sociopath?"

Her mouth puckered. "The worst."

"What made him so bad?"

"I don't know what it is. The lies, the feeling of being manipulated, like it's all a game. But it's something else too, I mean patients lie all the time. But sociopaths scare me. I was so happy when they finally took him to jail. I probably shouldn't be telling you this."

"I'm glad you are, but . . . I've got to level with you. And I don't know how to do this without your thinking I'm nuts. So I'm just going to dive into it, because I don't know how else to do it." I reached into my breast pocket and pulled out the folded sketches I had drawn to replace the ones that Susan had. I smoothed them out in front of her.

"Oh my God!" She blanched.

"Is that him?" I already had my answer.

"What are you doing here?" She pushed back from the table. "Oh shit! You just sat here and lied to me, didn't you?"

"I had to. I'm sorry."

"Why? What are you doing here?"

I half-expected her to push the panic button that would summon the guards and aides to take me away.

"Carol, I'm really sorry, but I have to know who that man was."

She looked at me, her eyes grown cold, all trust gone. "I think you should leave."

She was right, but to have come so close . . . "Is there anything I can do to make you change your mind?"

"Just leave, Chad. You shouldn't have come." Her voice was sad. "I don't know why you did this; I guess you have your reasons, but it was a really shitty way to do it." She stood by the open door, no longer looking at me. Suddenly, I remembered her, the hair wasn't blond then or as severely cut. I remembered her kindness as she'd talk to me in a normal voice while I was tied to a metal bed.

I got up to leave, replacing the drawings in my pocket. I could think of nothing to say. I followed in silence as she unlocked the unit door.

Halfway through, I turned around. "Thank you, Carol."

As she closed the door, she said, almost to herself, "You used to be so sweet." And the lock engaged, shutting me out, leaving me in the dingy hallway in front of the elevators.

I wiped my eyes on my jacket sleeve, her parting words resonated within me—that, and the total mess I had made of this. At least I knew the man existed;

211

she'd called him a sociopath. Still, I had no name, but the connection was growing.

I strayed out onto First Avenue, the day far too hot for a jacket. I spotted the herd of patients coming toward me, returning from their walk. I stopped to let them pass. The chattering aides, like armed guards, kept them together, their voices assaultive in their cheerfulness.

The same man as before pleaded, "Just one more cigarette?"

"John, we don't want to be late for art therapy." Her voice brooked no opposition. She noticed my attention, our eyes met; she smiled.

I smiled back; the condescending acknowledgment of two sane people. I stood transfixed and watched them slowly get sucked into the blackened brick building.

I don't belong here. But there was a pull, an urge to become that patient, that "grandiose and delusional" madman. The clinical words of my doctor—she'd called him Philip—hurt. I knew they were only half true. But long ago I gave up expecting people to understand. My experience was not something reasonable. But the truth, the horrible twisted fact was that when I was in Bellevue and my life was falling to pieces, I had never felt more alive and powerful. The other side of "grandiose and delusional" is that I was touched by God. I was a creature of light and incredible strength. Even now, to think of it, was to feel loss. I long ago recanted my experience. "Oh no," I said, to my doctors and my parents—I smiled with remembered embarrassment—"that was madness." I kept the memories to myself.

But still, those words in my record. I felt betrayed; no wonder they didn't like us looking at our charts.

I pictured a younger Dr. Sturges hurriedly writing, flipping through chart after chart, his patients reduced to symptoms and diagnoses. In his haste to move us on, he had confused the folder of the manic-depressive with that of the malingering sociopath. It's a wonder we made it to our appointed destinations: I to Glendale and he to jail.

Chapter Eighteen

As I moved from under the shadow of Bellevue, I thought about my next step. It seemed obvious; the question was how to go about it?

As for Dr. Sturges, his words; it was his job. I was never meant to see those notes. Was that really me on the printed page? I struggled with the split between how I saw the world and how others saw me. The chart merely widened the gap in that particular chasm. But that was for later.

My unseen nemesis grew more real. Like coordinates on a graph, I had a place and a time where our lives intersected; all that remained was discovering his identity.

Without thought, my walk pulled me back to the West Village, overshooting Fifth Avenue and Pamela's apartment. The thinking part of my brain struggled to be heard: *What do you think you're doing?* I refused to listen and quickened my pace. *What did Marvin say?* "Do you want to fuck her?" Not that. Yeah, yeah.

I turned the corner and stared down a row of parked patrol and undercover cars. Like a hive of navy-blue bees, policemen buzzed in and out, singly and in pairs, from the nearly windowless precinct building.

I took a breath and entered the hive.

Inside, a receptionist moved busily about her desk, rearranging papers and sorting documents into a tower of metal trays. A quick glance at the clock sped me along; it was four forty-five on a Friday afternoon. Quitting time, or at least change of shift.

"Excuse me," I said.

"Yes," she answered, not missing a beat in her task.

"I'd like to see Detective Bryant."

"She may already have left for the day. I could check if you like."

"Please."

"Hold on." She tucked the receiver under her chin, punched the number, and attacked another pile of papers.

"Hey, Marge, it's Alice; has Detective Bryant left? . . . Uh-huh, yeah, there's someone wants to see her . . . Hold on." She smiled. "Your name?"

"Chad Greene."

"It's a Chad Greene . . . Oh, okay. I'll send him up." She put down the receiver. "Do you know where her office is?"

"Yes." I was already moving toward the stairwell. An internal battle raged. In the back of my mind I remembered an exercise from an acting class I had taken some dozen years ago. It was about objectives; right now mine was clear, and the quickest way between two points was a straight line, unless you were Einstein in outer space, in which case it could be curved. I tried to focus my thoughts. *What is it I want to say?*

Her door opened before I could knock.

"Chad. This is a surprise."

"Can I come in?" God, she looked good. I wished to hell Marvin had kept his mouth shut.

"Sure. You certainly look a lot different."

"Yeah, the Bloomie's makeover."

"It suits you, a little more corporate than I might have thought. But you're not here to talk about clothes."

"No." My thoughts spun faster, struggling for the right gear.

"Do you want to sit?"

"I'd rather not; I have something I need to ask, and I don't know how to go about it. Let me just go for it. Here it is. Remember the drawings I showed you? You still have the sketch pad."

"Right."

"Well, I figured there was too much coincidence, and it all seemed to go back to when I was arrested and went to Bellevue. That whole mess. So I went back there."

"You what?"

"I just came from Bellevue." I paced faster. "I don't know exactly what I was looking for. But there was a man there, the man in the picture, and Dr. Sturges was his doctor, and I don't know . . . this isn't making a lot of sense. I got another one of those postcards, and I remembered the first one, and it had to be done by someone who knew me when I was crazy, really crazy."

"Like someone at Bellevue?" Her voice was slow and measured, something people do automatically as I start to rev.

"Exactly. I was looking through my chart and the last note was a mix-up. I got his note and I guess he got mine."

"Who?"

"The man I drew."

"How do you know that?"

And for the next ten minutes I tried to give a cogent account of my afternoon's endeavor.

"So what is it you want from me?" An edge of irritation had crept into her voice.

"His name."

"Chad, sit down."

I tried to oblige, but my body seemed to be vibrating; my feet needed to move.

"Look," she said, trying to capture my attention. "You've got to stop this. I promise I'll look into it. But you've got to stop doing this."

"Why?" A wave of rage rushed to the surface. "What am I supposed to do? Wait around till someone shoots me? Or until you decide I'm the best bet for a conviction? I am crazy, after all. Lock up the lunatic, fuck the evidence!"

"Don't talk to me like that." Her face flushed. "I'm not putting up with that sort of bullshit. And the crap you're pulling might get you killed. What do you think is going on here? This is a murder investigation;

it's not an art show, or a Hardy Boys mystery. Stay out of it."

We stood there, our faces red and our breathing heavy. We stared at one another across the desk.

I didn't mean to, maybe it was the incongruity of her expression—the fire—but a smile forced itself to my lips, then a laugh. I tried not to, wanting to respect her growing bewilderment. And then she saw what I saw, two people who had lost their perspectives and their tempers, and she smiled. Her face lit, touching something inside of me. She laughed, the sound rippled and soothed. We struggled to contain ourselves, but fresh waves overtook me and pulled her in. Tears popped in the corners of her eyes.

She looked away, trying to gather her breath. "This is not good."

"What?" I tried to find a semblance of seriousness.

"This. All of this."

"What are you talking about?"

"Let's get out of here. It feels worse in here." She sensed my confusion. "I'll tell you outside."

Obviously, I was missing something essential. She gathered her pocketbook and a stuffed black leather valise. She punched two digits on the telephone. "This is Detective Bryant. I'm going on the service now till Monday. I have the long-range beeper . . . thanks." She looked around quickly. "Come on."

I followed her, aware of the change of shift, the

sudden decrease in personnel as the weekend over-took the precinct house.

She moved quickly toward the door, not stopping for more than a cursory "See you on Monday" or "Have a good weekend."

Outside she immediately hit her Olympic stride, not slowing until we had turned the corner, so we were no longer in view of the station.

"What am I doing?" she said, almost to herself.

"You going to let me in on this?"

"I don't know if I should."

"I can't read your mind."

"Good thing." She attempted a smile. "I can't even make sense of things. I just know this isn't good."

"What?"

"At first I thought it had to do with Barbara, that's my sister."

"The one who gets sick?"

"That's right. She makes me crazy. There are times I could just shake her, when she stops her meds or starts to drink. It's like she never gets it. And then her voices start again, although she once told me they never really went away."

"I remind you of her?"

"I don't know, maybe a little." Our walk took us far-ther south. At Houston Street, the divider between the Village and SoHo, we crossed. I saw the banner for my show in the distance.

"How is she?" I asked.

"All right, I guess. She lives in a group home, is on a new medication. For her it's pretty good."

"I'm not her."

"I know." We stopped outside the gallery. My show was still up, all of the paintings spoken for. Either Serge or Pamela had clipped a number of reviews and placed them in Lucite placards. I read them, as always curious to see how others interpreted what I paint. It's odd trying to make sense of the intellectualized theories about something I consider intuitive and emotional. At least the critic from *Architectural Review* picked up on my love of light's effect on color.

I followed her inside, where tourists and shoppers peopled the gallery. It had a much different feel, like a carnival after the season, everything closed down, awaiting the next wave of business. A young redheaded woman at the reception desk, with a bob and crimson lips à la Louise Brooks, recognized me. I smiled at her, putting a finger to my lips.

The space where Dr. Sturges's portrait had hung was unfilled. The emptiness sat as powerful as any of my paintings. *I wonder where it is?*

Susan joined me. We stared at the blank wall, mesmerized by its potency.

"It's odd, isn't it?" she asked.

"Yes." I was glad that she finally understood.

"I mean, all of these other pictures are sold too, but they're still here."

"Exactly. That's how it works. Or at least how it's supposed to work. When the show comes down at the end of the month, they'll all be crated and shipped. But for whatever reason, they let the portrait go. I never even got around to photographing it. It's like it never existed. But, I guess when money talks, paintings walk."

"Do you know where all your paintings are? Obviously not the stolen ones, but the ones you've sold through the years?"

"Some. I know Pamela tries to keep track, particularly as pictures go up for auction or make it into galleries. She has a mailing list. That way anyone who's bought before gets invited to the next exhibition."

"You've been with her a long time?"

"About nine years."

"Ever thought of switching agents?"

"No, in fact, I'd never really thought about having an agent until I met her."

"Do you trust her?" She stopped at the podium with the visitors' log.

"I've never had reason not to."

"What about the portrait sale? Doesn't that bother you?"

"It did." I watched her flip back through the pages to the night of the show.

"Could you get me a copy of this?"

"Sure." I imagined Marvin's face turning deeper shades of apoplectic red. I took the book over to the receptionist, who readily agreed to make a copy of the ledger. When I returned, Susan was absorbed in *Park Scene Number Four*, it was a painting of an elderly couple walking down a hill in Central Park. Behind them, a pair of half-naked Rollerbladers began the necessary shifts with their bodies to avoid knocking them down. A squirrel, his attention pricked by the rumbling wheels, stood on his haunches and stared out through the canvas. It was an actual scene that had struck me at the time, something in the eyes of the woman skater, a recognition of things to come. The young man was less aware, caught up in the exhilaration of speed and the threat of losing control.

"What are you thinking?" I asked her.

"I can see why people want your paintings. This is beautiful, and sort of sad. It draws you in." Her voice was distant. "You need to be careful, Chad."

"Why?"

Our conversation was interrupted by the high-fashion receptionist returning with my copies. I handed them to Susan, wishing I'd asked for a second set, but I could always get that later. "Let's get out of here," I said.

"Okay." Her eyes lingered on the painting as we wandered out the door.

It felt good, her admiration. Without a receptive audience a painting was just so much gesso, pigment and canvas.

Outside the gallery she seemed distracted, lost in thought.

"What is it?" I asked, noting the fineness of her bones, her deliberate attempts to conceal an attractiveness that could easily flame into beauty.

"I want one."

"One what?"

She smiled up at me. "You're like the goose who lays the golden eggs."

"Come again?"

"Your paintings . . . out of thin air you make beautiful things." She stopped on the sidewalk. Her tone was serious as she said, "Why do you think people commit murder?"

"I don't know. Different reasons, I guess, not the sort of thing I think about."

"It's easy." Like a teacher instructing a pupil, she continued, "It's money, sex, jealousy and rage. Spur-of-the-moment stuff is usually jealousy, rage and sex. If it's planned you think first about money. Then, of course, you get different combinations of the four basics, it's usually not all one or the other. Take a contract killing; at least from the assassin's perspective, it's purely financial. But if you step back from him, or her, you get to the next level and the true motive; which may have little to do with money."

"Do you think Dr. Sturges was killed that way? That someone was hired to do it?"

223

She gave me a sideways glance. "It was clean. Whoever did it had planned things well, didn't leave any physical evidence, nothing the lab has come up with . . . yet."

"So what's the motive?"

"Wish I knew. But here you are in the center of everything, this sudden gold mine, making more and more people more and more money. You've got to be careful."

"So you said."

"You're being stalked, Chad. These things don't often end well."

"What do you recommend?" Our walk delivered us to the outskirts of Chinatown. We got swept up in the thick crowds on Canal Street. The air was ripe with smells of squid, roast duck, subtle spices and fresh fish. Hawkers extolled the virtues of their wares from sidewalk stands. My stomach answered the call, growling. "You hungry?"

"Always," she said.

"You know Wo Hop's?"

"Sounds good."

We steered a path toward Mott Street, forcing our way through the crowds.

We descended into the cool basement restaurant and were immediately seated. At the next table a group of Chinese men in kitchen whites rapidly stuffed and twisted wontons from a mountain of filling and poker-chip piles of flattened rounds of dough.

"I've been thinking about this," she said. "If I had a

woman victim who'd been through what you have with your dog, and the robberies, and these postcards, I'd recommend she'd keep a low profile. In fact, I'd probably tell her to get out of town." She looked at me, a half-smile on her face. "It sucks, but stalkers escalate. There's no question this person can resort to violence. And, for the sake of discussion, if it is the same person who killed Philip Sturges . . ."

"What do you suggest?"

"Keep out of it, Chad. Let me do my job."

"Is this part of it?" I looked at her dead-on. She began to reply when the waiter returned with our food.

"That's a cheap shot," she said, breaking the gaze. A hint of rose colored her cheek.

"Is it? I don't know anymore."

We ate in silence, both deep in thought. Several times I wanted to say something, not exactly certain what. I stole glances across the table, trying to figure the attraction. Our unspoken feelings for each other, like a herd of Disney's pink elephants, danced across the table. We both knew it was there, but to speak of it might start a stampede.

"Chad."

"What?"

"Let's make a deal. I'll look into your man from Bellevue if you stop your sleuthing."

"You wouldn't look into it otherwise?"

"No. I would. But as long as this person is out there, I just wish you'd keep out of it."

"Will you at least tell me his name?"

"I don't know his name," she said.

"I realize that, but it should be easy enough to find."

"What would you do with it?"

"Put yourself in my shoes," I said. "Wouldn't you want a name? Here's someone who knows all about me, goes into my apartment—twice at least that I know of—shoots my dog, and I'm like a sitting duck. Of course I want a name, and as far as keeping a low profile . . . Look at me, I'm hard to miss."·

"You're going to get yourself hurt, or worse."

I pushed away my plate. "I'd rather not get hurt, but if you think about it, not to be melodramatic, but . . ." I stopped myself. *Now there's a thought, not entirely repugnant, but something I'd rather not voice.*

"What were you going to say?"

"It's better left unsaid."

"You're a strange man."

"Tell me something I don't know." *The truth is, if given a choice between a life in hiding, forever fearful of an unknown assailant, and being dead, I'd rather be dead. Zack could get the insurance money. My longevity as an artist would improve. Only my parents would be truly grieved. And even there, though they would never say it, would be a sense of relief.*

It was dark by the time we walked back to Pamela's apartment. "Well"—I fumbled for words like an adolescent on a first date—"thanks for walking me home."

She smiled, acknowledging the role reversal. "I

should probably get going." Her feet were anchored to the spot.

"Yeah." The rumbling of elephants came closer. "Susan?"

"What?" Her face shone silvery in the streetlights.

I took her hand, feeling its softness and warmth. And, before I could stop myself, had pulled her slowly toward me, our eyes locked, her lips parted. The heat between our bodies grew. "I want to kiss you."

"I can't, Chad." Her hands against my chest, she pushed back. "I'm sorry."

Reluctantly, I let go.

"I should go." Her voice rang deep and breathless.

"Yes."

Neither one of us moved.

Then, remembering who she was, and where we were, the spell broke. "Good night, Chad."

"Good night, Susan."

And she turned away, heading north up Fifth Avenue.

CHAPTER NINETEEN

Detective Bryant walked quickly back to her apartment on West Eighteenth Street.

That was close, she thought. Wondering what a judge would say if she'd actually kissed him. *Very close.* Of course, it was easy to deny the whole thing. After all, he was psychotic. It was only a matter of time. The pieces were falling neatly into place. He had motive, opportunity, and the lab already knew that the blood found on the clothes wedged into the back of his closet was human. Once a match was made they'd have enough, more than enough, for the arrest. *And what was all that shit about Bellevue? Conspiracy theories—got to love it.*

He scared her—the photos of his wife taken in the emergency room, her body laced with fresh bruises, gave testimony to his potential for violence. *The woman was in her third trimester, how could someone do something like that?* Now, she'd watched his temper flare and subside, no real rhyme or reason as to what could set him off. It was all too familiar.

Kind of sad, really. Not your problem, she reminded herself. If he got away with this, he'd be incredibly wealthy. Even if convicted, his paintings would be worth a fortune. It's amazing, she thought, how depraved we've become. It didn't matter how you got famous, as long as you got your picture in the paper. Shoot your dog, shoot your shrink, it didn't matter.

CHAPTER TWENTY

I startled from a dream of guns and unseen as-
sailants. My mind raced through image fragments.
There was an old woman, someone forgotten from a
hospitalization years back. She was a white-haired
terror who flew into daily rages. Her neck veins
would pop as burly aides wrestled her to the bed and
strapped her down. In one of her lucid moments she
told me that she had lived in the state hospital for
twenty years, that they had taken away her children
and given her shock treatments. She was trying to
say something—in my dream. It was a warning, but I
couldn't hear.

The lighted orange dial of the alarm clock read
2:30. *I should try to sleep*, but the near total blackness
of the room and the shadowy silhouette of my half-
finished canvas pulled me out of bed. I stumbled to
the open window and yanked up the shades. A cool
breeze filled the room, bringing with it hints of color
carried on city lights. The moon had long passed, its
silver glow replaced by the dirty yellows and oranges
of tungsten filaments and halogen gases.

I slipped quietly to the kitchen and put on a pot of

coffee. Pamela muttered from her open bedroom door. I looked in to see her fast asleep. An old adage popped to mind, something from Ben Franklin: "Both fish and guests begin to stink after three days." We barely saw each other, but still, this was no place for me to stay. It was certainly no place for Ching, who, if further medical mishap hadn't occurred, could leave the vet's and his tiny metal cage later today.

The coffee gurgled and dripped, the aroma and the rhythm calmed my thoughts. *Now is not the time for anxious rumination.* With a final belch, the last of the water filtered through. I filled a mug, savoring the smell and letting the first hot bite hit my tongue.

Back in my room I felt a familiar resistance, the trace of doubt. It didn't bother me, just a reminder that while this was my passion, it was also my work. There was more, too, a daily fear that when I looked inside, there would be nothing there, nothing to draw upon.

I worked in the dark, half guessing at the colors as I globbed them onto my palette.

I repositioned the started canvas, alive with its groping hands and swirling bodies, to catch the streetlight. I painted. Without conscious thought, I gave features to the faces in the maelstrom. All people I knew—Susan, Pamela, my co-workers, the woman from my dream, the nurse at Bellevue. Fear filled me as my hand struggled over an unformed face. Experience had taught me never to resist a creative impulse, and so I gave in, immortalizing my stalker. Another figure rose out of the center and took the form of Dr. Sturges. Tears fell as I painted.

Daylight came. I pushed back from the canvas. My brush was still poised, but I knew—*it's finished.*

"Good." It was now eight o'clock.

I refilled my mug with coffee, now distilled down to a muddy consistency. I put on a second pot and washed my brushes in the sink.

Pamela stirred fitfully in the distance. "What time is it?" Her words rode on a yawn.

I told her.

"How long have you been up?"

"For a while."

"You're insane. You want to close my door? I want to sleep some more."

I did as she asked, and passing by the bathroom, stopped to take my lithium.

It was over a week ago that this all had begun. What is my goal for the day?

The phone interrupted my revery. Rather than wake Pamela, I picked up. "Hello?"

"Bubee, have you seen the morning paper?" I immediately recognized Marvin's voice.

"No. Why?"

"You're making this very hard for me. Didn't I tell you to stay away from reporters? What were you thinking?"

"You didn't say anything about reporters."

"Right. Don't be a smart-ass. We were talking about

the detective you want to shtup. Okay, so now I'm telling you to stay away from reporters."

"What are you talking about?"

"Chad, you're making yourself look guilty as hell." His tone was somewhere between amusement and annoyance.

"Look, Marvin. It's early. I don't now what you're talking about. Let me get a paper, and I'll call you back."

"No, it's my day off. Just keep your mouth shut and call me on Monday. And for the love of God stay away from the police and reporters."

"What paper am I looking for?"

"I think you'll figure that out."

"Okay, bye."

He hung up.

I sat trying to figure his annoyance. *Glad I didn't bring up my dinner with Susan.*

At the corner newsstand, I scanned the row of papers, stopping at the two-inch headline of the *Post*. My heart beat faster as I read:

TOP ARTIST
SEEKS SHRINK SLAYER

Then, in smaller letters next to a large photocopy of my sketch and two smaller pictures of yours truly and Dr. Sturges:

Major Manhattan Painter asks, "Have You Seen This Man?"

"Oh my God." I grabbed a copy, paid the man, and then ducked into the Olympia Diner.

I took the corner booth farthest from the window, ordered a coffee and buttered bialy, and read the copy on page three.

Manhattan Post Exclusive

ARTIST SEARCHES FOR INSANE KILLER OF VILLAGE PSYCHIATRIST

BY HAROLD SCHLEMER

The shotgun slaying of Dr. Philip Sturges, a prominent West Village psychiatrist, has turned up the spotlight on artist Chadwick Greene, a longtime patient of the now dead doctor.

Mr. Greene's recent SoHo exhibition, which netted high into the six figures, included a portrait of the psychiatrist, which sold to a mysterious buyer for $10,000. The painting subsequently vanished. Based on witness accounts of the sale, the artist made the above sketch of the buyer. Mr. Greene contends that this man is a mental patient whom he recognizes from one of his own hospitalizations for manic-depression ten years ago.

Detective Susan Bryant, heading up the

investigation through the Sixth Precinct's Homicide Bureau, offered "no comment" as to Mr. Greene's allegations. The darkly attractive Bryant added, "The investigation is in its early stages. We are following all leads."

The web thickens with the million-dollar theft last week of paintings and sketches from Greene's downtown loft. Ever the artist, he commented, "A lot of them were done when I was a student . . . I should have burned them long ago."

Jennifer Sturges, the grief-stricken widow of the doctor, commented, "It's just not sinking in. Why would somebody do this?" Ms. Sturges, a stunning blonde, added, "I hate to think it, but he did work with so many insane people . . ." When asked specifically about Chadwick Greene, she stated, "I knew he was a patient, but I never met him."

An anonymous co-worker of Greene insinuated, "His career is taking off. Who knows, maybe a scandal would push it further?"

That question will be answered in one week's time, when two of Greene's paintings hit the auction block. A spokesman for the tight-lipped Christie's conceded, "I wouldn't be surprised if the paintings establish new highs for Mr. Greene."

Clearly, the murder of Dr. Sturges is tangled in the fortunes of Chad Greene. Answers, at least according to Greene, may lie with the mysterious purchaser of the portrait. This man, Greene insists, has secrets, buried along with his own, in past psychiatric records."

"Oh, great." I read and reread the copy; the words dripped with innuendo, as though I had killed Dr. Sturges to manipulate the value of my paintings.

I stared at the picture of his wife, with the caption, "SUDDENLY ALONE: Jennifer Sturges bravely confronts her future. 'All I want is for them to catch whoever did this.'"

I didn't recognize her. In fifteen years with the doctor, I'd never seen his wife. He had no family pictures in the office. And aside from the fact that he wore a gold wedding band, I had no knowledge of his outside life. She was attractive, with a face not likely to be forgotten—her dark-blond hair tied up and back, her bone structure patrician. It was a look I associated with *Town and Country* or the Upper East Side.

I wondered how wise it had been for Dr. Sturges to have his office in his home. If I were a psychiatrist, I wouldn't want my patients to know where I lived. What did she think of that? Did she watch us coming and going through the small wrought-iron gate? Every hour someone new arrived to tell her husband about their lives, their problems and their hopes. I never saw his children either; I didn't know of their existence until yesterday.

The waitress came to refill my coffee.

"No, thanks, I've had enough." My insides churned and my thoughts felt muddled. *I can see why Marvin is pissed. What good does this do? Everything about it seems poisonous: the jealousy of co-workers, the intimations of guilt, and the prejudice.* ". . . so many insane people."

What had I done? Well, it was out there, no taking it back. I turned to my drawing on the first page. Would anyone really be able to do something with that? The face was generic, not near the quality of the ones Susan had. Why didn't I take more time with it? Done is done.

I paid my bill and left. Outside, the slowed commerce of a Saturday morning buzzed forward. *What is my goal for the day?* Without much thought, I turned north. I wanted to pick up Ching; after that, I didn't know.

At the corner of West Tenth Street and Fifth Avenue, outside one of the many NYU dormitories that sit semi-camouflaged in the raiment of now defunct hotels, an idea hit. As I looked up Fifth, I was struck with a familiar image. I changed directions. Like the "horse that knows its way," I took the well-trod route to therapy.

I'd avoided this block of West Twelfth Street, with its million-dollar town houses nestled behind wrought-iron gates. I caught sight of his house, a four-story brownstone with offices in what used to be the cellar. I stopped, still at a distance, as though seeing it for the first time. I'd never been in the house proper, always went in through the servants' entrance, where we patients would come and go.

He must have had money; he'd always lived here, as far as I knew. For fifteen years this is where we'd meet. When I started, he hadn't been in practice long. I knew that from Dr. Adams; they'd graduated from the same residency class.

I stared at the darkened windows, bits of curtain visible in the upper stories, a profusion of hanging cacti obscuring those on the lower level. *What lies inside? Two children and a wife, so I've come to learn. Although it is odd, in all these years I'd never caught a glimpse or even heard his family. My appointments were always after school; where were his kids?*

I was startled by seeing the heavy brass door handle begin to turn. Instinctively, I stepped back under the shadow of a tree and watched a woman emerge. She looked younger than I would have guessed, at least from this distance. She was dressed in black sweats, her blond hair pulled tightly back under both a headband and earphones.

She checked the door behind herself and did hamstring stretches, bracing her upper body against the iron railing. *I should move on.* But I couldn't help myself, I wanted a closer look. I watched as she deftly grabbed her ankles and touched her nose to her knees.

So lithe, she moved like a young woman. *She can't be more than thirty, closer to my age than to his.*

She began to jog west, her feet cadenced to music I couldn't hear. She turned south at the end of the block. Without thought, I followed.

CHAPTER TWENTY-ONE

/

My better instincts, if such existed, told me to stop. I couldn't. I mentally triangulated Jennifer Sturges's progress and followed. She turned west on Twelfth Street; I jogged the parallel block. She went south on Hudson; I tailed behind.

My train of thought was oddly puritanical. *A week after her husband's murder and she's out jogging? Shouldn't she be with her children? Shouldn't she be mourning? Of course, she is wearing black.*

She disappeared onto Christopher Street. I stopped at the corner, letting her lead grow. Her toned figure jogged in place at the distant end of the block, waiting out the traffic on the West Side Highway. The light changed and she crossed.

For the next forty-five minutes I shadowed her. *What is my goal for the day? To stalk a total stranger. Wonderful.*

She stopped outside a small breakfast café nestled incongruously in the meatpacking district, an area I'd avoid if I were a woman alone. Not that it's overtly dangerous, just deserted—a series of warehouse-lined blocks thick with the smell of blood and butchered flesh. Ching loved it here. In recent years, a series of chic after-hours clubs and trendy restaurants had sprung up, like mushrooms in a pile of dung.

I watched from the corner as she removed her headset, did a final round of hamstring stretches, and entered the restaurant.

I argued with myself. *Do I go in or do I stay out?*

You shouldn't be here.

True, but I am.

What will you do if you go in? Try to talk to her?

Don't think. Act.

I crossed the street and went in.

Even at that hour, the Barbie Café was full. The noisy clientele, many in black leather or nightclub garb, were obviously still working on the night before.

The decor consisted of thousands of Barbie dolls and her various male and female plastic-molded friends. They hung from the ceiling in sequined trapeze costumes and frolicked in candy-apple sports cars encased in the clear Lucite furniture.

As I approached Jennifer Sturges's table, uncertain of my opening line, I was struck by her resemblance to the doll. Her face was the Californian ideal, perhaps less tan, but otherwise wholesome and unlined.

She looked up from her menu and saw me. She seemed perplexed. "You're Chad Greene?"

I froze, caught in the clear cornflower-blue of her eyes.

"You are Chad Greene?" she repeated, almost like an accusation.

"Yes."

"And you know who I am?" she asked.

"Yes."

"What are you doing here?" She looked around, her expression nervous.

I couldn't think. *What is my goal?* Words failed me.

"Have you been following me?" she asked.

I nodded. "I wanted to talk to you."

She was trying to decide whether or not to call for help, to have me thrown out. She looked up at me. "Haven't you done enough?"

"It wasn't me," I said, trying to keep my voice soft. "I just want to talk."

"Great." She looked at the table, then back at me. "What the hell."

I took it as a yes and slowly sat down. "Thanks."

She edged her chair backward.

"I'll just have a cup of coffee and then I'll go."

"I see."

A man wearing a plastic-molded blond wig and a parody of a 1950s blue-and-red housedress took our order.

Jennifer smiled as he left with his skirts rustling behind. "I used to have that outfit . . . for my Barbie, I mean."

"How did you recognize me?" I asked.

"You're not hard to spot." She sipped her water, her voice drifted. "I feel like I'm getting to know all sorts of people I've never met."

"I'm sorry about your husband."

She looked up, her eyes misting around the edges. "Are you?"

"Yes."

"That was pretty rude, wasn't it." Silence. "How did *you* recognize me?" she asked.

I wasn't prepared. Somehow I didn't think telling her I had been trailing her all the way from West Twelfth was the way to go. "I saw your picture in the paper this morning."

"Really? That's just what I need. Which one?"

I handed her my crumpled copy of the *Post*.

She read the headline, her expression grew terse. Her hands began to shake. "I don't believe this shit!" She pushed away the paper, spilling her water. The liquid soaked into the newsprint, the stain spread and distorted my sketch of the portrait buyer. "I never said that . . . God, what a little shit." Angry tears squeezed from the corners of her eyes.

She looked across at me. "What is it you want?"

"I don't know . . . to talk."

"Look"—she struggled to keep her composure—"I don't know why you're here, but I wish you'd leave . . . now."

What could I say? "I'm really sorry about this, about all of it." I got up to leave. "Your husband helped me a lot and I miss him."

She looked up at me. "Do you? Really?"

"Yes."

"Poor Philip."

The waiter dressed as housewife Barbie returned with glasses of fresh-squeezed orange juice and two coffees. We stood frozen in tableau as he chattered on. "I can't believe it," he said with an easy familiarity, "he just calls out sick and I'm supposed to cover his tables. I am *just* one woman." He wrenched a smile from Jennifer. "I have to warn you, it may be a bumpy ride. If you want more coffee, don't be shy, the pot's over there." Without giving us time to respond, he was off to bus a vacated table.

"I didn't order orange juice," I said to her, still standing.

"I know. I didn't have the heart to tell him . . . you might as well sit down and drink it."

I felt as if I were with a stray animal, that any sudden movement would scare her off.

"You're awfully quiet for someone who wants to talk," she said.

"I'm not sure what to say."

"Let me start." Her tone was hard. "There seem to be a few questions everyone wants to know. Like, did I kill my husband?" She paused. "Or did you kill him?"

"That wasn't what I had in mind."

"Sure. Statistically speaking, I'm the number-one choice and you're probably number two. I fit a pattern. I try not to think about it, to keep everything business-as-usual. It doesn't work, though, does it? I feel like a fish in a bowl. Everywhere I go there's that policewoman, or a reporter, and now you. I can't think straight. I mean, seriously: Why are you here?"

I paused before answering, fighting back the quick rejoinder. "I met with your husband, once a week, for fifteen years. I know nothing about him. I know that he kept me out of the hospital on at least a dozen occasions, and more than once he stopped me from destroying years of work. Who knows, I might be dead if it weren't for him. And then someone kills him, and somehow I'm involved. It doesn't make sense. And I can't push it away."

She nodded. "That policewoman showed me your picture. Asked if I knew you. I wonder what she'd think of this meeting?"

"Not much."

"Probably assume . . . I don't know."

"Can I ask you something?"

"It depends," she said.

"Okay. You seem a lot younger than Dr. Sturges."

"Second wife."

"Oh."

As if she were reading my thoughts, she said, "Two kids and the first wife live in Scarsdale."

Transvestite Barbie returned with Jennifer's waffles. "If you need anything else, just holler." He looked at me. "You're that artist, aren't you?"

"Yeah."

"Really? That's what Vinnie said." He looked around the packed restaurant. "I never do this, but . . .

could you scribble something on a napkin for me? Nothing much, just anything and I'll pay for your meal, for both of you . . . tip included."

I stared at him, looking like some overwound giant toy, racing to keep up with the crowded dining room. "Sure." In spite of herself, Jennifer smiled. "But you got to bring me a plate of what she has. And I'll need a pen."

"You got it." He pulled out a felt-tip from his patch pocket. "It doesn't have to be much."

"You're getting to be famous," she said after he left.

"So they say."

She looked on while I drew a cartoon of our waiter. I thought back to my sisters' Barbie dolls and the little booklets that came with them. My impromptu composition combined one of those classic poses with an updated Lautrec café scene.

"That'll be worth a lot more than our meal," she said.

"I know. But at least he'll appreciate it."

Her cheeks flushed, she was struggling with some unnamed emotion.

"Are you okay?" I asked.

She clutched the sides of her face. Tears welled up. I wanted to hold her, to comfort her. "What is it?"

"Everything," she said, biting her lip. "I don't know what to do." She picked at her waffle. "I'm pregnant."

I wanted to say, I'm sorry, but somehow that seemed wrong. So I kept silent.

The Portrait

"He didn't really want another child. He said he'd already been through that. Why am I even telling you this?"

"Sometimes strangers are easier to talk to."

"Maybe. That sounds like something Philip might say. It's such a mess. We had all these plans, and none of them got done. I just can't figure out what I should do. I've even thought about an abortion, but that would be killing him all over. I just don't know."

"Time. You need time."

"Maybe. I'm going to have to do something, though. I can't go back to work full-time if I have a baby, and I can't pay for the baby if I don't go back to work."

This surprised me. "Is it that bad?"

"It's not good. He never changed his will. He was going to. I sometimes thought about it, but it's hard to tell someone. You know. 'Gee, what if you die? I won't get anything.' His family already thought I'd destroyed his life, was some sort of gold-digger nurse. His children won't even talk to me."

"You're a nurse?"

"It's how we met." She made eye contact. "I'm a psychiatric nurse. Kind of a cliché, huh?"

"No, it makes sense. You work with someone, things develop. It makes sense."

"They were already separated. So it's not like I broke anything up. Of course, that's not what his ex said. Funny, isn't it? After all this, she gets her way."

"What do you mean?"

"They'd been fighting over tuition. His oldest girl starts college this year. In the settlement they were supposed to split the cost. Dolores thought he should pay the whole thing. So she would call, or her lawyer would call. It was always like that. Even before the tuition, there was always something, some excuse. And now she pretty much gets everything. I've already been informed by her lawyer that I have thirty days to vacate."

"She gets the house?"

"Not exactly. It goes to the children, but they've already decided to sell it. They're going to sell everything. He really loved that house; it's been in his family for over a hundred years. It's like her revenge."

"Where will you go?"

"I have friends, for now. There is a little insurance money, so it's not totally bleak, and maybe it's best. The house takes a lot of upkeep, and without him . . . Maybe I'll move out of the city. It doesn't seem the best place to raise a kid."

"Did you tell the police this?"

She smiled. "Yeah, talk about your motive. She really cleans up. And the more I think of it—she's just crazy. The sort of things she'd say on the phone . . . I'll be happy if I never hear her voice again."

Barbie returned. "For me?!" He snatched up the signed napkin drawing. "And for you." He replaced it with a steaming waffle topped with a mountain of strawberries and whipped cream. "If you want anything else, just holler."

"Thanks."

"No, thank you." He studied the picture. "This is fabulous."

Jennifer watched our waiter show Vinnie his prize. "I really would miss New York, though," she said.

I smiled. "No place like it."

CHAPTER TWENTY-TWO

/

Susan Bryant reread the faxed laboratory results. It was a positive match. The blood found on Chad's clothes belonged to Philip Sturges.

Well, she thought to herself, that about does it, more than enough for probable cause: the wife hears the argument, Chad admits to the fight, he had motive, he was there, and now this. Almost too easy. Not enough for conviction, not yet at any rate, but a good start. Of course there's still the problem of the accomplice. She thought of her partner's suggestion: "Cherchez la femme," he may be right. That Pamela woman makes out pretty well with all of this; of course nothing solid connects her . . . not yet, at any rate, just a whole lot of money.

She pulled out a blank arrest warrant and called her secretary to arrange fifteen minutes with the judge.

She looked at the paperwork; all of this felt a little too close to home. Last night's phone call from her mother was not what she needed.

"Barbara has stopped taking her pills again," her mother said. "She stayed out all last night. I think the group home is going to kick her out. They want us to come in for a meeting . . . She can't live with us, Susan. We just can't handle her."

"I know, Mom. Do you want me to come with you and Dad to the meeting?" She hoped the answer would be no.

"If you could. You know how to talk to these people better. We just can't have her back here. With your father being sick and everything, I just can't handle it."

"Don't worry, Mom. Did they actually say they want her out of the home?"

"No, but I can tell something is up."

"Okay, let's not jump to any conclusions."

By the time she hung up with her mother, the anger had started. How many times has this happened? Why don't they just keep them in the hospital?

Later that day she stood outside the Village Veterinarian, the signed arrest warrant in her pocket. Her thoughts raced. He bolted. He took the dog and bolted. Shit! I should have seen this coming. Got to think, Monday afternoon. Where is he? He's gone to see his shrink. And then the awful thought came: Is he at risk? He's already killed one psychiatrist. Oh God. She pulled out her cellular phone and dialed her partner.

CHAPTER TWENTY-THREE

I lay in the too-small bed staring at the fluorescent alarm clock dial. *Yes, it's Monday. Do I really want to paint this morning?* Before I could rationalize myself into a couple more hours' sleep, I threw back the covers. The cool air hit my bare skin, forcing me out of bed. I dug through the Bloomingdale's bag for a T-shirt and sweats.

I fumbled to the kitchen and started the coffee. My thoughts flitted anxiously through the day ahead. *It's a tight schedule: three hours to paint, have breakfast, teach my classes, check on Ching, catch the train to Boston, see Dr. Adams, call Susan, call Marvin. Why do I do this to myself? It's like some masochistic urge to make myself as nervous as possible. Each thought cranks up my tension a little higher, like flicking your tongue over a throbbing tooth; you know you shouldn't but you just have to play with it, make sure it's still there, make sure it still hurts.*

What's your goal for the day?

That's right, focus. If you could only do one thing, what would it be?

Find the name of the man from Bellevue.

Good, and how will you do that?

The Portrait

I poured my first cup of coffee and walked back to the guest room mulling over the question. How do you find someone without a name? I thought of my hospital chart: At the top of each page were my name, date of birth and Social Security number. On the last page, where the notes had been switched, was it my information stamped on that page? Did I even look? What if it was his? The thought of going back filled me with dread. Would they even let me in? Of course, Marvin would say they had no choice. I put that on my list of things to do.

I painted. As brush connected with canvas, my fears evaporated. It was like an on/off switch for the nervous part of my mind.

I heard Pamela shuffling in the kitchen. "Morning," I yelled out, putting down my brush and opening the door.

"Did you sleep last night?" Her voice was gently accusatory.

"Yeah; could have slept more."

"Why didn't you?"

"This is when I paint."

"God, I don't know how you do it."

I joined her at the kitchen counter, waiting for the second pot of coffee to finish dripping. My attention focused on bare hooks where several framed photos used to hang. The empty spaces reminded me of my plundered loft. "What happened to your pictures?"

"Oh. I'm having them rematted. You want some breakfast?"

I picked at some toast, showered and got myself down to the studio.

It was a frustrating day. Between classes I tried to get hold of Susan—she didn't return my calls. At Marvin's office, Velma told me he was in court all morning and couldn't possibly get back to me before three o'clock. So much for my daily goal. To top it off, I forgot to take my lithium and Trilafon. Usually I popped them after my morning painting, but for whatever reason—sin of omission or commission, I didn't.

And now, sitting on the twelve-fifteen train to Boston, I couldn't shake the feeling that someone was watching me. I nonchalantly took inventory of my fellow passengers, half expecting to see my letter-writing nemesis in some Woolworth's Halloween disguise. Unfortunately, the seats obstructed most of my view.

I told myself I was being ridiculous. Try to take a nap.

Yeah, right. Like I could sleep with this certainty that someone on the train is out to get me.

I got up and walked toward the bathroom, peering down each row of seats as I passed. I tried to be discreet, but it was difficult for someone my height to get a good face-on view of every male passenger.

An AMTRAK ticket taker approached from the opposite end of the car.

The Portrait

A man in a baseball cap and T-shirt glared at me from his seat. "What you looking at?" he asked as I stared him fully in the face.

"Sorry, I thought you were someone I knew." And I hurried past, trying to brush by the uniformed attendant.

"Ticket?" He blocked my path.

I fumbled through my pockets. "I must have left it at my seat. Oh, wait, here it is." I retrieved the purple stub.

People stared at me as he punched the ticket.

"Thank you," he said, looking me straight in the face. We stood there staring at each other. He cleared his throat. "I need to keep moving."

"Sorry." I realized I was blocking his way down the aisle. I felt paralyzed. *Do I go forward or do I go back? Move.* I returned to my seat. *God, I wish I'd taken my pills. How could I have been so stupid?*

I stayed put, pretending to be asleep, all the time fighting off the sense of being watched. For the uninitiated, here's what paranoia is—an ego trip gone bad. It's like being on a stage surrounded by an audience that hates you.

I peered through lidded eyes. *Is there really anybody out there?* All I saw were the backs of heads and a little boy curled up on the seat across the aisle.

I tried to sleep, listening to the rumble of the train. My head began to nod.

"Prepare the Way."

My eyes shot open, darting around for the source of the voice. *Oh shit, it's starting again.*

My nerves were jangled by the time I made it to Dr. Adams's office.

"How you doing?" he asked, taking the seat across from me.

"I've been better." I decided to fess up at the start. "I didn't take my pills this morning and right now I feel like I'm about to jump out of my skin."

"I could call the pharmacy on the corner and have them delivered up," he offered.

"Could you?"

"No problem."

I listened as he phoned in my medicines. Like ordering a pizza. "Pharmacist, please . . . Yes, this is Dr. Adams for Chad Greene. Trilafon eight milligrams twice a day, Ativan one milligram twice a day as needed for anxiety, and lithium carbonate six hundred milligrams twice a day. A fourteen-day supply. Could you read that back? . . . Great, and if you could deliver those to my office. Thanks.

"So." He returned to his chair. "What's going on?"

"I'm losing it."

"That's not good."

"I feel like shit. Everything's going too fast and I have that feeling like there are people watching me. Which it would be great if I could say, 'Chad, that's just your paranoia, you crazy boy you.' But it's not, because there really is somebody who broke into my apartment and tried to kill my dog and leaves death threats in the mail. I'm like a puppet. 'Do this, Chad; now do that, turn around; now let's get some voices going. Watch out, somebody's behind you. Oops, only kidding, there's no one there.'"

"You're hearing voices?"

"A little—they're not bad."

"Are they telling you to do things?"

"You mean like smash mirrors?"

"For instance."

I smiled in spite of myself. "No. How long till my drugs get here?"

"They're usually pretty quick. It's been a rough week."

"Tell me about it. I go from thing to thing and I can't really figure what I'm doing. Like I went to Bellevue to look at my old chart." *Is that his eyebrow going up?* "And I almost kissed the police detective; remember that song, 'Love Potion Number Nine'? where the guy kissed the policeman?"

"You're losing me, Chad."

"Am I making any sense?"

"You're a little loose. I've seen worse, though. Try to focus on one thing and tell me about that."

"That's a good idea. Do you mind if I stand?" I was already out of the chair. "I need to pace."

"Sure."

"Too much is happening at once. It's not all bad. Like I got my own office, can you imagine? I wonder what's taking my pills, I could really use an Ativan about now . . . One thing, you said, focus on one thing. Let me think. Bellevue, that's probably what I should talk about, 'cause at this rate, that's where I'm going to end up. I'm just kidding about that, at least I hope I am. God"—I shook out my arms—"it's like every nerve is firing with some sick yellow energy." I looked at him sitting there, watching me. "Do you think that's it? Maybe whoever's doing this wants me to go crazy. Maybe that's what this is about. What a strange thought. Maybe that is it, and maybe what I need to focus on is staying sane." I looked out through the plants hanging in his window and saw a man carrying a small paper bag headed in this direction. "I think the pharmacy man is coming."

Dr. Adams met him at the door. I took the bag and swallowed my pills dry.

"Thanks for doing that," I said after the man had gone.

"Don't mention it. I noticed when you talked about 'staying sane,' something about that seemed calming."

"Yeah, isn't that funny? That one thought is worth a milligram of Ativan. Maybe it's too simplistic, but maybe that's what I need right now—simple things to hang on to. All I have to do is stay sane. I can do that. What do you think?"

"I think it's important and I think you do have some control. I also think it's going to force you to confront whatever it is that keeps you struggling with your medications and your illness."

"Like why didn't I take them this morning?"

"Exactly."

"And why didn't I have some with me, like four thousand nurses have advised me?"

He smiled. "By George, he's got it."

"I'm not Eliza Dolittle. But it fits, doesn't it?"

"What fits?"

"When I was growing up, my parents had a record of *My Fair Lady*, it's Dad's favorite. On the cover is a caricature of Henry Higgins pulling the strings on Eliza Dolittle. That's me. Everyone tells me what to do and how to do it. Most of the time, I go along. Whenever I don't, it's like 'Oh, there goes Chad acting up again.' But maybe that's the problem. I'm always either passively going along, or actively fighting against it. There's got to be a middle ground."

"What happens if you cut the strings?"

"I don't know. Fall over or stand on my own."

"Right."

"It's more like Pinocchio."

"You're switching metaphors."

"I know, but he had strings too. I was thinking of what he wanted—to be a *real* boy. That sounds good—to be real, to be like everybody else, to be normal."

"So what's normal?"

"To not take pills, to not be scared of what might

pop out of my head or out of my mouth. To not know what the inside of a locked ward looks like. That would be normal. To be a father to my son, to have my own father want to spend time with me. To not feel like I've been a total disappointment to him. That would be normal." I looked across at him. He was smiling. "What?"

"How to say this?" He paused, searching for words. "What you're describing the way you feel now, *is* normal. It's the human condition, to want the approval of your father, to want to be a better father to your child. This is normal."

"But I'm not normal. I'm a mental patient."

"That's your choice."

"Don't do that to me."

"Do what?"

"Twist things like that. I can't help it that I've got mood swings. You told me yourself it's probably genetic. You've been telling me that since I was seventeen."

"True, you have manic-depression. It runs in your family. It's also true that every time you go into the hospital, at least some portion of it, is related to your dropping out of treatment, or stopping meds, or getting overwhelmed with stress of your own making."

"That's not fair . . . Or maybe it is. It's just like what he said."

"Who?"

"Dr. Sturges. I told you I went to Bellevue and

looked at my chart; that's what he said in the note, that it was my pattern to 'stop my meds and become psychotic.' I'd like to argue with that, but I really can't. He was right and that's what makes me not normal. I'm like a time bomb always set to go off."

"What about someone who takes insulin? They can never stop."

"Not the diabetic analogy. Do you know how many times I've heard that? 'Chad, manic-depression is an illness just like diabetes or high blood pressure.' But diabetics don't get hauled off to the nutty bin for stopping their insulin."

"True, they get admitted to a medical ward. And the person with high blood pressure has a stroke or a heart attack and dies. The point is they've all got medical conditions for which there is no cure, only daily, ongoing, treatment."

"It's still different. People aren't afraid of diabetics or hypertensives; 'Oh God, get him away from me, his blood sugar's too high.' They are afraid of mental patients. And after seeing that chart, I understand why. It said I assaulted my pregnant wife. That's not what happened. What I did was bad enough, but I never hit her. But it's there in writing for all time, and even better, the last note isn't even mine. It's from someone who got sent to prison, but it's in my chart, so anyone who reads it is going to think I'm a sociopath. That's not like having an out-of-whack sugar level or blood pressure that's too high. It's different."

"You're right," he conceded.

"I know I am. Even though I had nothing to do with getting sick, now that I have my illness, whatever it really is, it always sets me apart. Other diseases just affect the body, don't they? People see me and they see a defect of the mind. They don't understand. 'What do you mean, you get manic? Can't you just stop it?' Or the helpful hints when I'm depressed: 'Gosh, when I feel down I tell myself to snap out of it.' 'What about exercise?' 'Do you get enough vitamins?' 'How about watching a funny movie?'"

"So, you have no control? Your illness will always pull your strings?"

"I don't know. Maybe I've overstated things—I do that sometimes. Maybe I'm just pissed at myself for screwing with my pills. It wasn't intentional, not this time at any rate, but it's no excuse."

"I'm not your father, Chad."

"What has that got to do with it?"

"You want to apologize to me for not taking your medicine, as though I might punish you somehow. It's your business whether or not you take your pills."

"I know. It's like there's a part of me that's stuck at seventeen, and if I could just make it out of adolescence . . ."

"Who are you rebelling against?"

"Well, my father, for one—but truthfully, we've been doing okay. And then I think of the pills, and maybe that's it, the thing that I've never been able to really accept. That for all my life I'm going to have to take medication. And even then, there are no guarantees that I won't flip out and destroy years of my life. It's like a wolf at the door, always ready to devour me."

"How does that fit in with not taking the pills?"

"If I don't take them, maybe I'm not really sick."

"What do you think of that statement?"

"Pretty stupid."

"It's your biggest wish—to be free of your illness. What you're describing is denial. The pills are a very real, twice-a-day reminder of your illness. If you forget them, maybe you can forget your disease. The problem is, the more you forget them, the higher the risk of relapse."

"I know, and this is where I'm supposed to say, 'You're right, I've got to accept my illness and go on.' Hell, it's been twenty years. But I'm not there. I don't want to give up the wish." And to myself: *Maybe I don't want to give up the mania.*

"Then don't," he said. "We're talking about hope, which is necessary. All I ask is that you look at a self-injurious pattern that decreases your chances of getting your wish."

I sat trying to focus on his words, maybe catching half of them. *It is ridiculous that after so long I can't fully accept my diagnosis—the evidence is overwhelming.*

"What are you thinking about?" he asked.

"What you said about denial. I think that's right. I don't know how you get beyond that, but I think that's where I need to go. And speaking of going, aren't we out of time?"

"Don't worry about it," he said.

I don't want it to end, but he's already let me run over. I feel a little calmer, and it's not just the pills. Some tremendous thought was struggling to be born. "It's not fair to you," I said. "I've been here two hours, you need to get home. I'll be fine."

He looked skeptical.

"Don't worry," I said. "I promise to call if I have any problems."

"Would you mind if I called you tomorrow?" he asked.

"To check in, huh?"

"Yes."

I felt a twinge of annoyance and the hint of a Disney tune, "I've Got No Strings."

"Fine. I got to get going." I shook the bag of pills. "Don't worry, I'll be fine."

I felt his eyes through my back as I left his office. *I wonder if he's watching through the window?* I resisted the urge to turn. Overall, I felt lighter, my perspective realigned, my brain humming at the edges of an awesome truth.

Outside, storm clouds had started to gather, bringing an early dusk. The last wave of commuters scrambled toward the subways. I followed, my thoughts drifting. Images of the man popped into my head. I pushed them away, only to have them return. I walked faster as the first rain fell.

What was that? I thought someone had called my name. I looked around. *I should have taken a double helping of Trilafon.*

It's just your imagination. I braced myself against the lamppost by the Boston Gardens, waiting for the light to change. A dark panel van glided by. *It's not following you, Chad.*

Sirens screamed in the distance. Two police cruisers skirted the Commons and vanished into the maze of Beacon Hill from where I had just come.

I crossed the street, trying to keep my thoughts occupied. *The face,* everywhere I looked, *the face.*

As I hit Washington Street and the Combat Zone, I realized the van was still with me. *It's a different truck, Chad, you're just imagining it.*

I stopped, amid the prostitutes and the pimps, and stared into the open window. I stood frozen to the spot. There, beneath a wig, beard and glasses, was the face darkly illuminated in the fading light.

He smiled, aware that I recognized him. He crooked his finger, motioning me closer.

I moved back, I started to run. *I've got to call the police. I need to get somebody.* The lights glittered like shiny daggers, I couldn't get my eyes to focus. *I need a phone.* I felt him follow.

"Chad!" a voice yelled out.

I heard the rattle of a chain. *Oh God, no.* The sound was too familiar. I froze and turned on the spot.

The van had pulled up next to me. I looked in, and saw him jangle something silvery.

Oh God, it's Ching's collar.

He motioned me to the window.

I obeyed.

"I have your dog," he said. "We need to talk."

Before I could react, he dropped the chain and pulled a chrome-plated pistol from inside his flannel jacket. He pointed it at my head. "Get in."

I did as he said, my eyes trapped by his.

Sweat broke out on my forehead as I climbed into the too hot cab. *He really exists.* I studied the contours of his face, the flare of his nostrils, the shadow where his ersatz beard met the curve of his chin.

"Where's my dog?"

His pupils constricted and his finger twitched. I felt a sharp jab, like a bee sting, over my heart. I grabbed my chest and found a small metal dart dug through my shirt and into my flesh. "What the fuck!"

He smiled and gently reached across my lap, pulling my seat belt taut. "Tranquilizer gun," he whispered. "We've got a long ride ahead of us."

A powerful sedative washed over me. "Who are you?"

The Portrait

"I thought you knew. I'm Allen Broadhurst. I thought you never forgot a face."

"I don't." I struggled to keep my eyelids open. "I'm not good with names." My last thought before I fell unconscious was: *I got my daily goal.*

CHAPTER TWENTY-FOUR

It's a bad dream.

"Wake up, asshole," a voice barked. Something hard dug into my belly. I grabbed for it and felt the jab of metal handcuffs scraping raw flesh, holding me back. I remembered. *It's no dream.*

"Time to paint," the voice said.

What? I struggled to kick off the fog of drugs that clouded my brain. A light shone in my eyes, it blurred the outline of my captor's face. Smells of rancid meat and blood filled my nostrils. My lips were parched and my tongue lay thick and dry in my mouth.

What am I doing here? My shoulders protested as I tried to sit, every movement hard-won through pain.

"Get up, asshole."

I pushed against cold cement, struggling to sit, my legs shackled in front of me, my hands cuffed behind my back.

Wincing in the light, I watched his form come into focus. He sat sprawled in an overstuffed chair looking across at me, a dark sticklike object in his right hand. His hair was medium brown and buzz-cut short. His features were full, his cheeks and eyelids sagged under the heavy shadows.

"Get up, Chad. Want some encouragement?" He leaned over something dark lying by his chair.

And then it hit me. "NOOO!" I struggled to my feet.

"Too late." He laughed and jabbed the stick into Ching's motionless body. Ching jerked, whimpered, and then was silent.

"No," he said, "he's not dead. Not yet." He stood, well out of the circumference of my tethered range.

"What do you want from me?" I asked.

He stared. His eyes glittered in the dull lights, black and hungry. "I brought you presents." He pulled a black cloth off a metal table. "What do you think? Nothing but the finest for the *great* artist."

The tabletop was buried under shiny tubes of Windsor and Newton paints and bristle-hair brushes.

"I asked you a question. What do you think?" He came closer, wary of my limits. He poked the stick toward me. I stared at its jagged metal edge, so like the filament on a lightbulb. His eyes met mine, smiling behind his weapon. "Pretty neat, huh?" He feigned with his left and jabbed at my gut with his right.

Searing pains shot through my body as the cattle prod connected with flesh. My legs buckled and I fell to my knees.

"Thought you'd like that." His breathing was heavy and excited; I heard the trace of an asthmatic wheeze.

I didn't move. I struggled to make sense of the situation, to focus through the waves of surging adrenaline.

My hands and feet tingled through the pain. My throat grew tight as though it might close off.

He lunged again with the prod.

I shifted instinctively, my shoulder ducked below his arc, sending him off balance. I pressed the advantage, lifting up underneath his arm. He tripped and fell hard against the wall. My arms strained against the handcuffs. *If only I could reach him—squeeze his neck, crush his head into the dust.* My hands strained slick and sticky from the blood that oozed from my wrists. I hurled myself toward him, ignoring the chains. I tried to ram him with my head.

"Jesus fucking Christ!" he screamed and scuttled backward, like a giant crab, across the floor. He broke free of my range.

"Fucker!" He scrambled to his feet. A trickle of blood tracked from his nose to his mouth. He wiped it away and looked at it, mesmerized. He sucked the blood. "Well, that was certainly something." He walked back toward Ching.

"What are the paints for?" I yelled, desperate to avert his attention.

He stopped and looked back over his shoulder. The hint of a smile. "Right. That's a little better. You need to show the proper interest, Chad."

He disappeared into the shadows, his footsteps echoed from the dark. The space was larger than I'd originally thought, some sort of warehouse or factory.

I heard a scraping sound as something wooden was dragged across the concrete floor. He reappeared in the light and began to assemble a massive, homemade wooden easel—a type I'd constructed myself when painting oversized canvases.

I looked at Ching lying on the floor. His fur was matted. An IV tube connected to a plastic bag dripped a clear liquid into his veins. I held my breath watching him, looking for the steady rise and fall of his chest— at least he was alive.

"What's the matter?" Allen's voice intruded into my thoughts. "The dog is fine. Whether he lives or dies is entirely up to you."

"What do you want?"

"A painting." He stepped back to reveal an eight-foot-square canvas that glowed sickly yellow under the bare bulbs.

In spite of myself I felt a surge of excitement staring at the blank canvas. "You stole the paintings from my apartment."

"Of course. But you yourself said they weren't your best. I have to agree. That won't do. Besides, you owe me. Yes," he said under his breath, "you certainly owe me." He looked at me. "Aren't you curious as to what your greatest, and perhaps final, work will be?"

I didn't answer.

"I see." He sank back into the chair, his hand resting on Ching's head. "You're going to paint my portrait."

I stared at him, the face I'd drawn a dozen times; I wasn't far off.

"What are you staring at?"

"You."

He got up and came closer. "Go ahead and look." He turned his head to display each profile. "Tell me you've never had a better subject." He waited for my reply, his eyes bored into mine. "I see. Cat got your tongue?"

A jolt of electricity shocked me to the floor.

I swallowed hard, trying to catch my breath. I looked up at his figure haloed in the dirty light.

"When I ask a question, Chad, it's a good idea to answer." His voice softened. "If you do what I tell you to, everything will be okay. This isn't hard and you're not stupid." He cocked his head. "You're just crazy . . . now, get up."

I did as he said, each movement filled with pain.

"Now, this is how we're going to work. You're going to paint and I'm going to pose. It's not very hard. Simple as pie."

"I need my hands."

"Do you think I'm stupid? Let me show you how we're going to work. Over here." He stepped into the shadows. "I have a gun." He returned with a long-barreled chrome-plated pistol. "It's a pretty gun, don't you think? Very shiny . . . I'm waiting."

"For what?"

"I asked you a question. Please don't forget what I tell you. Do you need some reinforcement?" He tapped the gun to the cattle prod wedged in his belt. "Perhaps a few quick jolts into puppy would increase your learning curve. Now, I asked you a question: Don't you think the gun is pretty?"

"Yes."

"Yes what, Chad?"

"Yes, I think the gun is pretty."

"It is, isn't it?" His voice softened, and like an actor, he stepped into the light's hot spot. "Now where was I? Oh yes, how we play this game. I sit here"—he gestured broadly to the torn upholstered chair. "And you—paint there. It's not a hard concept. It's easy to grasp. Are you ready?" He smiled, coming closer.

"Yes . . . I'm ready."

"Much better. Just a couple rules. Should you try and run away—I kill the dog and then I kill you. Or maybe the other way around. It doesn't really matter, but somehow I think it's just richer to kill the puppy first, don't you think?"

"You're sick," I said, unable to stop myself. I braced for the jab of the prod.

"I see." He stepped back. "Of course I'm not the one who beat up his pregnant wife, am I? Did you kick her? Did you make her bleed? Inquiring minds want to know."

"It was an accident."

"Not what I heard. But then again, men can be such scum, can't we? But let's not argue. There's been too much of that already. Back into the corner."

I obeyed; my legs tangled and clanked in the chains. I watched as he pushed the canvas and easel over to the edge of my freedom.

"Good. Now come here." With his right hand he fished a key ring out of his pocket, his left hand held the gun. "Turn around."

The handcuffs fell noisily to the floor.

"That's fine." He stepped away.

"Turn around."

My wrists were swollen and bloody, my fingers tingled and throbbed as the circulation returned.

He backed into the room, the gun raised. He reached overhead and pulled the cord on a reflector lamp that dangled over the tattered velvet chair. A pool of light spread from the single high-wattage bulb. "I know you like incandescents, thought I'd oblige."

The added illumination flooded the room, revealing a vast space broken up by concrete pillars and stacks of wood-slat packing trays. The only furniture consisted of his chair and two small metal tables, as in an operating room. One held the paints and brushes, the other, partially concealed by the chair, was covered with a collection of vials, intravenous bags, syringes, and another gun.

He noticed my attention. "Do you think this should be in the picture?" He wheeled out the table, displaying its contents. "I wasn't sure. Props can be distracting, don't you think?"

"It depends."

"Right. Of course, who am I to say? After all, *you* are the talented artist. And that's why I want you to do my portrait. It wouldn't do for just any old hack. I want a Chadwick Greene. So what do you think? Is the chair okay?"

"It's fine."

From out of a brown-paper shopping bag he pulled a tweed jacket, a white shirt and a red silk tie. He changed in front of me, revealing a strong torso that had spread in the middle. "I thought conservative would be best," he said. "It makes it more timeless."

"What are the drugs for?"

He smiled. "Shame on you. I'm the one who asks the questions . . . Well, maybe this once." He cinched the knot on his tie and checked his reflection in the barrel of the gun. "All right." He pushed the table closer. "A good working knowledge of pharmacology is indispensable, don't you think?"

"I guess."

"You guess? I give you too much credit, Chad. But that's my shortcoming; I always expect too much from people—just leads to disappointment. So"—he flourished a plastic syringe—"something for everyone. But you know the real trick, the thing that most people don't get?"

I shook my head, all the while pushing against the

leg shackles, wondering if they could be snapped from the two-inch iron ring embedded in the floor.

"What's good for doggy is good for Daddy. One drug fits all. Of course, the problem with phenobarbital is how much? Usually you go by weight, but everyone's different. If you give too much . . . well, it's a problem. Doggy doesn't want to wake up. In fact, it might"—he lowered his voice—"die. And then Dr. Anderson gets all upset, and we can't have that. He's such an asshole. Then there are the other things, like ketamine and Amytal. You'd think they'd keep better tabs on the stuff."

My stomach lurched as I made the connection to the veterinarian. "How do you know Dr. Anderson?"

He smiled. "I'm the night assistant—have been for almost a month." His face was inches from mine. "I watch the puppies on the graveyard shift. Lots of time, all by myself, to try things out. That's how they do things in medical school. You always practice on a dog, or a little kitten, first. Why do you think your dog wasn't waking up?"

I remembered Dr. Anderson's confusion, his search for an explanation, something about Ching being a slow metabolizer of the drug.

"Yeah, I know," he said, as if reading my thoughts. "He never caught on. I just kept shooting him up with more and more phenobarb; it was pretty easy."

"Why? Why are you doing this?"

"Oh, I suppose"—he looked at his watch—"just this last question and then it's time to paint. Why? Well, I needed to keep my eye on you. As long as I had the dog, it was easy. It's important to plan ahead."

"How did you . . ."

"Know you'd bring the dog there? Is that what you were going to ask?"

I nodded.

"Because you showed me. I've been watching you and the good doctor for three months. I know everything about you—monthly visits for clip and groom, that *nasty* bout of kidney infections. You spend more time on your dog than you do on your son." His eyes burned into mine. "Everywhere you go, when you paint, how you paint, who you meet, who you want to fuck; I'm there. You're a very predictable man. It's just like pulling strings on a puppet . . . Isn't that what you told your shrink?"

"How did you . . . ?"

He interrupted, looked at his watch. "I'm sorry, time's up. Got to paint."

He pointed the barrel of the shiny pistol at Ching's head. I couldn't move. *Do what he says, Chad.* I forced my body into motion and set to work. The smell of the paint and the feel of the brush in my hand helped to ground me.

"Where would you like me?" he asked, relaxing his gun hand.

"The chair is good."

"That's what I thought. You like the lighting, don't you?"

I framed the composition in the discrete pool of yellow light. "It's fine."

I slipped into a familiar track and let the horror of the situation wash through me, distilling it inside my body. *If I die and this is my last painting, it must all be there on the canvas.*

My eyes flew back and forth between Allen and the canvas. I sketched the parameters of the composition. The dome of illumination provided a natural hot spot and focus. It would be a study in light and dark. Ching's inert reddish blackness off to the side gave balance to the glint of the stainless-steel table with its pharmaceutical vials and shrink-wrapped syringes. In the middle sat Allen, caught up in his own trance. He held perfectly still, staring off into darkness, the gun held primly between folded hands.

I lost track of time. The spell broke with the beeping of his watch.

He blinked twice and turned to look at me. There was a moment of recognition, as if he really had been somewhere else.

"Good," he said and got to his feet. He picked up something small and metallic from the table and loaded it into the other gun. Without hesitation, he pointed and fired. I felt the sharp jab, like a bee sting piercing my flesh. I grabbed at my chest, finding a small stainless-steel barb. I pulled it out as the potent mix of tranquilizers hit. My knees gave. I tried to speak as darkness engulfed me. The last thing I remembered, through half-closed eyes, was a hazy form in jacket and tie standing over me looking at the canvas.

I sleep. I dream. In one, I am a weaver whose tapestry signals horrible destruction. Rather than finish the intricate hanging, I unravel it with one hand while working the shuttle with the other. In the background, an unseen evil lurks, waiting to catch me at my deception.

The scene shifts and I'm with Ching, on a hillside overlooking the ocean. Below us, two figures spread out a picnic lunch. I want to join them, but can't find my way off the mountain to the beach below. One of them waves to me, and I realize they're Zack and Jocelyn. I try to wave back but my hands are bound; I can't raise them above my waist. I shout, and my words get tangled and lost in the wind.

Then it's no longer a beach but an isolation room in a psychiatric ward. I'm wrapped and shackled, but this doesn't bother me as I lecture to an assembled crowd of doctors and students. "It's all very easy," I told them, "finding the way of the superior man. You just need to go faster, and if that's not enough, go faster still."

I woke to darkness, my body pressed against cold cement, my hands cuffed behind my back and my legs twisted in their chains. "Hello," I yelled into the silence. My ears strained for street noise, the sound of voices, anything. *"Hello!"* I heard Ching whimper softly in the distance. *"Can anyone hear me? Help me,"* I shouted, the words echoing inside the blackness. I screamed until my throat burned and my voice went hoarse. And then, a certainty inside my head: *You're here to die.* I rolled into a sitting position, my mind increasingly numb to the pain. My eyes picked out shapes and shadows. A familiar voice tickled from deep inside. *"It's time."* I felt the shadows coalesce, I watched them move, acquiring glimmers of light and color.

"Chad," I said out loud, "don't do this. Stay sharp." But still the shapes gathered. They stood around me. They began to murmur. I tried to ignore them and traced back the chain to an unyielding iron ring anchored in the cement. Peals of derisive laughter surrounded me as I kicked at the ring. I turned toward the sound, expecting to see my captor, but all I found were the shadow people growing clearer. "You're not real." My voice pushed them back.

Then, from somewhere in their midst: *"We are real. We've always been real. You can't ignore your destiny."*

"Don't do this, Chad." But it was too late.

CHAPTER TWENTY-FIVE

Allen returned and, still shackled, I painted.

He was all smiles today. He wanted to talk. "I bet you want to know why I killed the shrink."

My body is wrapped in a cloak of light, the canvas has become a giant portal. Odd, that after so many years, this certainty should reveal itself now. It wasn't the mirrors and it wasn't the glass; it's my painting. This is the vessel.

"Listen to me, you freak." He rose out of the chair.

I looked at him, more curious than afraid. *Am I really catching the man hiding behind the eyes?* I stared deeply into his head, glimpsing random images of blood and fire. I felt the heat of his hatred, the force of his envy.

He turned away, smiling. "You really are crazy, aren't you?"

I returned to the painting, wanting to transfer the images from my mind to the canvas.

"What did you say?" He stared at me.

My lips were moving, mouthing steady incantations; the portrait had become an intricate spell. "I'm giving you a painting. It's what you want—a portrait painting." How close "portrait" is to "portal," I thought.

He stepped back, examining me from a distance. "He was right about you."

"He was often right."

"Do you even know what I'm talking about?" I noticed a glimmer of fear as he sensed my growing power.

"Dr. Sturges." Allen's thoughts telegraphed into my brain. "You wanted to tell me why you killed him."

"Just shut up." He walked back to the chair and fidgeted with the bottles on the table. He muttered and drew up a syringe. "For later; I guess it wasn't enough."

I followed his actions, the voice in my head oddly benign. "It's never enough, is it?" Snippets of hospital scenes flashed to mind; nurses arguing with doctors: "It's too much. The book says not to give this high a dose." The harried resident's reply: "Well, nothing else is working. Just give it."

My hands moved quickly as they sketched in the under-drawing for his face, like bones beneath the skin; it was an intuitive X-ray. His skull appeared ever clearer, an image of death with eyes that burned.

"He said you were psycho." He sank back in his chair.

"The word is psychotic," I said, my brush flying ever faster.

"Whatever." He scratched the back of his shaved head, the stubble was dark and uneven. "Sturges didn't recognize me, not at first. He thought I was some poor sap out to blow my money on a crying jag. 'Oh, boo-hoo, my wife tried to leave me. So I whacked her.' That's just what I said. It was beautiful." He went on, savoring the memories. "Gave him all the details, just like it was yesterday. He was real calm, putting on his little shrink games, like the minute I turned my back he wasn't going to call the police. I could see him itching to do it. 'What do you mean by whacked?' he asked.

"'Oh, you know,' and I smiled real big, took off my wig, took off the glasses. Just beautiful, watching him squirm, checking out the distance to the door, to the phone.

"What do you think you're doing?" he asked.

"Don't you remember me?" And then I stood and took out my gun. So beautiful. 'Let me refresh your memory. It's 1987 and the flowers are in bloom. I come home from a hard day of work as a fuckin' lab tech and my bitch wife decides she's had enough and wants to go home to Mommy. Well, I think about that and I think about it some more, and it doesn't sit right. Know what I mean? It's not like she hadn't pulled this shit before. So I smacked her, not too hard, just a little tap to help her regain the proper perspective. But you know, Doc? It wasn't enough. She got all huffy and tried to go for the door. Well . . . you just don't do that to Allen; it gets me upset. I tried to tell her. I couldn't really stop myself. She should have known better. But the truth'—and here I got real close and whispered in his ear—'she was pretty stupid. Remember now, Doc?' I could feel him shaking. It was *so* beautiful."

I stared across at him, bathed in the yellow light, the lines of his face darkly rimmed with dripping shadows. A smile played at the corners of his full lips. "I put the gun to his head, like this." His eyes shot open and locked with mine. He placed the barrel of the dart gun to his right temple. "Can you picture it? It was a feeling you can't imagine. I'd thought about if for years, every day I was locked in that place, but it just never equals the real thing. I'd picture how I'd do it, over and over. You know, and I can tell you 'cause I'm sure you won't tell, it gets me hard . . . just thinking about it. About how *superior* he was, lording over me, like some fucking imperial doctor. Put me in his little 'quiet room' all tied to the bed. I knew what he wanted, watched him get off on it. That was his first mistake. Might have forgiven that, maybe not. You never know. But then the bastard had the cops come. Said I 'wasn't appropriate for the ward.' Well, that's the kind of thing that's sort of hard to forgive—mistake number two.

"It just got better and better. Now, I ask you, what had I ever done to him? Didn't know me from Adam, guess some people can't help but mess with other people's business. They tried to send me to jail; he testified at my arraignment; called me a "sociopath," all dressed in his gray faggot suit. Mistake number three. And then, his biggest boo-boo, and I suspect the one that killed him . . . he put the wrong note in my hospital chart." He laughed, snorting through his nose. "Don't you love it? Well, my lawyer certainly did, and the jury did, and the other two psychiatrists, who were pretty easy to snow, did. I wasn't a sociopath at all, I was, and I quote, '... a floridly psychotic manic-depressive who attacked his wife in response to delusional stimuli.' And before you know it, I was unable to stand trial by reason of insanity. And ... just like on a TV game show, I was off for an all-expenses-paid trip to beautiful Whitestone Forensic Psychiatric Hospital. Ten years as a nutcase. My lawyer said it would be two, maybe three. But he'll get his turn.

"Ten years of letting assholes shoot me up with Thorazine and Haldol until I couldn't walk, until I started drooling and shaking and falling asleep on my feet. Ten years of twerp shrinks asking me, 'Are you taking your pills? Do you have any thoughts of hurting yourself? Any thoughts of hurting anyone else?' Well, yes, now that you mention it, I'd love to plow a knife in your belly, something long, maybe a serrated edge—better for traction.

"But I was good. And you know what? *I got better.* All that nasty manic-depression—it went away. They didn't have a clue. With all their fancy diplomas and BMWs, they didn't have a fucking clue. Just amazing. Makes you wonder how we spend our tax dollars. They were sure it was the pills. 'See how much better you're doing. You must always remember to take your pills.'

"And I'd agree, 'Oh yes, Doctor. I feel *so* much better. What a horrible thing I did to my bitch wife, naughty, naughty.'" He laughed through clenched teeth. "'It must have been that nasty manic-depression' . . . that, and a seventeen-ounce ball-peen hammer. Details, details."

I stared at him, watching waves of red heat pulse from his body. The lines of his face melted, forming and reforming.

"What are you looking at?"

His words were lost in the distance, my attention riveted to a church bell ringing softly inside my head.

"What are you looking at?" He closed the gap, the dart gun pointed at my chest.

I felt his thoughts batter at my brain, his skull glowed translucent beneath the stubble.

"I asked you a question."

"Prepare the way."

"Yeah, right. Back up," he said.

Still holding the paintbrush, I moved back to the iron ring, dragging my chains, the noise of scraping metal like the clanging of bells. "Dingdong. Dingdong." Unable to stop myself, I started to chant. My feet rocked from side to side, my body felt incredibly light. "dingdong, dingdong, dingdong."

"Jesus." He was torn between the half-formed image on the massive canvas and my growing noise. *"Shut up!"*

"Dingdong, dingdong, dingdong, dingdong."

He raised the gun. "Shut the fuck up!"

The Portrait

I rocked faster, keeping time with the bells pealing in my head: "*Dingdong, dingdong, dingdong, dingdong, dingdong.*"

He pulled the trigger.

CHAPTER TWENTY-SIX

Very convenient, Allen thought, mulling over the information he'd pumped out of Helen at the change of shift. Of course, that is the way it was supposed to go, the cops think Chad grabbed the dog and split town.

"They were looking for him," she said. "It was that lady detective again."

"Oh, really." His indifference spurred her on.

"You know what?"

"I have no idea."

"I think they're going to arrest him."

"How would you know that?"

"I heard them talking."

"Uh-huh."

"No, really, I overheard her say something about his running away, maybe going to Boston." She paused. "She wants to talk to you."

"Oh, really?"

"Yeah, they want to know if he said anything to you when he picked up the dog. Maybe said where he was going. I told them you worked nine to eight; I think she kind of lost interest when I said that."

"Whatever."

Everything fell into place. If it weren't for that damn newspaper article, it would be perfect. Even with that, his face plastered on page one, no one was going to make the connection. Or, by the time they did, he'd be long gone.

They were easy to fool. He thought back to the job interview. "Yes," he told Dr. Anderson from beneath his short dark wig and colored contacts, "I was a medical student for two years." Then, after the dramatic pause: "It was then I realized I just wasn't cut out to be a doctor." A moment of introspection, a half-smile. "Of course I still am paying off the loans."

The truth was carefully blended with fiction. Even if Anderson checked with the medical school, all would be right as rain. He knew, he'd tried it himself.

"Yes," the bursar's secretary would say, "Allen Broadhurst was enrolled for two years." End of story, no mention of expulsion, of body parts missing from the anatomy lab, of unauthorized animal dissections, that's confidential. After all, who wants lawsuits?

Of course, the *real* reason he was called into Dean Harrison's office had been jealousy. At the time, he didn't realize this. The memory still burned. "I'm sorry, Allen," he had said, "but your behavior is unsuitable for the profession."

In the end, that's what it boiled down to—jealousy. True brilliance made people nervous. He remembered a line from Nietzsche: "Societies are built by the weak to protect themselves from the strong." Maybe, when all of this was over, he'd pay a visit to the dean. The thought made him smile.

Allen made his rounds, checking on the rows of kennels. It sickened him, the attention paid to these smelly things. *Just one more month, maybe a little longer. That should be plenty of time to separate his quitting from Chad's suicide.*

"What are *you* looking at?" He banged his hand against the cage of a bandaged cat. The animal hissed, its back arched. "Maybe another night," he said, not interested in his usual games.

"I have to think." He jimmied open the narcotics cabinet and removed two capsules of methamphetamine. He dumped the fluffy white powder onto the counter and carefully spooned confectioners' sugar back into the cellulose lozenges.

With a scalpel he formed lines and snorted the drug through a coffee stirrer. The speed hit his brain with a jolt. *Nothing like steady work. You've got to love the fringes.*

He paced the floor and recapped his progress. Months of planning, plotting out the good doctor's schedule. With his van parked outside Sturges's brownstone he tracked the flow of patients, eavesdropping on the sessions with a twenty-five-hundred-dollar listening device bought at the Espionage Shop. He recorded everything.

At first, it seemed the perfect blackmail scheme, an endless supply of teary confessions of infidelity, embezzlement, or worse. When the truth leaked out, it would ruin the doctor. He had imagined Sturges, in desperation, moments from arrest, killing himself. Or, if he wasn't so obliging, he'd help out—a perfect revenge either way. Unfortunately, it turned into one boring monologue after another about distant fathers and inadequate mothers. It was all he could do to stay awake.

Then he hit pay dirt. That first day he saw Chad enter the office—instant recognition, almost too easy. A chance for sweet revenge. And something more—a chance to make them pay. It was only fair, after all. Ten years in the nuthouse, what was that worth in dollars and cents?

Not one to believe in fate, it gave him pause. The paintings he'd taken years ago at Bellevue. The ridiculous art therapist who raved about everything Chad did, but couldn't recognize the power in his own, Allen's work. Just another idiot. Even so, he knew they'd be worth something someday. Who knew it would be that much? All those years rolled up in his "patient's belongings" bin along with his watch and his belt. The money from their sale primed the pump. *Got to spend money to make money.*

As for Sturges, he'd always been a dead man; it was only a matter of time and opportunity. And when opportunity knocks . . . That last session with Chad, he heard every word: their fight, his pretty little wife calling down to check on him. "Are you all right, Philip?"

His answer was too prophetic: "I'm almost done for the day."

How true.

He watched Chad leave the office, and after months of waiting, invited himself in.

He replayed his final scene with Sturges, the look in his eyes, the weight of the gun pressed against his temple. "Ohh." He closed his eyes and swayed, savoring the details: the pop of the bullet, the shotgun's recoil, the smell of burned flesh and the first blossom of blood, a sample of which he saved to be planted on Chad's clothes.

And after, his thoughts incredibly clear as he scanned the office, picking out the choicest bits of scattered evidence. *Too perfect.* He knew then, when he pocketed the invitation to Chad's opening, that he had to have the portrait. After all, well-documented provenance increased a painting's value. He wondered what a picture of a murdered psychiatrist painted by his killer would bring.

For now, it sat in a padlocked Jersey City storage container, that and a van load of other artwork, most of it crap, neatly wrapped and stacked. When this was finished, he'd leak the pieces out one by one.

The rest was simple—maybe not for a lesser mortal. But for those two days, his brain hummed with a furious speed. His appearance at the gallery, a quick in and out, and then on to Chad's loft. *They never caught on.* He tranquilized the dog and then shot him when he heard Chad coming up the stairs. *Didn't want him to bleed to death. That wouldn't do.*

Now, it was time to finish up. *Maximum impact*. The phrase stuck in his mind, *maximum impact*. It had to be high profile, and there could be no doubt, at least not much—a little conspiracy edge wouldn't hurt. The papers loved the story; he knew they would. The *Post*'s headline today screamed: SUSPECTED SHRINK SLAYER FLIES THE COOP. None of this hurt, every word pushed up the value of his hidden cargo. He just had to play it out carefully.

That day at the pier, it would have been perfect. He watched Chad from the parking lot. His receiver pulled in broken snippets of the conversation with his shrink. He was going to do it. Pity he didn't. But now, he thought of his captive, of his own unfinished portrait, drowning won't work. The police may be slow, but they wouldn't overlook the marks on his wrists and ankles; what to do about that? He paced faster. If there was a note . . . and the body didn't show up, at least not for a while, they might overlook a detail or two. He smiled and snorted the last two powdery lines. It was only human nature.

CHAPTER TWENTY-SEVEN

"Write," he said, dressed in the familiar jacket and tie, his pistol trained on Ching's head.

I picked up the pen, too tired to resist, my eyes barely able to focus.

"To everyone I've hurt," he said. "Write it down."

I did it.

"To everyone I've hurt, I'm truly sorry. Things have gotten out of hand, and this is the only way left. I couldn't survive in prison, and I won't go back to the hospital. Please try to forgive me."

He stopped and licked his lips. "That should do it. Now sign it and place it on the floor."

I let the paper fall.

"Now back away." He aimed the gun in my direction. "That's a good boy." He retrieved the note, looked it over. "Good, very good."

He studied the not yet finished canvas, and backed away. "You're taking too long," he muttered. "Decisions, decisions. It's nearly complete. What difference can one more day make?" He paced. "It's like those paintings in the hospital," he said. "All those surgeons and chiefs of staff. I used to look at them when I was a medical student, knowing that mine would be up there one day." His eyes bore into mine, red anger pulsed in waves off his forehead. "It has to be perfect."

I watched as he reached a decision. He grabbed the pistol off the tray, aimed it at me and fired.

Again I felt the sting of the dart and the drug, like a fist squeezed over me. I heard the sound of his leather shoes as I fell to the floor.

I lay there, not conscious, not unconscious, but suspended like a fly on the wall. *Am I dead?* I surveyed the situation with detachment, my chained body crumpled in front of the canvas, a pen in my right hand. Allen, his back turned toward me, viewed the half-finished canvas, torn between envy and admiration. I saw Ching, his body not moving. *How much longer can he survive?*

Desperation filled me and I hurtled backward into the deepening stupor of my body. *A chorus of bells lulls me deeper, a band of shadowy men and women surrounds me. They chant and keen in time to the bells. I walk with them. One of them takes my hand, and as he does, the face of Dr. Sturges materializes inside his black hood.*

"Chad," he said, "prepare the Way. The wicked must not inherit the earth. Prepare the Way."

I want to say something, struck by the inconsistency of his biblical stance; I thought he was a Freudian? I turn toward him and he vanishes. Brief flashes of remembered faces illuminate the blackness. They urge me toward action: Jocelyn, my parents, my son—Zack calls, "Dad, Dad, Dad." I drifted into unconsciousness.

My eyes blinked open, attracted by a tail of light, like a firefly that was there and was now gone. Now there was only darkness. I imagined scuffling noises in the distance. My mind flitted from thought to thought. *He never put back the handcuffs.*

Again I heard a distant echo, something hard scrambling over the cement floor.

"Help me," I croaked, my throat parched, my lips cracked.

Silence. I waited. *It was your imagination.*

"Help me. If there's someone there, help me," I yelled into the void.

Nothing.

At least I'm awake. The drugs are no longer strong enough for my revved-up system. I traced the chain back to the iron ring. I braced myself on my hands and kicked it, repeatedly. Pain shot up through the soles of my sneakers. I didn't stop.

"What was that?" I froze and muffled the clatter of my chains. It sounded like an animal, or maybe two. *"Help me. I'm down here. Somebody help me!"*

Silence. *It was just rats.*

"Please, help me. I won't hurt you. Help me."

There's no one there, Chad. I've got to think. Use your head. Use your hands.

"Prepare the Way."

Just shut up.

"Prepare the Way."

I scrambled on my knees in the darkness, surveying the borders of my tethered range inch by inch. My hands came up against the leg of the easel. I lay there grasping the splintery wood; it shook under my touch.

"Prepare the Way."

"Wait a minute, the canvas." I peered through the darkness, trying to judge the distance to the table. *Well beyond my reach, but maybe.*

I struggled to my feet, my legs were like rubber beneath me. I yanked the canvas free of the clamps and let it fall to the floor. It landed on a cushion of air. I trapped it with my foot to keep it from floating out of reach. A wave of dust swept across my face and into my nostrils. *Now, just maybe.* I dropped to my stomach and pushed Allen's unfinished portrait in front of me.

A voice started to chant, commenting on my progress. *"Portrait, portal. Portrait, portal."*

"Please, shut up." I tried to feel through the canvas, using it like a giant tentacle. I crept forward on my belly. *It's got to be there.* I held my breath as the wooden frame butted up against the chair.

"Okay," I moved it gently to the right, knowing I only had a single shot. *If I screw this up . . .*

"Portrait, portal. Portrait, portal."

I tried to breathe away the voices. *Please be quiet, just this once. Please, please, please.*

With a gentle metallic thud, the canvas connected with the leg of the surgical tray. *Okay, this is it.* I aimed the canvas and, with all my strength, pushed.

The table clanged to the ground. Its contents rattled and rolled across the floor. I fixed on the dull thud of metal. Holding tight to the canvas, I cast it out like a net, trawling for the scattered objects. I focused on a spot to the right of the fallen table.

On the third try I felt the painting catch on something heavy. I pulled it in. Like a train set on Christmas morning, it was all I ever wanted—Allen's gun.

"Now what?"

I cradled the cold steel pistol and rocked.

"Now what?"

"*Portrait, portal. Portrait, portal.*"

"Shhh."

A thought came. I traced back my chains to the metal ring. *I've never fired a gun.* I felt the outline of the thick iron, visualized it, and let my hand communicate the spatial relationship between it and the barrel of the gun. I aimed. I fired.

"Shit!" Shrapnel tore through my jeans and into my calf. "Goddamn!" My head rang with the explosion, my hand tingled. I gritted my teeth and felt for the ring. The metal burned my fingers. I yanked back on the chain. *I hit it; it's just not enough.* I took aim again, and fired. The bullet missed, sparking off the floor to the left.

The Portrait

"Okay, Chad, calm down." I felt the ring. I fixed it in my mind. I pulled the trigger. The chain shuddered.

A door slammed open.

"Hold it right there!" Allen's voice filled the room. A light went on. "Drop the gun. Or I put a bullet in your dog."

I froze. My hand clamped to the pistol.

"Drop it, Chad."

He moved closer. I could see that it wasn't the dart-gun in his hand, but an evil-looking snubnose handgun.

"Prepare the Way. Portrait, portal. Portrait, portal."

I let it fall to the floor. My eyes were riveted on the metal ring. The damage to it was nearly complete, the shaft ninety percent sheared off from its base.

"Get up."

I turned and faced him.

"Kick the gun over to me."

As I did, I positioned my body in front of the ring, hiding it from his sight.

He retrieved the pistol and tucked it into his belt. Then he saw the fallen canvas. "What did you do to my picture?!" He stared at his portrait. The image was smeared with filth and splattered with sugary liquid from a dripping intravenous bag. "You couldn't follow directions, could you?!"

"Prepare the Way." I looked at Allen, the gun in one hand, the other curled into a ball.

"Prepare the Way." I saw Ching.

"Prepare the Way." I felt the cold metal chain in my hand.

"Prepare the Way." I twisted the links around my fist. I dug into the floor, my muscles strained.

"Prepare the Way." The metal gave, and then it snapped. Without thought, I swung the tethered weight into the air.

He pivoted at the clatter and the whistle. *"What the fuck!"*

Our eyes locked. Dad's instructions on how to use a sledgehammer popped into my head. "Keep your eye on the target, that way you'll never miss."

I didn't.

It happened in slow motion. The realization on his face, his eyes wide. Metal connected with flesh and bone. It caught him behind the ear. He staggered back and brought the gun in line with my chest.

Too late. The chain whipped through the air. *"Prepare the Way!"* Eye on the target. Die, die, die.

He grunted as the ten-pound weight slammed into his skull. Bone shattered and he crumpled to the floor.

A scream pounded in my ears as a pillow of sticky blackness spread behind his broken head. The sound, like a warrior's cry, echoed, and then I realized it came from between my lips.

How long did I stand there?

"Prepare the Way."

"Portrait, portal. Portrait, portal."

Images burned themselves into my brain: Allen's

face with its staring eyes, the growing halo of blood. I couldn't move.

✔ "Get the dog."

Somehow, I disconnected Ching from the intravenous. His body was hot and limp in my arms.

Still dragging my chains, I found my way out of the basement, up two flights of stairs, and onto the street.

"*Prepare the Way.*"

It was mid-morning in the middle of the meatpacking district. My eyes burned in the sunlight. Workmen stopped and stared. They whispered viciously, their thoughts transmitted into my head.

Someone took my picture. I stared at him, not certain what I should do.

"*Prepare the Way.*"

Then, from the corner of my eye, I saw something familiar—a restaurant. I crossed the street, not stopping for cars. Horns blared and then fell silent.

There was a line of people waiting to be seated in the café. They fell away as I pushed through the outer doors.

A man dressed as a woman came toward me with a coffeepot. He stared at me. I knew his face.

"Come with me," he said.

And I let the voices sweep over me.

CHAPTER TWENTY-EIGHT

I lay in bed, mesmerized by the steady drip of intravenous antibiotics and fluid as they worked their way down the plastic tube and into my vein. Sharp pains stabbed at my wrists, my ankles, and the four spots on my abdomen and legs where the surgeon had removed shrapnel. When the nurse asked if I wanted Demerol; I politely declined. "It's not that bad, thanks." I even smiled.

I made sure they gave me my lithium, and even a little of the Trilafon. The voices were quiet, so maybe I wouldn't need it much longer.

A lot was hazy. How I got here. That first walk in the sun, Ching, bleeding, wrapped in my arms. I remembered the Barbie Café, and the waiter with his black-plastic beehive hairdo.

"What happened?" he asked.

I couldn't answer, my eyes fixed on the gold buttons of his sheath dress. "Help me." It's all I could manage. He called an ambulance and the cops. He took Ching and told me he'd take him to the vet.

Yesterday, they sent up a psychiatrist, an earnest young man, probably a resident. I could have used someone to talk to, but I knew that wasn't his purpose.

He was there to give me a diagnosis and see whether or not I needed to be admitted to the psych ward. I gave him limited information, enough not to be labeled "guarded and paranoid." I assured him that I would meet with Dr. Adams as soon as I got out of there. That, at least, was the truth. All the time he was in my room I wanted him gone. What business was it of his whether or not I was hearing voices? But I knew that one wrong word, or turn of phrase, and he'd lock me up. At least the cops need a warrant.

I looked at my wrists, bandaged like those of a failed suicide. I pushed back the image of handcuffs, but too late; Allen's face and the dungeon flooded into my mind. My throat tightened and my heart pounded. I tried to slow my breathing. *Let it go, let it go.*

A bright spot in my day: Daryl, the waiter from the Barbie Café, stopped by after checking on Ching at the vet's. Apparently, my dog and I are both getting a course of antibiotics and a heavy helping of fluids. Ching's going to be okay, at least physically.

The other stuff, the things I dragged out of Mom and Dad . . . the things Marvin told me, well, that was just harder. I feel like a retarded child sometimes, or like Charlie Brown, who persists in his belief that Lucy will really hold the football when he goes to kick it. *She was going to arrest me.* She had the warrant.

I made Pamela show me the headlines. SUSPECTED SHRINK SLAYER FLIES THE COOP was one. When I got out of there, I'd look at them all, maybe do a collage.

It was strange seeing Susan—Detective Bryant, yesterday. I could feel her disappointment.

Marvin was there, cautioning me to answer simply.

She took my statement, asking occasional questions. "How did you know Allen Broadhurst?"

I kept it simple.

"What is your relationship with Daryl Taylor?"

"He waited on me at the Barbie Café."

"Why did you go there?"

"It was the first thing I saw."

"He says you made a sketch of him. Do you do that for all your waiters?"

"He asked, and paid for my meal. Let me ask you a question." I didn't give her a chance to refuse. "I know you were going to arrest me; is that still your intent?" I felt Marvin's hand on my shoulder.

"No."

"Good. Just one more question. After I gave you all that information, the drawings, after all those talks, did you even try to look into it? Try to find out who he was?"

She said nothing. I had my answer.

After she left, Marvin said it was for the best. "What, she's going to press charges now, after she botched the entire investigation? I don't think so."

The papers and local news shows were having a field day with the story. The picture of me dragging chains and carrying Ching was on the cover of all three dailies. The evening news ran video clips of the warehouse where I was kept. An outcry over the release of violent criminals into the community was sounded. Of course, that's not how it was heard. The nurse's aide who changed my sheets confirmed that.

"You're the artist fellow, aren't you?"

"Yes."

"I know, 'cause I've seen you on the TV." She smiled. "Actually, people talk around here, you know."

"Sure."

"I think it was really brave what you did to that guy. I get so scared thinking about all those nutcases out on the street. I mean, if someone's not right in the head, they shouldn't let them out around normal people. It's just not fair. I mean, I know they're people and all, but they really should be locked away, as much for themselves as for everyone else."

"I have manic-depression," I told her. "Sometimes *I* hear voices."

She knew I wasn't joking. I saw fear in her eyes as she finished the last hospital corner and fled my room.

Pamela said her office was flooded with interview requests. Marvin said I should probably decline. For once, I was going to listen to his advice. I'd like to put this behind me, if that's possible.

It was strange, but in some ways, even with all this pain, and the flashbacks, my thoughts were clearer. Almost losing my life had made me reevaluate it, look at what mattered.

I finally reached a decision, one I'd been struggling with for the past two days.

I picked up the phone and dialed.

A boy answered.

"Zack?" I said.

"Yes."

"This is your dad."

PAUL CARSON

BETRAYAL

Frank Ryan knew his position as Chief Medical Officer at high-security Harmon Penitentiary was dangerous. After all, his predecessor had been murdered. But Frank never expected what happened to him the night he got that mysterious emergency call.

As he left his apartment he was
KIDNAPPED,
BEATEN,
DRUGGED,
and interrogated for six days.
Then, just as suddenly, released.

Now he can't find anyone who believes him, and his girlfriend has disappeared without a trace. His desperate search to find her—and some answers—lead Frank deeper and deeper into a sea of conspiracies, lies…and danger.

ISBN 13: 978-0-8439-6145-4

DOUGLAS MacKINNON

President of the United States Shelby Robertson is in the third year of his second term. Four-star general Wayne Mitchell is the man in charge of the nation's land-based nuclear arsenal.

For the past few years, both men have shared a common belief—**the apocalypse in coming.**

And they are determined to hasten the process.

Unless someone can stop them in time, they will set in motion a chain of events that could wipe clean the face of the earth.

THE
APOCALYPSE
DIRECTIVE

ISBN 13: 978-0-8439-6088-4

☐ YES!

Sign me up for the Leisure Thriller Book Club and send my
FREE BOOKS! If I choose to stay in the club, I will pay only
$8.50* each month, a savings of $7.48!

NAME: _____

ADDRESS: _____

TELEPHONE: _____

EMAIL: _____

☐ I want to pay by credit card.

☐ **VISA**   ☐ **MasterCard**   ☐ **DISCOVER**

ACCOUNT #: _____

EXPIRATION DATE: _____

SIGNATURE: _____

Mail this page along with $2.00 shipping and handling to:
Leisure Thriller Book Club
PO Box 6640
Wayne, PA 19087
Or fax (must include credit card information) to:
610-995-9274
You can also sign up online at **www.dorchesterpub.com**.
*Plus $2.00 for shipping. Offer open to residents of the U.S. and Canada only. Canadian
residents please call 1-800-481-9191 for pricing information.
If under 18, a parent or guardian must sign. Terms, prices and conditions subject to
change. Subscription subject to acceptance. Dorchester Publishing reserves the right to
reject any order or cancel any subscription.

11/22/18 → 11/29/18